XL

CHUTE #3

**Center Point
Large Print**

**This Large Print Book carries the
Seal of Approval of N.A.V.H.**

CHUTE #3

Mackey Murdock

CENTER POINT PUBLISHING
THORNDIKE, MAINE

This Center Point Large Print edition
is published in the year 2007 by arrangement with
Golden West Literary Agency.

The text of this Large Print edition is unabridged. In other
aspects, this book may vary from the original edition. Printed in
Thailand. Set in 16-point Times New Roman type.

ISBN: 1-58547-896-2
ISBN 13: 978-1-58547-896-5

Library of Congress Cataloging-in-Publication Data

Murdock, Mackey.
    Chute #3 / Mackey Murdock.--Center Point large print ed.
        p. cm.
    ISBN-13: 978-1-58547-896-5 (lib. bdg. : alk. paper)
    1. Texas--Fiction. 2. Large type books. I. Title. II. Title: Chute number three.

PS3613.U694C49 2007
813'.6--dc22

2006023792

Dedication

An old cowpoke friend once toasted a crescent moon outside a country dance hall near Haskell, Texas. His comment covers my feelings for the dedication of this book. He raised and tilted his bottle to the moon. "Here's to all the broncs I've rode and all the ladies I've knowed."

I'll only add,
And to all those rowdies who have taken a deep seat in the saddle, tugged at a hat brim, and hollered, "Turn him loose!"

Acknowledgements

A hearty THANK YOU to my editors
Ron and Caryl McAdoo of Longhorn Creek Press
and the DFW Writers' Workshop members. Your
continued support and confidence improve my efforts.

1

Bedsprings squeaked like a distant windmill on a lazy day. The sound froze Guthrie's poised fist. He waited to rap the screen porch door. The noise came from inside the small, open windowed house. Barely audible, it tied a knot low in his belly and brought to mind yearlings facing a castration squeeze chute. He resisted the urge to bellow his rage, maybe just walk away. Instead, he dropped his hand to his side, tilted his Stetson to the back of his head, and looked beyond the tree's foliage.

Of all fathers, why did his have to think himself God's gift to womanhood? How one weather-beaten, old used-to-be cowpuncher could end up in so many different beds remained a mystery, especially in a town where the stores outnumbered the churches by only one. Jesse Sawyer had a fast fly. Being his son was a load.

Guthrie rolled a smoke, studied the tree's shade, and judged the time near eleven a.m. He'd left Pampa an hour before light then later crossed the tracks and hit the Main Street of Saddle Horn in time to stop at Alvin's Café and chew fat with the midmorning coffee drinkers. His mom had sipped coffee in her own kitchen with both hands on the mug while he prepared fried eggs and bacon. He learned as a youngster that Cora Sawyer cooked breakfast once a day, early, and you ate then or fixed your own.

His second place finish at Pampa failed to interest her. He did his dishes then soon tired of dodging specifics about his past three weeks' activity outside the arena. Conversation came hard, even finding common ground with a schoolteacher mom, when you'd molded her vision for her son from that of a brain-surgeon to a potluck rodeo bum. In all fairness, she had listened to his third reference to the dry weather before suggesting he went to town to find his father.

Guthrie lit his cigarette. Well, he'd found him. And from inside, it sounded like the windmill's fan had caught a breeze. "Jesse, you in there?"

Silence greeted the question, but he knew the answer. The old Dodge pickup sat in back of Rita's "Café & Wreck Room". Though the misspelling of recreation was an honest mistake, it gave an even more honest description. The room served up more scars and stitches than the combined wrecks of both horses and automobiles in the Panhandle.

"Guthrie, thought you'uz in Pampa. You alone out there?" The first of his dad's sentences held a touch of aggravation, the second, major concern.

"No, I got the Lady's Home Demonstration Club with me." Sweat on that.

Jesse's chuckle sounded relieved.

"Back door's open to the café, Guthrie Hon. Why don't you go over there and have yourself a beer? We'll be along directly." Rita's voice held a feline quality. The only animals he had no use for were cats. They reminded him of fur balls and the discovery, at a young age, of what the smelly, little mounds near the radish plants covered.

"No, I'm going. Jesse, Mom said for you to get your ass home by noon for dinner. Think she thought we might want to visit."

"Wait!" Jesse said.

Kicking his heel against the raised brick of the narrow walkway offered Guthrie little relief. He stepped carefully down the walk and around over-ripe mulberries. Constant breeze had lodged most of the fruit in the sand-filled cracks between the bricks. More berries littered the hard windswept ground beyond the yard fence. He'd as soon have front-yard chickens as a mulberry tree.

Guthrie stopped, turned, then looked at the little shotgun house and shook his head. Next, he faced the street and studied the support post for the picketed yard gate. Its age appeared to match his quarter-century. Some would hold that to be past prime for a gatepost, but right-on for most in his profession. His aches and the post's lack of weathering put the lie to that assumption. Perhaps, the stanchion owed its longevity to being planted here along the Texas Cap Rock where little moisture fell to cause timber decay.

His own creaks and groans leaned more on rank saddle stock and their difficulty in staying upright on the slippery, mountain-goat footing along those same Cap Rock's eroded and treacherous brakes. Only a few of those spills tended to accelerate the loss of youth for hard-riding cowboys. Still, the opinion might be sound for he'd tell the world he'd lost no edge, and that post did tilt.

The gate swung inward to open. A few years ago it did so automatically when unlocked. In those days, the weight added to the chain pulled down, and it opened a full ninety degrees. Now, the post's angle forced the gate into the ground when it half-opened. Fat folks turned sideways to enter. Guthrie stepped through straight.

His '57 station wagon sat in front of Rita's café. He strode toward it across the gravel parking lot taking the short, choppy steps high-heeled boots encouraged. Nearer the vehicle, metal bottle caps enriched the gravel, and Guthrie scuffed his boot soles to dislodge any stubborn mulberries clinging in their high arches.

He sat behind the steering wheel and stretched. He leaned back and sighed. Loneliness more painful than the smoldering anger from finding Jesse with Rita closed around him. He plucked a match from his hat-band, stuck it in his mouth, then pulled his makings out and manufactured a cigarette.

After a backward circle, he drove onto the pavement heading for town a half-mile away. He didn't know why he bothered coming back by this way. Jesse always disappointed him. His being home seemed to aggravate his mother, and all his friends were long gone, married, or both. Well, he'd hit the road by sunup.

At Main Street, Guthrie turned north. He waved at old man Reeves in front of the post office. Gossip maintained the aging druggist bought his store thirty years ago and dispensed sodas, patent medicine, and contraceptives in about equal portions. He'd moved to Saddle

12

Horn from New Hamburg saying he preferred a good Protestant town for business reasons. Reeves proved his commercial astuteness during the war when prophylactics were in short supply and shotgun weddings flourished. He started stocking shotgun shells and competing with the Dry Goods Store for the diaper trade.

A block-size park occupied the opposite side of the street from the east-facing businesses. The courthouse, located in the northwest corner of the park, was square, two story, and unpretentious. South of the center of government, a domino game was underway in the shade of an elm tree. Guthrie parked sideways to the low cable that prevented high school kids, drunken cowboys, and palsied oldsters from driving on the park's lawn.

Historians allowed the first settlers founded Saddle Horn in 1895. Wits said the domino game started the next fall, after the crops were laid-by and the yearlings shipped.

Guthrie steadied himself with one hand on the open car door and stooped. He smoothed the tight fitting Levi's deeper into his high, gun-barrel boot tops then approached the game at a slow saunter. You didn't want to blind-side these old gents when they concentrated, especially if the thinking had to do with count-laden hands.

Even if the welcome his folks offered left something hanging on the line, the good-natured banter generated by this game always lightened his pack. He didn't have to be a big city shrink to know the same held true for

13

the participants. In a land where drought reigned and your livelihood depended on moisture—a land where you made your living with muscle and guts and only had to think on occasion, a fellow thirsted for mental exercise. In Saddle Horn, his friends slacked that thirst in the elm's shade. Keen opponents brought laughter.

He could have closed his eyes and found the game. The crack of dominos slapping the table sounded across the park, and the frequent shuffling mimicked a slow freight on a long grade. Some of the men there probably hadn't spoken to their wives twice in three days, but now they babbled like schoolgirls at their first dance.

Guthrie stepped to the shade. "Who's rules yawl playing by today?"

An old timer with wisps of a short-cropped snow bank peeking beneath his narrow-brimmed Stetson looked up and grinned. "By God, boys, look who's here! Guthrie, how you been? Rules? They same as always, Bible belt and simple: no money, no booze, no guns, no women, and no fights. Made 'em up just to keep you Sawyers out." He picked up a hand full of face down dominoes and held them shoulder high for Guthrie to see.

"Fine, Mr. Hefner. You're looking fit." He studied the hand then the penciled slashes and Xs on a nearby tablet. "Looks of that tally sheet, you got the gate closed on this bunch."

"They're pretty gentle alright, all except old Bud there. Have to watch him close, or he'll start a new spinner."

14

The man playing in front of Hefner had a round stomach and a short cigar. To his right sat Bud, a bare-headed, sun darkened man wearing spurs and western shirt buttoned cuffs to collar. His big sweat-stained, felt hat rested in an empty chair. His forehead's sharp sun-line branded him cowboy as distinctly as a bald face on a red yearling spelled Hereford. One of the others wore overalls, and the fifth player, Coach Weaver, sported exercise shorts and a T-shirt. Among this crew, the coach's tennis tan paled.

Guthrie nodded and spoke to each in turn as they took time out from fiddling, spinning, and spouting their peculiar sing-song adding machine chatter of, "Trey-deuce'll get you ten" and "What'll you take for that double-five?"

"How'd you do at Lubbock, Guthrie?" asked Bud.

"Got lucky. Caught a good draw and scored an eighty-seven. Who told you I'uz there?"

"Aw, we keep up. That get day money?"

"Yeah, took the whole show."

Bud looked at Mr. Hefner and wagged his head. "You know old Guthrie's making us all famous."

"That so?" The older man frowned at his dominoes. "Whose play is it? Ain't surprising. Like daddy, like son. What'd he do? Pass out and make an obituary somewhere then list Saddle Horn as his place of birth?"

Bud suspended a blank-four over the five-blank. "Last Monday a Cadillac, long as that block, pulled into Bully's station." Bud motioned at the tablet. "Give me fifteen! An old geezer was driving and the gal with him sure wasn't his granddaughter. Heard her telling 'Sweetie Pie' that this town was where that cute, curly headed, bronc rider was from, 'Didn't he remember?'"

"Cute, huh?" Mr. Hefner snorted.

Guthrie laughed.

The sixth man, maybe fifty-two, stood behind Coach Weaver watching the game. Guthrie shook hands with the lone observer. The man fit in with the group, except that his clean western garb was designed more for sitting behind a windshield than on a horse. His white hat was white. His hand, when he shook with Guthrie, felt smooth, though hard the hand of a man who might carry a couple of pens in a shirt pocket with his cigars and not bolt at the sight of an adding machine. Such a hand might be found on a person who owned a livestock sale barn or perhaps a feed lot. Ira Walker owned both.

Ira's grandfather neighbored with Charles Goodnight and helped settle the country. Ira helped himself to whatever suited his fancy. Guthrie had no idea what tipped him off, but for some reason, he'd always sensed bad blood between Jesse and this number three Walker. On this issue, he trusted his old man's judgement.

Ira frowned, raised his eyebrows, and looked at Guthrie. "What'd you do, give 'em that showboat, stand-up, tip your hat dismount?"

Bud looked up from his dominoes, started to smile, but met eyes with Guthrie and lowered his gaze back to the spots.

All the anger directed at Jesse earlier returned with

interest, Ira now its target. "Showboat's a strong word, Mr. Walker. I work hard, not always long, but always hard, at what I do, and 1 put it out there for the world to see. I don't run-up the bid on my own stock, and I don't salt any weights. If it's all the same to you, you can put that showboat garbage to rest. Okay?"

Ira turned red. He clamped his jaw, took a step toward Guthrie, and then froze.

Old man Hefner knew everyone in town. He knew Ira, and he'd known the Walkers before him better. At the moment, he stood arrow straight and fiery. "Hold it, Ira. Let it go. You goosed the boy, and he didn't take to it. Thing for you to do is pay him some respect and heed his words. Looks of him, he might just rip you apart, but either way, this town ain't big enough for you to let this grow. You hear what I'm saying?"

Ira stood for a moment, his gripped fists at his sides. He wheeled on his heels and walked away.

Guthrie spat, let his anger burn.

The coach started to play an ace-deuce on a trey then his tan deepened to beet-red, and he put the count back in formation with the rest of his hand. He found another domino. "Is Cora enjoying school being out?"

Jesse's Dodge moved down the street. He slowed, looked toward the game, seemed to hesitate, then continued toward home. Guthrie forced civility. "We really ain't visited much, but I'm sure she is. She had a pot of beans working earlier." He looked at Mr. Hefner, at least fifty years his senior. "Boys, hope I didn't dampen your game. I'll see yawl again." He nodded at the rest of the players and pointed at Bud.

Guthrie's anger cooled on the way back to the Chevy. Its intensity startled him. Always easy to rile, even he was surprised at how quick that blowup occurred. Aw well, he wouldn't lose any sleep over it.

That old-man Hefner was a scrapper, though. Jesse had told him how tough the old man used to be before a bad horse killed his boy and Jesse's best friend. It happened about the time of Guthrie's birth. The old man substituted the Baptist church for his lost son and his own hard ways. He hadn't missed a sermon, drank anything stronger than lemonade, or passed a bad word since they tamped the last clod on his boy's grave.

Peculiar, he wondered what the old gentleman meant by "let this grow".

2

The aroma of simmering red beans met Guthrie at the front door, and a TV weatherman's voice struggled to make hot and dry sound like news. In the living room, Jesse dozed oblivious to the set's distorted picture. The popping and sizzling of grease said his mother turned frying chicken to supplement the beans. He sat in her chair across from his dad. The couch offered comfort, but sat too low for easy escape.

Jesse grunted, closed his mouth, and blinked.

"Guess I'm getting to be a real pest, huh?" Guthrie said.

A mirth starved smile crawled across Jesse's face. He

lit his own then offered a Lucky to Guthrie. "Every-body's got to be somewhere. I been the one outta place."

Guthrie contemplated the disadvantages of Bull Durham versus a free Lucky and forked the ready-roll with his fingers.

His mother's voice came from the kitchen. "That you, Hon?"

"Yeah, it's me." He lit the smoke.

"You had a late breakfast. You probably aren't hungry."

"Mom. Ever know me not to eat?"

He had overtaken his dad's five-foot nine frame his senior year of high school. Since, he'd added another two inches. However, on all measurements other than vertical, the older man still had him beat. The last time Cora mixed the laundry, Jesse's denim jacket contained a couple of inches too much material to go in Guthrie's closet, and the same was true of his Levi's.

Sitting or standing, the family resemblance wasn't that great. The connection evidenced itself in speech, movement, and facial expressions. Guthrie worked hard in his youth to get the walk just right and spent hours in front of the mirror practicing the crooked smile. That was before he aged enough to understand the admiring looks the old man received from the ladies and the envy in the men's voices when speaking of Jesse Sawyer did not all come from his dad's exploits on horseback.

"Staying awhile?" Jesse got up and turned off the TV.

"Just till morning. Abilene show's starting Thursday."

"Need any money?"

"Naw, I'm flush. Lubbock and Pampa treated me pretty good."

"That so?"

"Uh-huh."

"Wal, that's good." Jesse slid his footstool into position and stretched out. "I'm glad. Want'a work this evening?"

"What you got?"

"A main line leak over near the school. Planned to see if Lightning and Caleb wanted to sweat a little, but I'd as soon pay you if you ain't afraid of the wrong end of an idiot spoon."

Guthrie nodded at the set Jesse'd just quieted. "He said ninety-eight. That's pretty hot."

"Yeah, but we'll be digging down hill."

"It ain't the digging. It's the shoveling, and less I'm confused, that's uphill."

"I'll get Lightning."

"No, I'll do it. Leave you and old Lightning alone, you'll start pulling on a bottle, and one of you'll forget the other'n and end up burying him in that hole." Generally, Jesse curbed the bottle while working, but tasks done afoot just moved faster if oiled.

Jesse had been raised a cowboy and the right hand man of a self-taught father who practiced animal doctoring. The first years of his and Cora's marriage, they fared better than most with her teaching and him working at his hand-me-down trade. The third year, the state passed a bill that outlawed folks practicing Jesse's chosen profession without a license. Since he couldn't spell veterinarian, he became Saddle Horn's city-water man.

Didn't pay much, but in a town of seven hundred and fifty, the job gave him time to pick up an extra dollar or two helping neighbors work cattle during periods of peak ranching activity. Jesse provided fodder for a lot of bench warmed and sewing circle gossip, but no one ever connected his name with sullen or lazy.

Cora peeked around the door. "It's ready." Each took a seat around the small table set in the kitchen.

His parents joined Mr. Hefner and others at the Baptist Church most Sundays. Jesse even gave thanks for both dinner and supper on the day of rest. When, during his questioning years, Guthrie asked why they restricted the blessing to the Sabbath, Jesse said he figured God was tired as anybody during the week. Far as he knew, his mother never pushed the issue. Now, she passed food and looked sharply at Jesse.

Guthrie heaped his beans over two slices of cornbread, speared the pulley-bone from the chicken platter, then added scallions and tomatoes to his plate. He sensed his mother's eyes and took the gravy bowl she held toward him. "What do yawl hear from Jack and Irene?"

Though three years his senior, his sister getting married and moving to Oklahoma City after her high school graduation proved a milestone in Guthrie's life. With one less pair of Sawyer eyes to keep tabs of his escapades, the world, comprised of Saddle Horn and

21

fifty miles in each direction, lay at his feet.

When Irene said, "I do" and headed for the tin-canned car, he embraced his new found freedom like a litter's bully nuzzling front tit. The window dressing for his new life included school, sports, and front-room parties. He'd spiced the pattern a little to include bootleggers, car chases, and some backseat wrestling. Guthrie's youth had been happy. Adulthood proved more binding.

Cora passed the chicken to Jesse. "They're doing fine. Jasper did have another bout with his throat, and the doctor's talking taking out his tonsils."

"He has 'em out, yawl going?"

"I'll probably go for a couple of days so Irene doesn't have to miss any work." She looked at her husband. "You need pepper sauce, Jess?"

"Don't you reckon they can manage?" Jesse asked.

"You don't have to go. I can drive myself."

"You know that ain't it."

"Well, when there's sickness, I'd rather be busy helping than sitting here worrying."

"He's right, Mom. Why don't yawl not go the first few days, anyway. Otherwise, you'll be sitting there rocking through the night while old Jasper's dreaming about pulling pig-tails and eating freezer cream."

"Sitting with the sick doesn't tire me."

Jesse looked at Guthrie with an expression of futility showing. "Hon, I know that. Just seems you might want to ease off some. You ain't no spring chicken, you know."

"Humph! Why not? You're still acting like you're cock-o-the-walk."

The old man's color drained. Mom knew! How'd she know? Guthrie lost interest in food. He stirred the beans on his plate then took a drink of tea. Jesse's bull-like shoulders slumped. He added pepper to an already seasoned tomato. Cora held the cup towel before her mouth, chewing slowly.

Who said silence was golden? Seemed more like a lead weight in the pit of your gut. There it was. That voice inside jumping up and down for him to carry the conversation. "You know, I met a guy in Lubbock the other day. A bull dogger from Cortez, Colorado. He said they don't eat beans. Feed 'em to the stock. Bet the fool never had any this good."

"You know that's true." Jesse nodded vigorously.

Good, they were going to let it slide. "Almost had to pop Ira Walker in the mouth a bit ago."

"That so? The man does have a way, don't he?" Jesse had found a shell and wasn't coming out.

Cora's expression didn't change, hadn't changed during the entire meal. "I'm buying groceries this evening. I'll get round steak if you're gonna be here a few days."

"Naw, I'm leaving for Abilene in the morning."

"Abilene? Time for that already?"

"'Fraid so. Third weekend in July."

Cora looked at Jesse and gasped. Tears welled in her eyes, and she put both hands to the cup towel. "It's the twelfth. Oh, today would be Christina's birthday." She

23

looked from one to the other. Tears ran down her cheeks. Her shoulders shook. She made hurt puppy sounds.

Jesse put a hand on her arm and leaned toward her.

She stiffened.

Christina had died at thirteen months of age, seven months before Irene was born. Her illness started with dysentery and soon progressed to dehydration, fever, then death. With modern medicine, the sickness would have meant inconvenience. With that of the 1930's, it meant death. His mother had seen to it that he and Irene stayed well informed of the tragedy, and that was all right. But why did she torture herself so?

She stood stiffly and turned her back. "Would y'all excuse me, please? I think I'll start that ironing." She stepped to the hallway and stopped, holding the door facing, her back to them. "Late this evening, after we eat, maybe we could all go to the cemetery."

"Sure, Hon, we'll all do that." Jesse looked at Guthrie.

"Yeah, Mom. It'll be cooler then." He washed and Jesse dried. He covered leftovers then stuck them in the Frigidaire.

Minutes later, Jesse had trouble getting the Dodge started. The engine sputtered then fired roughly, missing on a few cylinders. He let out on the clutch, and the pickup jumped, coughed, and died. "Coldest natured thing I ever saw."

"Cold! In this heat? How long since you changed plugs?"

24

"Don't know. I remember you did in high school. It'll crank next turn, I bet." He was right. Jesse coaxed the Dodge into high gear just in time to switch back to second to make his first turn. In the back, shovels, picks, and an assortment of pipe wrenches and boards added to the leaky muffler's racket.

"Does she ever nap?"

"Who?"

"Mom. Does she ever nap?"

"If she does, I ain't accusing her of it."

"It ain't a sin."

"To you and me, maybe."

The first foot of hard, dry dirt tested them. Jesse brought out picks and a grubbing hoe to go with the shovels. A leak dampened two-foot block within the grave size plot offered little resistance. The picks enabled them to lower the balance of the rectangular down to where the shovels, with the aid of a little boot shoving, worked nicely.

The sun beat down, and Guthrie's clothes became soaked. Jesse set a slow, even pace, seldom talking. Shadows from drifting clouds offered brief relief. An occasional breeze stirred. At knee depth, his old man crawled out and headed for the shade of a Paradise tree and the water. Guthrie joined him without invitation.

Jesse held the water bag by its upper corner and spout. Tilting it, he stopped halfway up and spoke around the side of the spout. "These old trees are proper named, ain't they?"

Guthrie looked for his tobacco. He'd put it here

25

somewhere to keep dry. "They do come in handy."
There it lay, by the big feeder root. He took his turn
with the water bag, squatted cross-legged, and leaned
his back against the tree. The nearby yard with its circle
of green in the withering, drought-dormant lawn held
his attention only a moment then his thoughts returned
to his mother.

"I believe it bothers her worse each year."

"What?"

"Christina. I believe time makes her death get harder
for Mom to handle."

Jesse went to the Dodge and leaned the backrest forward. He returned with a pint of Seagram's Seven, took
a generous drag, then offered the bottle.

Guthrie shook the gesture off.

With the pint tucked inside his waistband, Jesse
chased the whiskey with water. "You're right, her
pining just gets worse. Them that say, 'time heals all
wounds' are wrong. You'd think it'd ease it some, but
time's ruthless. Wears on you. Seems like, the more of
it passes, the nearer you are to where you started.
Losing the little girl took its toll, and every year adds to
the burden." Jesse lit a Lucky and squinted through the
smoke.

"Your messing around don't help." There, he hadn't
thought to say it, but since it was out, okay.

Jesse's eyes turned steel cold. He returned the pint to
the truck cab. His boots drug sand. Turning toward the
shovel, he fixed Guthrie with a hard look. "Boy, your
mother and I've been together thirty-four years. There

26

ain't nothing about the other'n we don't know. What you say may be true, but I ain't ready to hear it, not from you or nobody else. Now, let's finish this hole."

Later, a faint pallor around Jesse's temples and forehead tempered the heat's flush. He straightened. "That's enough. I'll finish it tomorrow. Let's go wash up."

3

Refreshed by a cool bath and shave, Guthrie managed to get to the couch. A twenty-minute nap left him groggy. Still, he did his part with the noon leftovers that served as supper. Cora had the table cleared and dishes soaking by the time he'd pulled on his boots, brushed his teeth, and combed his hair.

"Y'all ready?" Cora tied the ends of a scarf beneath her chin.

The trip to Christina's resting site took only minutes. Jesse drove the Chevy across the vacant lot where the church once stood and stopped in front of the cemetery. The double gates were constructed of welded pipe reinforced with long-obsolete, metal wagon wheels. Above, an arched sign dispelled any doubts that this was indeed a place of burial. The surrounding fence joining the gates consisted of five strands of barbed wire.

Returned energy brought problems of its own. Guthrie fidgeted. In town nine hours now, and his yearning to move-on had him champing the bit. He stepped from the back door of the Bel-Aire and rolled a cigarette.

"Know why they fence cemeteries?"

To pull that old line, Jesse—somehow the word Dad had sharper edges today—must not be too at ease. Guthrie couldn't remember the first time he'd been asked the question, but he well recalled how filled with manly pride he'd always been while laughing with his hero at the thought of people just dying to get in.

"Spare me," he said.

Jesse grinned while holding the gate for Cora.

Christina's stone, small and lonely, occupied a plot large enough for others to be placed beside her at some future time. The marker's shadow in the late sun dwarfed its actual height.

A summer breeze rippled cedar branches in the trees scattered among the headstones, and the earth radiated warmth through the worn leather of Guthrie's boot soles. Looking at the dust tinted stone, oblivious to the outside world, he fought an internal blizzard.

A vision of rows of crosses at Washington National Cemetery bobbled, floating on the cold backwaters of his memory. Even the desert wind and the hot Texas sun failed to penetrate the frigid barriers of his hidden spot. Seemed longer than a year since he'd escorted his best friend's body from Vietnam to its final rest.

Receiving his own discharge shortly afterwards, he'd fought bad broncs and worse odds trying to forget those torn away by death. He'd grown up in the shade of this shadow cast by a stone-marked grave. God, how often he'd found it in his sleep. His mother's perpetual grief exposed what dirt attempted to cover. In spite of other's attempts at levity, she'd made sadness a virtue. He vowed to chart a different course, not allow his own private wars to take control.

She knelt and dabbed at her eyes with a Kleenex. Jesse stood, bareheaded, staring hard at the stone. His fingers hid in the hip pockets of his creased Levi's. His hat rested on his right buttock, squeezed at the brim by his thumb.

"Jess, she'd be thirty years old."

"Uh-huh." He knelt beside his wife.

What! The world was crazy! This morning Guthrie'd hollered the old rapscallion out of another woman's bed. Now, here Jesse was, obviously torn by emotion, consoling his wife of thirty something years, who—unless Guthrie was nuts—knew the whole deal. And Cora, durned if she didn't act like he was the Baptist equivalent of the Pope.

"She was so beautiful. She was, wasn't she, Jess?"

"She looked just like you. Remember how she used to squeeze my thumbs?" Jesse's expression softened. He traced the tip of his finger along Christina's name.

Guthrie clamped his jaw, looked at the low sun, and blinked. He turned from the grave and searched for his grandfather's stone. He moved slowly among the markers. They were as different as the names they preserved: small, tall, narrow, wide. A couple of sculptured World War One figures stood erect with rifles at their sides, their war identified by the design of their headgear. Seeing a stone tree trunk, he wondered at it then recalled it representing a group called the

29

Woodsmen. Perhaps he imagined that.

He struck a match with a thumbnail, lit his smoke. Prepared to flip the dead light, he thought better of it and scraped off the burned portion on a boot heel then found a home for the remainder in his hatband.

Yeah, there'd been a lot of last good-byes spoken here. He looked at the adjacent vacant church lot beside the farm-to-market pavement and remembered its popularity as a teen parking spot. Come to think of it, there'd been a few hellos whispered over there. Slowly walking back toward the car, he searched for the site's earliest grave.

His parents joined him. They held hands. Jesse guided Cora through patches of stickers in the dry grass and pointed. "See that'un over there? That's Mr. Hefner's folks' spot. A few months ago, the cemetery committee decided everybody would gather with hoes and clean graves. They asked Mr. Hefner his thoughts on it." Jesse's eyes seemed to fasten on Booger Hefner's grave beside his grandparents.

Guthrie waited, but his dad made no sign of continuing. "What'd he say?"

"Said go ahead, chop all the weeds they wanted on his folks' plot, but don't touch the grass. His father was a cattleman."

Cora nodded toward a nearby plot. "Jess, want to go by your mom and dad's?"

"Naw, we'll leave 'em be."

Guthrie surrendered to the itch to join their conversation. "So, where's Mr. Schofield's?"

Jesse nodded at the oldest grave. It belonged to one Mr. Arnold Schofield, dated, on a hand-carved, sandstone marker, April 1, 1893. Legend held Arnold as a circuit-riding minister of Presbyterian persuasion who made the fatal error of attempting to convert a trio of X-slash-bar (X/-) riders.

At the time, the punchers celebrated April Fool's Day by working on a leftover fifth from the night before. Intrigued by the reverend's top hat, the jovial riders tossed it in the air for target practice. After emptying their six-guns, one of the boys returned the somber article intact to Brother Arnold.

A God fearing, but devil scorning advocate of fire and brimstone, the reverend purportedly drew himself erect on his bony mount, waved the unscathed hat toward the Heavens, and commanded the Lord to, "Forgive these fools, for they know not what they do".

Perhaps Charlie Lasater took offence at the word 'fool', or maybe he thought his aim had improved from the earlier practice. At any rate, historians all pretty well agreed his bullet took off the top of the preacher's head. He was one of the last men hanged in the Panhandle, but swore on the gallows that he aimed to send the stovepipe to Glory, not the old sin buster.

A few minutes later, Jesse drove toward home leaving Christina and Mr. Schofield's resting sites behind. Beside the Chevy, swirls of dust capped boot-high, wind-driven waves of sand along a cotton field turn row. The school and football field came into view. An asphalt track encircled the field's sidelines and extended around the goal posts. The facility, unfenced and flanked with low benches, stirred memories. The lush field invited him, and the dry breeze wasn't unpleasant.

Jesse and Cora discussed stopping for an ice cream. Guthrie asked to be let out at the athletic field. He'd watch the youngsters working out on the track then walk the half-mile home. Jesse stopped the Chevy and raised his hand in a silent see-you-later gesture.

Guthrie stepped out and put his hand on his mom's elbow.

She patted his hand. "I'm glad you were with us, dear."

4

Guthrie watched the car move away then walked to the bleachers. Four high school boys rounded the dirt track, too distant to be logged into their proper family trees. They did more shoving than running and traveled at a slow-mile pace. He satisfied himself he had three of the runners' ancestries properly matched, but the handle for the remaining maverick escaped him.

At the fourth row, he picked up a breeze and turned to seat himself. A small boy thirty feet away on the track caught his attention. The kid glanced toward him, but avoided his effort at eye contact. Guthrie sat, unsnapped his starched shirt pocket, and from its tight quarters, made a two-fingered scissors maneuver to retrieve his tobacco sack.

The youngster limped badly on his right foot, walked on his toes like he had a tender heal. He did not, however, allow it to slow him. Industrious as an ant, he moved hurdles from the field's sideline onto the track.

Guthrie had a good view of the sun nearing a rest on the horizon, and off to the southeast, distant shadows traveled to the far reaches of Wild Mule Canyon. Somewhere out beyond the edge of town, a coyote yapped, and a chorus of town-mutts responded.

The high school boys made minute adjustments to the hurdles, straightened some and checked the number of steps between each. They tousled the youngster's mop of brown hair and thumped his ears. In general, they made him aware of the great privilege he enjoyed by being allowed in their company. Having positioned everything to meet their approval, they spoke to Guthrie, two called him by name. The four stripped to running shorts.

One of the boys motioned with his head to the kid. "You gonna give us a start, Flap?"

"Yep."

"How? You gonna count?" asked another.

"Nope, I'll wham with that old broken bat down there. I'll go ready-set-wham. Okay?"

Guthrie fetched the indicated broken bat and handed it to Flap. "I don't think we met. I'm Guthrie Sawyer."

"Hidy." Flap moved away, obviously unable to afford time for a grown-up while in the presence of teenagers. He turned to the high school boys' chatter.

The tallest of the four youths sat on the first row and

retied his sneakers. "I'll raise my hand when we're ready."

The hurdlers walked thirty yards down the track and stretched, took practice starts. Guthrie followed the kid to the starting end of the bleachers. He'd earned glory here as a miler, but none of these guys remembered that far back. What would they have been, third or fourth graders?

"Who'll win, Flap?"

The kid pointed. "Alfred."

"Alfred." Guthrie awkwardly tried to identify the chosen lad by aiming along the pointing finger.

"Alfred." Flap said it slowly, like he trained a pup. "The far one. He's faster'n greased lightning."

"Hey, I told you my name, but you've been sorta close lipped. What's your full handle?"

The boy looked Guthrie over like he might be a refugee from a UFO. "Well, they know you. Guess you ain't no stranger."

"Don't talk to strangers?"

"Maybe here. Not home. I'm John Robert Walker, but you can call me Flap."

It couldn't be! Could it? Well, maybe. It'd been about that long. Boy! That'd make a fellow grab for leather. "Where's home?"

"F-l-a-p!"

"Ready? Set." Flap walloped the bat on the seat with a loud bang. His eyes sparkled, and his face matched the setting sun's brightness. Wheeling to watch his heroes, his last word barely carried. "Houston."

It was true! He was Erilee's boy. The racers cleared the first hurdle as Guthrie mired in memories. Yeah, the age tallied. He graduated high school the week she had the boy a little more than seven years ago. A year older than Guthrie, she'd married that blamed Lane Walker, and they'd moved to Houston.

Flap ran to the track swinging his stiff foot in an arc and pumping his fists through the air. Guthrie cringed at the peculiar slapping sound accompanying each of the boy's steps. No doubt about how he earned his nickname. The kid bent with hands on his knees and watched Alfred cross the finish line a few steps in front.

Keeping his gaze off Erilee's boy proved hard. Part of what he saw on that face you'd expect to see plastered on the window of an ice cream store or looking at a litter of pups. Longing might describe it, but more. A touch of worship flitted there. Flap added a third ingredient. A look not unlike what you might see around the chutes when a hundred-and-fifty pound cowboy made the last tug on his John B's brim and eased to the back of two-thousand pounds of death dealing hurt. Rodeo promoters and pulp paper writers tagged it determination.

Whatever words used, what he saw on the boy's face jolted Guthrie worse than a stiff-legged bronc. The sadness of the moment squeezed him like a flank girth. What could tear at your innards more than a crippled kid pushing so hard to run? A child, a mere baby, but there he stood, telling the world without words that fact was not fact, the impossible, possible.

The plains' sun would set there in the west. Shadows might deepen in Wild Mule Canyon, but here in Saddle Horn, a much larger drama unfolded. The heroics of others faded from this six-man football field. The curtain raised on the courage and scope of a seven-year old.

Guthrie stepped back to the stands and sat on the first row. He made a smoke and watched the older ones ignore the kid. Something about Flap reminded him of Erilee. Probably that air of independence. Whatever, the memory of her excited him. She'd taught him smart cowboys didn't ride off into the sunset, girls weren't always fragile, and ultimately, that lonely fostered a lot of stupidity and battled time on even terms.

The four teenagers piled into an old truck and drove away. Flap walked among the L-shaped hurdles flipping them over so they were no longer upright, but still presented an obstacle a few inches in height.

"Need help?"

"I got 'em."

"Okay if I watch?"

"Suit yourself."

Flap tipped over the last hurdle and limped to the starting line. He faced Guthrie. "Drop your hand and say, go."

Guthrie held his arm high and complied. "Go!"

Flap's face adopted a killer's look. He shuffled down the track, cleared the first over-turned hurdle, and let out a shout of approval. A fall and two stumbles later, he cleared the last obstacle. From his knees, he threw both clenched fists skyward. "Yeah!"

Guthrie didn't remember standing, but found himself on his feet hollering whoopee. His hat drifted ground-ward not far from Flap.

The kid grinned.

"You done good."

"I'll do better. I'm going to run in the Olympics. There's an operation for this foot, you know."

"No, I didn't know. That's good. I'll be rooting for you." He stepped from the bleachers. "You through?"

"Yeah, once I get these hurdles up. Yonder comes Mom."

Guthrie lent a hand. "Yawl still live in Houston?"

"Dad does. Me and Mom are gonna live with Grandma Kramp and help her awhile."

Guthrie stored the last hurdle. A car's tires crunched gravel behind him. He turned then tried to swallow his heart, hoping to not make a fool of himself. At sight of her, he knew it was hopeless. If he opened his mouth, whatever came out would be sophomoric.

She still had that year of age on him, and having a baby added a maturity that all the broncs in Texas failed to provide. She'd always affected him that way, gave him a sense of being laughed at. Funny how some women could butter a fellow up like pancakes and never receive the time of day in return. Others, gals like Lee, sometimes made him feel a fool, and he always kept coming back. Maybe it had something to do with wanting the hard to get. Lord! She was beautiful.

She beamed. "Guthrie!"

37

"Lee." It wasn't much, but at least she'd know he wasn't brain-dead. He walked to the car's door, opened it, and held out his hands.

She hesitated, seemed uncertain. "I didn't think you were around anymore."

"I'm not. Get out. Let me look at you."

Lee stepped from the car. Her straight, brown hair hung shoulder length, shorter than he remembered. The wind blew it back from her face. There'd been a time when she pulled it forward more, achieving that sultry look of the heroines in the Friday night movies.

He sank in the whirlpool of her gray-green eyes, pulled under, powerless. She moved toward him, took his hands, then stood leaning back from him. He began to understand Jesse more every second.

Her nearness unlocked hidden corridors of his mind, released odors of chalk, high school gyms, and chemistry labs—released them to drift and swirl in his mind, blend with her perfume and the pungent aroma of sweat from aroused, back-seat bodies. He felt the light kiss of his last football game's powdery snow on his face and, from later that same night, tasted the salt of her tears when she told him she carried another's baby.

And now this woman was married to the father of that child. He gave a slight pull, almost unconsciously, and suddenly, she was in his arms. Her head rested on his shoulder, her body pressed against him. Maybe, old Lane didn't have a gun.

Guthrie squeezed her, rested his face against her hair, and then glimpsed Flap's sullen expression. Instantly, he moved back, caught Lee's eye, and nodded toward the boy.

Concern crossed her face, and she turned toward her son. She brushed her skirt. "Y'all've met, I see. John Robert, Guthrie and I are old friends. We went to school together. He ran track."

John Robert looked straight ahead, his expression unchanged.

5

"Johnny? Did you hear what I said? Guthrie won district in the mile."

"Well, whoop-de-do!" Flap flashed Guthrie a jaundiced look. "My dad played football for Childress. They played eleven-man ball. You hicks played six-man."

"That's right."

"You know my daddy?"

"Yeah, I met him. He was a little older'n me."

"Still is."

"J-o-h-n-n-y!"

Guthrie caught Lee's eye and shook his head before she continued.

Lee bent forward, face to face with the boy. "How about it? You ready for that hamburger?" She looked from Flap to Guthrie. "I promised him a Dairy-Do treat. You afoot?"

"Uh-huh, Jesse and Mom dropped me off. We'd been out to the cemetery. Matter of fact, I think they were stopping by the Dairy-Do themselves, but I'll just hoof it."

"Hop in. We'll give you a lift."

"Maybe not. I don't think John Robert's too keen on it, and I don't want to lose a pal."

"Nonsense! Get in. You don't mind do you, Johnny?" She gave the boy a hard look.

"Suit yourself."

Lee held her seat forward. Guthrie squirmed into the back.

He propped a boot on his knee and studied mother and son. Her earlier expression of reprimand washed away as soon as it served its purpose. Sincere interest replaced it. She obviously reveled in the boy. "How'd you do?"

"Got over every one. Only fell once. Guthrie threw his hat in the air."

"All right." She motioned thumbs-up.

Guthrie caught her eye in the mirror. "He'll get the job done."

Lee pulled to the drive-in window and ordered John Robert's burger and ice cream. Again the mirror served as go between, this time she caught his eye. "Coke?"

"Sure," he passed her a dollar. He had change, but getting into that front pocket while sitting offered a challenge.

From several inches and a glass pane away, Jesse stared into Guthrie's eyes. He and Cora sat with Mr. Hefner. The older man wiped at mustard on his chin, and Cora nibbled the last of a cone. His dad's eyes

40

darted from Guthrie to the front seat. He leaned back, grinned, and hooked a thumb indicating that Cora should look their direction.

His mom's eyes widened. Her glance turned toward the driver.

"Hello, Mrs. Sawyer," Lee mouthed aloud through the glass.

Cora smiled, looked past Lee at Flap. She raised her hand and wiggled her fingers.

Lee received the order, waved bye to his family, and pulled away.

Guthrie held John Robert's cream while the boy did a number on the burger and coke. "Do I get lick'ums?"

"Don't you touch it."

"You better hurry, then, Lee. We got a major melt-down going on here."

"I'll stop at Mama's."

At her mother's, she relieved Guthrie of the cone and shooed John Robert toward the back door.

Guthrie walked to a front yard hydrant, rinsed, then slung his hands dry. From inside came sounds of Flap bragging to his grandmother of his exploits at the track. Daylight faded quickly.

A porch swing hung from the pipe frame of an old swing set. He tugged at its chains and pressed weight on the seat with his hands. Satisfied, he sat and rolled a smoke more by feel than sight. Streetlights cast shadows along the main residential thoroughfare of Saddle Horn. Jesse and Cora drove by. Home was two blocks down. For a moment, his memory carried him back to a time when, like Flap, he knew the impossible created only a temporary inconvenience and the pain of Jesse's escapades played second fiddle to his own hijinks.

Erilee joined him. Her perfume told him she paid him the compliment of freshening up. "Guthrie, it's so good to see you. What's it been?"

"Seven years and eight days."

Silence followed his words. Her eyes closed, and her lips moved. She smiled. "You ought to be an accountant. I had no idea you were so thorough."

"Ain't generally. Most the time, I'm lucky to know what season we're in. Somehow, that little detail just stuck."

"I'm flattered. How are Cora and Jesse?"

"Fine, fine. Is Mrs. Kramp ill?"

Lee's eyes telegraphed her pain. "She's got leukemia. Maybe a year, year and a-half left. I thought when we lost Daddy three years ago, we'd suffered enough."

Guthrie took her hand. "I'm sorry." He leaned back. The evening star presented a solitary front to the ever-darkening sky. He toed the swing into noisy motion. A streetlight several houses down offered faint illumination. "So you're just here to see her through this then back to Houston?" He tried to keep the anxiety, the hurt, out of his voice.

"No, Lane and I are through. I won't be going back to Houston. I've a job teaching here this fall." She stared through the dim light, her head cocked to one side.

No question about it, he could clear the twelve miles

across Wild Mule Canyon in one easy hop. He had to be careful here. All these emotions were for a memory, a puppy-love romance mixed with the security of childhood, the hormones of adolescence, and the thrill of discovery. He didn't know this woman beside him, and she didn't know him. One thing though, he was a quick mixer.

She watched him. "Guthrie, right at the moment, I need a friend. Will you be my friend?"

He stood, paced a few steps back and forth, and then rolled another smoke. "Boy, you know how to make it tough, don't you?"

"Can I have that?" She pointed to the cigarette.

He handed it to her and manufactured another, then lit both off one match. "I don't think I can limit myself to friendship with you, Lee. Seems to me, I tried that road already. Got ten years of friendship—seven of it in absentee—and old Lane got you.

"You were the friend who made eternal, jungle nights longer in Vietnam. Every time I eat a face full of arena dirt, my friend's memory shows up laughing at me. You can't imagine how many boring parties I've escorted my friend to in the last seven years. No, no, I'm through being friends. It just won't cut it anymore."

"I'm serious, Guthrie. You haven't been exactly out of my mind all these years, but I've been through a rough time. It doesn't take the brightest gal on the block to see I'm in no condition to jump out of one fire into another."

Guthrie took her hands, and she stood before him, her

43

face barely visible. He smiled. "I guess for me you'll always be chickens one minute, feathers the next. Get your lipstick, and I'll buy you a beer. If you're real friendly, maybe I can get Sammy to play you a tune out at Rita's."

The Budweiser clock over the door to the hallway at the Wreck Room said nine forty-five when they arrived. Guthrie and Lee made the seventh and eighth customers sharing the momentary exit from reality. He held up two fingers to the bar man, mouthed the word Pearl, and seated Lee at a table near the small bandstand.

The music at Rita's came from Sam. No one knew his source. On a good night it would make you cry, laugh, and wish you weren't so sinful. Sam plucked his guitar, rode his bicycle, and talked only with great difficulty. It took him a minute or so to speak a short sentence, but when he sang, his voice rang snow-bank pure and flowed smooth as a mountain stream. Sam, his talent, and his handicap had shared forty-five years.

Rita met Guthrie's eye, took the beers from Abe, then brought the brews and a bowl of yesterday's popcorn to their table. "Hi, Cowboy. Erilee, I heard you were back. How's your mama?"

"Scared, otherwise almost normal. Thanks for asking."

When Sam wasn't picking, he smiled a lot. Music was a serious matter. He made music now, but smiled when he saw Guthrie.

"Sam, my man." He shook his fist at the musician and laughed.

44

Sam stopped playing and shook his own finger. "Pa . . . duc . . . uh." He nodded rapidly.

"Guthrie, Sammy. Guthrie!"

"Just . . . down . . . the road." Sammy slapped his knee and his thin body shook with laughter. When the musician laughed, bystanders forgot his pocked complexion, bad teeth, and that big nose. Hell, some forgot the drought.

Guthrie motioned at Erilee. "You remember Lee?"

"Mem . . . ber Francis." Sam's big grin covered most of his face. He cradled his guitar and returned to Harbor Lights. The grin faded into a look of reverence.

"Francis?" Lee raised an eyebrow then her beer.

Guthrie smiled. "Sammy lives pretty much in the past. You'll notice most of his music is from the forties and fifties. I could be guilty of a Francis or two, but I think that's just his way of getting me in trouble. About the time you think you've figured him out, he'll throw you a curve.

"Tell me about John Robert. He said his foot was operable."

"It is. We'd planned it for last April. The week before, Lane and Ira had a falling out. Since his granddaddy supported us, John Robert was the loser."

"Expensive?"

"Yes, and a matter of priority. Since then, I'm afraid, Lane's had other priorities."

"Huh!" Guthrie put rubbery popcorn in his mouth, watched Rita and Abe for an opportunity to get rid of it, then spit it into a paper napkin and threw it into a

45

nearby wastebasket.

Jesse stuck his head in the door. He made his way toward their table. From the hitch in his get-a-long, he must have been frequenting the pickup. "I told Cora, I bet yawl were out here. Abe," He looked back down to Guthrie. "What yawl drinking?" He checked their bottles. "Bring us three Pearls.

"Erilee, it's good to see you, honey. I'm sorry to hear about Evelyn's sickness. Cora just found out about it at the beauty shop yesterday." Jesse sat opposite Guthrie, next to Lee. He placed his hat on back of the empty fourth chair.

"Good to see you, Mr. Sawyer. Yes, she just learned for sure a week ago Monday. Is Cora not with you?"

"No, she's tired. Today would have been our first one's birthday. The cemetery's always tiring for her. But it's Jesse, Erilee, Jesse. My daddy was Mr. Sawyer. Just call me Jesse and him old Guthrie, but do it loud when dinners on the table. Right, Son?"

"You're right." Out of the corner of his eye Guthrie caught a glimpse of Rita bringing the beer. First one, our little girl, the baby. Why couldn't he honor her by using her name? Why wasn't he home where he belonged?

Sitting the beers down, Rita picked up an empty and put her hand on his dad's shoulder. "Howdy, Jesse."

"Rita." He shook a Lucky from his pack with an unsteady hand. Two extra cigarettes fell to the table and rolled into beer bottle condensation. He aimed then tossed them toward a spittoon near the bar. He missed.

Sammy hit an outcropping of musical pay dirt and earnestly picked the vein toward the mother lode. Conversation hushed.

Lee smiled, caught Guthrie's eye, and then exaggerated her expression telling him to loosen up and not be so serious. He grinned like a clown, and she chuckled. Didn't she know serious was spelled J-e-s-s-e? But, what was going on with the old man? He'd hit the bottle all Guthrie's life, but with few exceptions, he'd stayed on top. Tonight, he'd lost both stirrups and scratched leather with every move.

"Lee, let's dance." Surely, he wouldn't follow them out there.

"I'd love to. Excuse us, Mr. uh, Jesse."

"Yawl go ahead. Don't blame you. Have fun." He mumbled something about indoor hats, picked up his, and with his beer in the other hand, joined Bud and a cattle hauler named Billy Odom.

The Wreck Room dance floor would accommodate three or four sober couples or a truckload of Rita's clients. Tonight, Guthrie and Lee had it to themselves. She put the side of her forehead to his cheek, her free hand on his shoulder, and allowed him to pull her close. He guided her across the floor, and Sammy's music carried them to thirty thousand feet above the badlands of New Mexico.

For the first time in seven years, with Lee in his arms, Saddle Horn seemed like home. Guthrie relaxed, let the music's rhythm control his moves. He treaded water and marked time in the warm pool of Lee's nearness

47

and Sam's artistry. This was the only girl who ever meant anything to him. No need for words. The bicyclist's music and the song did the talking.

Sam mentioned familiar scenes and a jealous cowboy, a cowboy who used a gun to kill another then had to run. At that point, Guthrie took note of the snug way that pelvis bone worked against his right pocket. It seemed to hunger for closeness. He had an answer for that, but everyone in the joint watched.

You might figure old Sammy would pick a song that ended when the dance was just beginning. The music stopped, and there they stood. The beer drinkers clapped modestly, and they held tighter. At the moment, the present offered too much to worry about that other time out in that West Texas town of El Paso.

6

Jesse handed Guthrie two Luckies on the way to the table then followed with three fresh beers. The ex-cowboy, ex-animal doctor, looked at Lee and winked. "I worked him pretty good this evening, but he didn't miss a step, huh?"

"If I remember, he's hard to beat at most things, Jesse. I think he's got a few moves left."

"Dancing and riding are two of them, huh?" Jesse laughed.

Guthrie finished off the beer he'd left at the table and started on the fresh one. Lee, the dance, the beer, or likely all three, worked to mellow him. Even the Old

Man acted better. "Jesse, that song of Sammy's ever give you the creeps? Make you wonder if death's waiting, like it says, out in El Paso?"

The beer's label seemed to fascinate Jesse. Guthrie wished he had the question back. "Naw, Son, you don't have to worry about that. It don't wait. When it's ready, it'll come after you." The fun vanished from the older man's face and bitterness replaced it.

"Jesse, ain't you tired? Go home. It's near eleven o'clock."

He tilted his beer instead of answering, drained half the bottle, then set it down. He looked at Guthrie. "Cora's the one tired. It's the little girl's birthday, it would be . . . You know." He let his chin drop and stared at the table's red-squared oilcloth.

Lee looked confused.

Guthrie sensed his morning anger returning. The day started with a sleep-around dad, progressed to an offer of friendship from a woman he'd had on his mind ten years, and now it looked like he'd spend the rest of the night getting his old man to bed.

He lowered his head, tilted his face even with his dad. "Christina, Jesse, her name's Christina." He brought his fist down on the table, harder than he intended. "She was your daughter. Why don't you just use her name? Christina!"

Jesse hadn't raised his head, but rolled his eyes upward to lock on Guthrie. They were close—inches apart.

Jesse's palm rocketed toward Guthrie's face. No

problem, he'd just dodge. The old man couldn't be that fast, especially after all he'd drank. The hand wasn't just huge, it was shod-hoof hard. Guthrie's nose crunched, his eyes closed, and the inside of his lips compressed around his teeth. He tasted blood, and his tongue hurt.

Somehow things had geared to low and were happening slow, like that car wreck in Cheyenne. He saw all the bad stuff, but couldn't change it. He'd been wrong about his Dad's quickness, terrible wrong. The old legend must've been all they said. The dance floor became the shuffleboard, his back its puck. His head hit the raised portion of the bandstand. His vision blurred.

Lee screamed, "Guthrie."

Fog dimmed his vision. Sam's music stopped. Through the haze he watched Lee shove Jesse, saw him struggling to get out of his chair then fall, rise, and grow larger coming his way. To one side, Rita talked into the phone, shock on her face.

He tried to get to his feet, but Jesse's shoulder hit him in the chest. He staggered backwards, stumbled into something. Sammy grunted. The musician disappeared somewhere beneath the pile. Jesse grappled for Guthrie who struggled to rise.

He stood, grasped Sam's arms, and pulled him erect. Jesse looked up from his stance on his hands and knees, the anger on his face now replaced with anxiety.

Sam's face displayed terror. Guthrie put a hand to his own head, wanted to cry for the simple man before him. "You all right, Sammy? Talk to me, man, are you okay?" He patted the musician's back.

A universe of confusion apparently separated Sam from speech. He put his arms around Guthrie, released him, then turned to Jesse and patted him. He helped the old fireball to his feet.

Jesse stooped with his hands on his knees looking from Guthrie to Sam. "What do you think, Guth? Reckon he's okay?"

"I don't know. Where's his guitar?"

"Over there, over there in the hallway. I see it." Jesse once again was light and quick. He handed the instrument to Sam.

Sunshine broke through the clouds on Sammy's face. He stroked the guitar. Jesse's forehead almost touched Sam's. They both looked down.

"Try it. Hit the strings. See if she'll chord. If they's anything broke, I'll buy you a new one." Jesse helped Sammy to a table near the stricken Lee. He brushed Sammy's shoulders then straightened. Guthrie held the musician's chair. He stood and wondered about Rita's call.

Jesse tackled him shoulder high, but this time Guthrie wasn't totally surprised. He'd recognized the taking care of Sammy as being only a lull in Jesse's rage, not the end. He went down under his dad's weight, got his feet into position, then kicked him up and over. Jesse landed on the bandstand with his head through a speaker box.

"Jesse! Y'all take that outside." Rita needed no phone, now.

Guthrie sprang for his back and tried to apply a half nelson, lost it, then the hammerlock that followed. Like a bull, Jesse broke every hold. The older man struggled to all fours then swung a fist. The blow caught Guthrie's shoulder and sent him reeling.

A chair tangled between his legs. He rolled to his feet, doubled his fists, and shuffled toward his father.

"Don't do it, Guthrie. Don't hit him. You'll regret it the rest of your days." Bud stood a few feet away.

Guthrie leaned forward, both fists swinging at arm length like pendulums. "Tell him that!"

"He's beyond talking to. Wrestle him if you want. When you two give out, holler, and we'll help you get him home."

"To hell with him. I don't care if he ever gets home."

Jesse lunged again and caught him in a bear hug. Guthrie's back met the floor. He got an arm around the older man's neck. Someway, he had to stay close, prevent him having room to use his fists. Jesse's arms moved to Guthrie's waist and applied pressure. Breathing became difficult. What'd Bud say, holler? What a deal, a lot of help he was. Things slowly swirled, darkened, he was sinking.

A steam engine blasted, and Jesse became a snowman. Frost covered the floor. The world turned white. Another sharp hiss sounded, and Jesse released him, scrambling to get out of the blizzard. Guthrie rolled to a sitting position, spread his arms wide and balanced with his palms on the floor. He shook his head, tried to see through the storm. His mom drifted on a cloud that seemingly moved across the dance floor. She carried Rita's big fire extinguisher tucked under her left arm, and her right hand swung its nozzle.

Guthrie had been flogged by nesting hens and gored by raging mother cows, but he'd never seen anything female this mad before. Lee stood a step behind Cora. She didn't look too friendly herself. If his mom became contagious, it would be a long hard night.

Cora spoke, but her lips remained in a straight line. "Look at you! If you two aren't a sight! Erilee, take a good look."

Jesse stumbled and clawed his way from hibernation. He raised to his knees. "Cora, let's go home. Or'ta be about time for the weather." He headed for the door speaking over his shoulder. "If they's any damages, see Guthrie."

Cora motioned at Bud. "Would you drive his pickup? I'll bring you back."

Jesse stopped and started to say something, but looked at Cora then handed Bud his keys.

Rita moved to the other side of the bar. "You're a good woman, Cora. He's lucky to have you." Her voice had dropped the purring quality and picked up a touch of honey.

"Oh, shut up, Rita! Why don't you go find a razor blade to slide down? Yeah, then maybe follow it up with a cool alcohol rinse." Cora's eyes blazed. She looked at Guthrie. "You want breakfast in the morning?"

He rubbed the top of his head. "No, thanks."

Bud took the fire extinguisher and hung it back on its hook. He waited for Cora. "Sammy, how about a few lines of 'When Old Shep Was a Pup' for this cheery group?" He closed the door behind he and Cora.

Rita came from behind the bar. Sammy picked the guitar, got through the line of when he "was a lad". Guthrie took a deep breath, caught Lee's stare, and realized he'd only reached the eye of the storm.

The door swung open. Cora strode purposeful toward Rita. The Wreck Room's mistress smiled and lit a cigarette. The gentle lady who used to sing him lullabies brought her fist overhead in a long, swinging, downward arc. The blow caught Rita flush on the nose. Her lighter went one way, the cigarette another. She took a step backward then sat between two stools. Her arms dangled one over each seat.

"Slut!" Cora turned and walked back through the door.

"C'mon." Lee had him by the arm. She held her other hand out, palm upward. "Gimme the keys."

"What're you talking about? I ain't had but four." Bottle caps and gravel crunched underfoot.

"I'm not sure you're safe sipping tea and sucking lemons. Gimme the blasted keys."

He handed them to her. What a day! Moments later, in the Chevy, he fought to keep from kissing the dash when Lee found reverse. The station wagon hurtled across the parking lot. She straightened him with the brakes then, swinging out of the lot, put him into an even more intimate relationship with the door. Gravel strafed parked cars behind them. Tires met the blacktop and squealed in an arch across the road before the car rocketed to a steady blast-off for Saddle Horn.

Bright lights blinded Guthrie. An oil truck shot past like a comet—barely missed them. Its air horns wailed, sounding near death defiantly.

"Stop down there at Blake's Texaco. Gonna clean up." Maybe if he stalled, bought a little time, they could talk this thing out. Silence louder than the horn's blast continued to the station. Lee pulled to a stop near the pumps, under the awning.

Guthrie tried the side restroom door, found it locked, then returned to the water hose between the pumps. He pushed the hose valve. Nothing. The hose connected to a hydrant a few inches above ground level. He opened it then bent the valve and directed water to his face. Completing his chore, he secured the water, and slinging his hands, searched for paper towels. No luck. He dried on his handkerchief.

He placed his hands on his hips, kicked gravel. His view dropped to the toe of his boots. "About tonight. Sorry. It started good, but guess it sorta fizzled there at the end, huh?"

Lee studied him through the car's open window. "How could you be so insensitive? Couldn't you see the pain on Jesse's face?"

He raised his hands, palms up, started to speak. He didn't remember hearing any pain in the Old Man's voice at Rita's this morning. "I. . . ."

"I'm sure you saw some tough times in Vietnam, but

you aren't the only one. I've seen enough stupid drunks for a dozen lifetimes." Erilee threw the car door open then jumped to her feet.

Guthrie took a step backward.

She stepped toward him. "You got any idea how big cockroaches get in Houston?"

"Cockroaches? No, no!" What did a cockroach's size have to do with anything?

"Well, let me tell you, they get big." She held her hands a foot apart.

He started to challenge her dimensions, but decided things were nuclear enough without it.

Lee dropped her hands then raised the left, palm down, to shoulder high. "Okay, you put drunks here, cockroaches here," She used the other hand and made a lower step. "Then you put cowboys along about here." She bent and repositioned her hand from the drunk's level to knee level for cowboys.

Guthrie started forward, thought better, and backed off a bit more. He raised his hand above his head. "Guess bankers and wealthy cow folks like the Walkers go up here, do they?"

Lee's shoulders shook. A sob broke from between her hands covering her face, and she turned and lurched for the car. She sat then burst into more tears.

Guthrie followed, bent, stuck his right arm through the window, and patted her shoulder. He reached with his left hand to touch her cheek.

She intercepted it, slung it away.

His knuckles banged against the side mirror, hurt. He

56

grabbed the hand and held it slightly above the knees, between his legs while massaging the injury and silently reciting a choice list of profanity. He shuffled straddle legged around the rear of the car to the other door and got in.

Lee drove slowly to her mother's. She was out before he could open her car door, but stood waiting. He walked beside her. On the porch, she stood with the screen half-ajar, the lock undone, but the door closed.

Did she invite him closer? He moved toward her.

She extended her right hand and shook his with a finality he could only associate with preachers and gravesites. Looked like the Sawyers' brawling had made his last chapter with Erilee Kramp the shortest.

He slept in the station wagon parked in front of his folks' house. He stripped to his shorts and lay on his sleeping bag glad the night had cooled. A breeze stirred enough to keep the mosquitoes at bay.

It seemed he'd slept only a couple of minutes when pounding on the top of the Chevy woke him. He made out Jesse's form against an awakening eastern sky. Guthrie rubbed his eyes, fought his hair. "What do you want?"

"Buy you a cup."

What? "I don't—you ain't eating breakfast here?"

"Don't seem too good an idea."

"Yeah, I'll catch you. Where you going?"

"Alvin's, see you there."

Guthrie tiptoed to the front bathroom. He came out a

few minutes later, groomed, awake, and revived. It'd been a short night, but he required little sleep. He angled the Chevy into the concrete walk in front of Alvin's and parked beside the Dodge. Mounting the high sidewalk with a braced arm on his raised knee, a half-stifled groan escaped.

Inside he straddled a stool beside Jesse. "Morning, Alvin."

"Guthrie. Breakfast?" The café man sat a steaming mug on the counter. "Take it black, don't you?"

"Just coffee. Yeah, this is fine. How come them old founders raised that sidewalk up so? They must have known they'uz in no danger of high water in this country."

Expression washed from the big man's face. He turned to his grill. "Never gave it no thought." He brought Jesse bacon and eggs. "More coffee?"

"If you got plenty."

"What kind of answer is that? If I got plenty! It's my business to have plenty."

"Just habit, Alvin. Don't talk so loud. My ears are sore. Guthrie, when these stores were put in, they wanted that sidewalk wagon-bed high. It'uz their dock as well as a place to walk."

The old man still had all the answers. "Jesse, about last night—"

"Let last night sleep. Anybody out of line, it'uz me. Far as the scuffling's concerned, wal, fighting's like a spring laxative. It cleanses a body up pretty good and gets rid of a lot of meanness."

Alvin scraped grease and bacon bits from his stove with something akin to a putty knife. "Guthrie, you seen Sammy? He's asking about you the other day."

"Last night. He's still got the gift."

"Uh-huh. See his new bike?"

"Naw, has he got a new bike?"

"Yeah, your dad went around passing the hat and making us all feel guilty till we coughed up enough to get it. You talk about proud."

Guthrie looked at his dad who sopped the last of the over-easy from his plate. Jesse Sawyer, a man as unpredictable as Panhandle weather. "Tell Mom love, and I'll see yawl in a few weeks."

"Abilene?"

"Yeah, then San Angelo. Maybe El Paso." Guthrie reached for change.

His dad shook his head and made an I-got-it motion. "Was Erilee mad?"

Guthrie turned at the door, wagged his head, then nodded and laughed a mirthless chuckle.

Jesse put money on the table. "For that, I'm truly sorry."

"Yeah, me, too." He shut the door then heard Jesse call. He waited by his station wagon until the old man came out.

Jesse lit his Lucky. "Son, remember, don't be afraid to skip a show if their pick-up men don't suit you."

Guthrie lit his fashioned smoke. "Thanks." He turned into the sun at the state highway and from the corner of his eye glimpsed Jesse still standing in the middle of the high sidewalk. Guthrie raised his hand above the top of the old fifty-seven.

7

Guthrie flipped down the station wagon's visor. The sun lingered low and the shade covered his eyes only when going down a grade. After a half-mile, he returned the visor to its up position and tilted his hat brim. In his rearview mirror, Saddle Horn's water tower marked the town's location. The buildings dropped from sight behind rolling hills.

The two-lane blacktop skirted the rim of Wild Mule Canyon providing an unobstructed view of miles of broken country, long cool shadows, and a maze of potential hideaways. He'd chased cattle over nearly every foot of the canyon, but still its sight stirred him deeply. Ex-President Johnson could have the limestone outcroppings and rugged terrain of the Central Texas Hill Country, but for his own rejuvenation, he'd take this raw, ragged, and razor sharp Cap Rock escarpment along the foot of the Panhandle.

Abandoning the canyon, his route turned south and stretched straight ahead through rolling grassland. In the distance, the road narrowed. Fence lines on either side merged to a single point, and the horizon devoured both. Beyond the roadway, pastures wore summer's khaki. Patches of powder blue sage clumped, motionless, awaiting the morning breeze for movement. Maverick thoughts accompanied him. He rode the ridges, drug the valleys of his mind rounding up yesterday's events and the disaster of his evening with Lee.

If Jesse had just stayed home, everything would have been fine. Initially, Lee seemed more than glad to see him, and the good Lord knew she made his day. How a woman could have a baby and still look that good was a mystery. Easy to imagine how she tired of honky-tonks and brawls living with old Lane.

And that Flap. What a cutter! The boy deserved a better dad. Well, next time would be different. He'd see to that. He'd failed to make the ante last night, sort of ducked his tail and faded away, but next time, he'd see to it that the only Sawyer she had to put up with was his truly, and he'd practice his best behavior.

He pushed the speed-o-meter to eighty-five. It was a good bet that old Flint would be in Abilene. Flint Payne hailed from Cloudy, South Dakota, rode bulls, loved life, and held up his part of whatever chore needed doing. He could make a party out of lancing a boil and go a week without sleep.

A year ago, in Cheyenne, he broke his arm in the morning and scored winning numbers on a bull that night. He combined fun and courage to the point of stupidity. And handsome? Both women and men flocked around him. Guthrie and the bull rider joined up for eight or ten of the same shows every year, and when they did, one was usually not far from the other.

Guthrie located day-old coffee and donuts in the back of the Chevy. Disregarding taste, freshness, and temperature, he pushed them down for a short breakfast.

Later, he ate chicken fried steak in Stamford, Texas then shortly before noon, spotted the sprawling city of Abilene. Miles beyond the town, Buffalo Gap's low range of hills wavered above shimmering mirages.

A Texas happening. A city where space presented no problem. If it had sprouted in New England, it would, no doubt, cover a tenth the area and have been built upward. It owed its birth to the railroad, its sustenance to livestock and oil, and any national notoriety it might enjoy to the air force. Unsure if it should be labeled city or town, Guthrie still liked it. A moment later, he passed the population sign saying 101,000 and decided it ranked the higher brand.

He skirted the city and within minutes drove through the rodeo grounds' gate. The show opened in three days, but the sparse grass had already allowed the soil to be worked to a powder by both hoof and wheeled traffic. His tires stirred dust to drifting clouds. He parked in an area marked 'Contestants Only'.

Before him, high, fenced lots joined the arena's chutes by intersecting alleyways. Livestock milled within the pens. A small building marked 'Office' occupied a spot beyond the lots. Guthrie headed that direction. Halfway down the alley, Flint's familiar form perched atop an upper railing. His black hat tilted up, encircled by a narrow band around its crown. The binding secured a jaunty, pheasant feather.

Flint whittled without looking while his eyes roamed back and forth over about twenty penned bulls. They milled. Some ate at the hayrack while others jostled, tested the pecking order. Two, one dark and tiger-stripped, the other a dirty brown, squared off and pawed the ground. Their tongues hung from frothing mouths. Both showed the muscled and athletic bodies so characteristic of their Brahma genes. Low, rumbling bellows seemed to strain from deep within. Their sides heaved, and bulging eyes followed every move the other made. Both were huge, horned, and panting.

Guthrie tugged his hat tighter and mounted the fence beside Flint. He settled comfortably then hooked his heels on a rail and worked on a cigarette.

Flint made no sign of recognition. He continued his study of the brutes. "Fellar told me one time Hindus think Brahmas are the God of Creation."

"Come to think of it, I've heard some cowboys use a Holy word or two in describing them." Holding his rolled cigarette in one hand, Guthrie held the other toward Flint, palm up. "Them two getting hot, huh?"

Flint continued studying the bulls. A moment later he straightened a leg in the air, fished a clip of bills from his pocket, and placed a ten in the extended palm. "I'uz hurting that night or you'd never of got her. How was it?"

"Even bronc peelers get lucky sometime." Guthrie laughed. "You know chivalry don't allow us Westerners to discuss a lady with riff-raff."

"Was she really a cheerleader for the Chiefs?" The bull rider worked the roll back into his pocket. The wager had been placed a month earlier in Wichita, Kansas.

"Guess so. She was pretty active."

Flint's voice carried over the bawling bulls and penned roping calves. He directed it at a man wearing a sweat stained shirt and straw hat. The puncher had just shut a gate on some calves and now stood in the alley. "Willy, you got two in here getting pretty hot. Some old boy's gonna want 'em fresh when he draws 'em."

Guthrie climbed down to the alley. "You paid up?"

"Uh-huh, go ahead, there's got to be a pet in here some where, if I'un just find him. You ate?"

"At Stamford. Catch you later."

"There's a game over at the horse barn tonight."

Guthrie acknowledged the invitation with a blind wave.

One of the women in the office gave him directions to a laundry and dry cleaners. After taking care of that chore, he climbed to the highest shaded spot in the empty stands and stretched flat on a bench seat. He placed his hat out of harm's way and realized yesterday's digging had brought on a little soreness.

He awoke to a lowering sun and the sound of cutting-horse men working cattle in the arena. After a little eye rubbing and memory spurring, he figured out again this was Tuesday, and the first show didn't start until Thursday night. He sat up, stretched, and admired the animals' work.

Their manner seemed to fit the canine species more than the horse kingdom. Small and agile, each mount approached the herd of cattle with dainty, slow steps almost identical to a bird dog moving to a point. Once

64

a yearling had been selected, the horse turned sheep dog, nipping the beeves' flank, spinning, and dancing sideways, whatever the calf s action required.

Guthrie indulged himself a few more minutes with the ballet before him then stood and made his way to the station wagon. He retrieved a small bag and carried it to a dressing room under the bandstand where he changed to shorts and running shoes. Six miles later, he returned, showered, then found Flint tossing washers in the hall of the horse barn.

When they poured the concrete for the barn's hallway, some politically savvy city father, perhaps with a brother-in-law in the cement business, instructed the workers to sink two tin cans twenty-five feet apart in its center. The man no doubt hoped to propel himself into the mayor's chair with a reputation as a washer loving Good-Old-Boy.

At some point in his life, he must have wasted too much time as a student of the game he promoted because he'd certainly given little thought to construction engineering. The project, long on political savvy and short on practicality, proved his undoing in pork-belly-politics. The cans rusted away in the first couple of months, revealing to all that the depth of the concrete was less than any standard would allow.

The remaining holes had a tendency to fill with horse apples, filthy liquid, and straw. Properly cleaned, they served their purpose, though those using them probably never cast a vote. Someone had cleaned them before the current game. Smart money said it wasn't the dandy, Flint.

The bull rider faced Guthrie. "When do we draw?"

"Two-thirty tomorrow."

Outside the barn, a group pitched horseshoes. From the volume of their banter, they must have been passing a bottle. Flint manipulated washers between the fingers and thumb of his left hand, waiting his turn. His Indian cheekbones and hawk-like nose shadowed a thin mouth and chiseled chin. A glint of mischief flashed in his eyes, and his mouth slanted when he spoke. "Them boys getting rowdy."

"Pay it no mind. Some failed to receive the genteel upbringing of you reservation boys." Guthrie squatted, leaned against a stall.

"Uh-huh. They're passing a bottle, and it's dryer than an August corn shuck in here. Anything I hate, it's a drunk when I'm sober."

"And a sober man when you're drunk," Guthrie finished.

"Since you bring it up, White-Eyes, how about you and me driving over to Impact soon as I finish whipping up on this bunch?"

Guthrie stood, pulled a knife from his pocket, then knelt again. He opened the knife and carefully trimmed a fingernail. "You got a slick tongue. You're on. Maybe some barbecue over at Fred's, later?"

"What's Impact?" asked a line-backer-built member of the washer contest. He stood near the opposite target.

"Walt, is this your first visit to old Guthrie's great state?" Flint practiced hollow swings.

"It is, and I don't see I've missed much."

"Wal, I'm disappointed in the one thing you have missed. Abilene's dryer than preacher's spit. You wanna buy a bottle, you go to Impact."

Walt made his toss, a sinker. "Abilene, Abilene, dear old Abilene, right next to Impact, Texas." When not tossing washers, Walt bulldogged steers.

An hour later, the steer wrestler made his way from the middle of Flint's pickup and dodged half-buried, steel posts. Only knee high, the barriers stood in disarray outside the plate glass front of Roy's Liquor Store. Their various angles suggested foresight and Roy's understanding of the driving ability his customers. Scrapes, dents, and surrounding bits of broken glass testified to the accuracy of his vision.

Flint and Walt fought their tight pockets while Guthrie paid for the fifth of Old Grandad. They each handed him bills on their way to the pickup. Flint produced coke chasers from his cooler, and Walt held a quarter in front of Guthrie. "Flip you for that outside seat."

Guthrie lost the toss, and they loaded into the truck. Flint drove toward Abilene.

Walt took the first drink, made a face, and smacked his lips. "Barbecue, huh? I may learn to like Texas."

8

A clean horse blanket served for a table, saddle pads for seats, and the bear-like trucker's deck of cards completed their needs. Near identical, cream colored horses, most standing with their heads protruding over the half door to their stalls, served as an audience.

Guthrie motioned his head at the palominos. "Is that Vernon's Santa Rosa bunch?"

"Uh-huh." Flint took his eyes off the trucker's shuffle only long enough to glance at his own dwindling poke. A single light bulb illuminated the immediate area, and another brightened the barn's front. Walt's wristwatch showed twelve-thirty. The fifth of whiskey sat near the center of the blanket. It contained one last anemic swig. Three empty six packs of Pearl resting on the waste barrel's litter were all that remained of a second run to Impact. Time lumbered like a waterlogged heifer on a hot day.

Five antes started each hand. The big trucker preparing to deal was named Ben. The New Mexico calf roper answered to Slim. A casual look at the trucker's poke showed him to be winning. He wore dark shades and a dirty cap with a logo above the bill advertising "Ace Oil Filters". Earlier, he'd unloaded a herd of stringy looking Mexican steers then parked his rig not far from Guthrie's station wagon.

Walt burped loudly and grabbed his stomach. He staggered to his feet. "I don't feel so good. I'm gone." He bent to pick up his last dollar, staggered, then walked directly across the blanket, almost stepping on Guthrie. His grab for the dollar missed by a foot, but he never slowed, just continued toward the front of the barn.

Guthrie started to rise and lend Walt a hand, but Slim beat him to it. The roper seemed anxious to be helpful or at least away from the ante. He grabbed his meager stash and Walt's dollar. "I'll see him to his trailer." At the last moment, he avoided the handles of a wheelbarrow and continued after Walt.

The trucker touched fingertips to his mouth, adjusted his shades, and dealt three hands of five-card draw. Guthrie's five dollars represented the last of his third fifty-dollar allotment for the night's gambling. The hundred and fifty equaled three days of digging with Jesse or a few seconds of hell in a whirlwind aboard some hammerhead bronc. On a good day, it was "easy-come—easy-go", but on a good day, the lady with the fickle temperament smiled broadly.

Tonight, luck seemed subsidized, and the bad smell he'd picked up didn't come from the trash barrel. He raised a dollar, drew two black cards to replace the two red ones he turned in, then took a moment to focus. He made out the clumsy figure of a club and his hopes for a spade flush joined the night's other unfulfilled fantasies. Flint called the dollar, took one card, and looked like he'd been snake-bit. Ben called then raised a dollar and took one card. Guthrie folded, but the Dakotan stayed in.

Flint tossed his dollar at the pot. He flicked the edge of a card and looked at the big trucker. "Ain't them specs a little dark this time of night?"

The man reached a hand to the glasses. His thumbs were like clubs, large even for his bulk. "These? Oh, I went to the eye doctor yesterday, and he put those drops in, what do you call it di-o-late? Anyway, I've been having some headaches. Thought I might need glasses." He turned over three aces.

Flint motioned disgustedly for him to take the pot.

"What'd the doc say?" Guthrie asked. The man lied. He'd seen him park his rig before the game, and he wore no glasses.

"Said nothing was wrong a little sleep wouldn't cure. You boys 'scuse me. I gotta go over to that john and see a man about a dog. Be back directly." He struggled to his feet and toward the back of the barn.

Guthrie's eyes followed him. He walked with no stagger. His bulk occupied about half the hall. "That sons a bitch's done robbed us blind."

"I know. He's seeing something through them damn lenses you and I can't see." Flint stood, tilting slightly backward.

Guthrie asked, "You drunk?" He'd never seen four one-dollar bills so hard to straighten.

"Who?" Flint glanced up and down the hall then giggled.

"Bet he's got his grease or dye or whatever on the frame of those glasses." He gave up on the ones and crammed them in his billfold.

"Welcome to the party. What are we gonna do? He's too big to fight. I'd rather him have my money than me a murder rap." Flint walked up and down the hallway drifted from one wall to the next, steadying himself against one then the other.

70

Out of sight, Ben seemed less threatening. Guthrie leaned against the wall. "Let's whip his ass and get our money back."

"Guthrie, how much you weigh, wet?"

"One hundred and fifty-eight pounds. What you looking for?"

"Ain't sure. There ought to be something around here to even things up a bit. With our boots on, we might total within ten pounds of that turkey." Flint kicked the gallon can of washers.

"Think he'll be back?"

"That's his grip over there against the wall." Flint worked at untying his neckerchief. "This might work. You got one of these?"

Guthrie pulled the red bandana from his hip pocket. He wore it around his neck only when competing.

Flint knelt to one knee, smoothed his scarf on the bare concrete, put a four-inch roll of washers in its center, and folded it diagonally. He rolled it then knotted it on either end of the discs. With the neckerchiefs loose ends gripped in his hand, he made a mild test swing at the palm of his hand dangling near his knee. Somehow the blow missed and smacked the kneecap.

Flint grimaced in pain. He stood and shook the leg then handed Guthrie the can of washers. "Go ahead, make one. It's an old navy trick. Makes a pretty good black-jack."

"Thought you were in the army?" A couple of minutes later Guthrie tested his homemade weapon. Satisfied, he tucked it under his shirttail. "What if he don't go down, and the law gets into this?"

"We'll show 'em that deck of cards." Flint pointed. "Put 'em over there in that foot locker."

"We better get him out of here before we start anything. There's too many shovels and things around for him to grab."

"Okay. We'll walk toward his truck with him. When we get out there where that ground slopes down to the other end of the arena, I'll ask him for a light. When he gets his hand in his pocket, you cold-cock him. Likely, he'll never know what hit him." Flint moved back and forth.

"More likely, he'll just get a bad case of washer dandruff then whip the stuffing out of both of us. Uh-oh, here he comes." Guthrie patted his homemade blackjack, making sure it was secure. He rolled a smoke and handed it unlit to Flint. The fool hadn't figured how strange it would look to ask for a light with a pinch of snuff in his fingers. At least, he'd concealed his weapon.

Ben walked around the horse blanket. "Where's my deck?"

"Deck? What deck?" Flint looked at Guthrie.

Hair on Guthrie's neck tingled. Apparently, the bull rider didn't realize the gate had opened. "Sheriff drove by. Asked if we'd been gambling. Course, we said no, but he said he was concentrating, confis—you know, taking them cards just in case."

"I didn't hear no car, you little misbegotten whelp of a liar!" Ben took a step toward Guthrie.

72

Flint jumped between them, crouched forward, his knotted fingers splayed, and shuffled side to side. The bandana swung back and forth. "You nor nobody else calls my partner a liar. You fat son of a dilapidated sea biscuit! You stole ninety dollars off me and more off him. You got exactly ten seconds to cough it up, or I'm personally whipping your jelly-ass."

Flint talked ten feet tall, but a blind man could see his words came from the bottled ninety proof. His five-foot-nine stature couldn't shake a shuck at the load he'd cut, and Ben wasn't buying. He crouched, grinned, and raised his doubled fists and elbows in a boxer stance. The trucker circled, facing Flint.

The instant the big man's eyes left Guthrie, he saw his chance. Jesse always said the first lick beat the last-at-bat. Guthrie welcomed his opening. The loaded cloth seemed awkward rising, then he swung it downward with adrenaline pumped force and the taste of mortal fear. This show needed to end.

Ben turned, got far enough around for the filter emblem on his cap to take the full force of the blow. His eyes froze then rolled. A loud thud sounded in the barn. The trucker lurched backward. His head jerked. Washers sprayed the air, fell, and rolled in all directions. The closest palomino wheeled and kicked the side of his stall. The animal's panic rolled like a ground swell through the barn's length. Horses snorted, stomped, and pawed nervously. Ben went to his knees and shook his head.

Guthrie examined his empty hands. He tossed the

73

ragged neckerchief to one side, clenched his fist, then moved forward, balanced, and swung a left. The hook caught Ben on the side of his jaw. The huge man went down. Guthrie moved after him. Someone pulled at him. Flint gripped his arms.

"Here, I'll finish him." He tugged at him.

Staggering to one side, Guthrie wiped his face on the back of a sleeve and stood, straddle-legged and swaying. This battle had an edge over last night's.

Ben rolled, spit, made a grunting sound, then rose, blocking a good portion of the light over the game's blanket. He advanced, swinging both arms and mouthing obscenities.

Flint's homemade club swung in calf roper's circles, fanning the air. Then, by chance, it struck the trucker's arm.

Through the haze of alcohol, Guthrie suddenly realized he and his pard were out-manned. He clamped his jaw and leaped toward the circling Ben. His shoulder landed against the trucker's ribs. He worked himself to Ben's back and grabbed around his neck. The giant had no stirrup, and the timers seemed to have lost the buzzer. He flopped on the driver's back like a headless chicken.

Ben bent, and his head and mane came into range. Flint connected with his washer-filled neckerchief on the man's head. The trucker crashed toward the floor with Guthrie on top. Somehow Flint's arm was in Ben's grasp. Another arm knocked Guthrie away from the struggle.

Both Flint and Ben rose to their feet. Flint's ineffective blackjack lay on the other side of the hall. The bull rider moved and landed a fist to the face that brought blood then took a lick that sent him sprawling against the wall. He slid to a sitting position, shook his head.

Guthrie grabbed Ben's shoulder, trying to turn him and land a punch. The attempt failed. He took a blow to the head from a ham-like fist that knocked him to his knees.

Flint made another rush and caught a blow to the face that flattened him. He lay face down, motionless.

The trucker straightened trying to tuck in his blanket of a shirttail. He staggered, picked up his cap, then grabbed a long handled spade. He turned.

Guthrie struggled to his feet looking for a weapon. A shop broom leaned against a stall. He grabbed it and stood his ground.

Ben stopped. Blood ran from a deep cut in his left eyebrow. He panted, swayed with each deep breath. "Get outta my way, cowboy." His huge hand waved sideways. "Outta my way, or you'll never ride another nag."

"Leave my hundred and forty-six dollars there on the floor and," Guthrie nodded at the unconscious Flint, "another ninety for him."

"You little punk, get outta my way." He drew back the shovel. "I'll kill your ass. Try to rob me!"

"You're doing the robbing here. The killing part's up in the air."

"What?"

"Who's going to get the flowers? It ain't decided."
Guthrie slammed his broom against a stall opening. The
brush broke off, leaving him holding a four and a half-
foot handle with a jagged point.

Ben feinted with the spade, stopped, and stared. His
face showed disbelief. The big man spat blood. He
shook his head. Blanching, he tried to chuckle, but only
managed a dry wheezing sound. "You'd do it. You'd die
for a hundred and fifty bucks."

"Not any, just mine."

Ben let out a deep breath. The spade rested in the
crook of his right arm, and his hand reached for his billfold. He counted the money then threw several bills to
the floor. He walked toward Guthrie, eyeing him
closely as he passed. At the door of the barn, he threw
the shovel to the floor. The metal rang sharply against
concrete, and nervous horses bolted, bounced off stall
walls, and turned cocked ears.

A garden hose connected to a hydrant at the end of the
barn. After washing himself, Guthrie caught half a
bucket and carried it to Flint. He located his shredded
neckerchief, wet it, and then squeezed water onto his
friend's face. Outside, a diesel engine fired. Headlights
swept the barn, then chains rattled, truck springs
squeaked, and slowly the noise faded.

Flint stirred, leaned over the bucket, and raised hand-
cupped water to his face. A large angry looking red spot
showed on his right cheekbone and swollen tissue
almost covered the eye.

Guthrie flopped back against the wall and rolled a

smoke. Flint pitifully administered to his battered face. Suddenly, the bull rider looked in both directions. "Where is he?"

Guthrie handed him ninety dollars. "We won."

"The hell we did! I don't feel like it."

"What's that, 'dilapidated son of a sea biscuit thing'?"

"Maw don't put up with a dirty mouth."

Guthrie started to laugh, but the pain sobered him. He tried to speak without moving sore lips. "She'd shore be proud tonight."

"Where is he?"

"Got in that old International and drove off. That's one time an Indian and a cowboy whipped a fat man."

"One-quarter Indian."

"Okay, one-quarter Indian and two cowboys."

"That don't come out right."

"You work it out. I'm going to bed."

9

Guthrie moved his tongue gingerly against the inside of his lip testing the soreness. Sunshine filled the opening of the station wagon's raised, rear door. Bawling calves substituted for an alarm clock. This was Wednesday, draw day, and his last day of idleness before show time.

His cooler surrendered a small, unopened can of cold orange juice. Moving to the tailgate, he rolled a smoke and stirred circulation by swinging his bare legs in the morning air. He wore only under shorts. Cobwebs seemed too benign to describe the clutter in his head.

Someone with more restraint or a better brand of hooch, one that left less of a hangover, must have coined that phrase.

Two barrel racers from the trailer a few spaces away giggled at his lack of modesty. Alternating between admiring the long thin muscles in his legs and thinking about his head, he'd not heard them walking by. They laughed and waved as he grabbed for his pants. They whispered and giggled, then oscillated from view. He decided to call Lee after breakfast.

Guthrie found Flint at the showers chanting a supposed Sioux love song. Later, the bull rider joined him at the Chevy for a lift to breakfast. Guthrie flipped on the ignition, hit the starter, and nothing happened. He stepped out and raised the hood. With a screwdriver, he arced fire from the battery.

"Starter, I bet. Saw a garage down by the interstate. Al's, I think."

"I got a chain in my pickup. Just a minute, I'll tow you."

Guthrie wore his hair cut above the ears, but considered himself a free spirit. The three-mile ride lashed nine feet away from the rear bumper of Flint Payne's pickup in seventy mile-per-hour, rush-hour traffic convinced him of the contrary. He really liked control, lots of it.

The Dakotan nursed a death wish. Maybe not for himself, but certainly for bronc riders from Texas. The man flitted in and out of traffic like a hummingbird. When finally he stopped in front of the garage, Guthrie was unsure if his knees would support his weight. He sat awhile without moving to catch his breath.

"You gonna roost in that thing or talk to the man?"

If not so glad to be alive, and if Flint's face wasn't such a mess, he believed he'd have hit him. "Just trying to acclimate to the altitude."

"What?"

"Never mind."

Later, Guthrie toyed with the stacks of change he'd carefully placed on the shelf of the phone booth. He mentally rehearsed his opening lead-in, formed her name carefully on his lips. The morning's knee weakness returned, this time driven by a desire to succeed. This needed to go right. Nothing was more important than for this to go right.

Lee's voice answered. "Kramp residence, Erilee speaking."

"Hi. It's Guthrie. How you doing? How's Evelyn?"

"I'm fine, and Mama's having a good day. She's making John Robert a pie. Where are you?"

Good, no anger! "Abilene. Look, Erilee, what you said, about being a friend I . . . I wanta be. And about the way I acted at Rita's night before last, I'm sorry. Don't know what got into me. Just lost my head, I think." There was a long pause. He realized he held his breath. "You're important to me, Lee. Just wanted you to know."

Beyond the phone booth, men and women carried musical instruments toward the bandstand.

"Guthrie, I'm so glad you called. I needed that. What

I said to you, afterwards, a lot of it I didn't mean. It's just that violence, any kind, makes me crazy, now. I don't handle it well. I said some stupid things."

"That'll be eighty-five cents, please."

"Yes, ma'am." He plunked in change from his stacks.

"You mean that part about cowboys and snakes?"

"You dog." She laughed.

Thank God, she laughed.

"I saw Cora at the grocery store yesterday morning. Then I went to the beauty shop. Guthrie, I know now you were hurting, and I was too wrapped up in myself to see."

"Me? Hurting? Not me! Why? What'd they say down there?"

"Aw, you know how gossip is. If you don't, let me tell you. They've got pretty long claws around those hairdryers. Somebody mentioned the sewing circle had a kitty. Said they were collecting to get Jesse a vasectomy. Sounds like he's still swinging a wide loop, and I know how that hurt you in the past. I'm sorry, really."

"Don't worry about it. I outgrew that a long time ago."

"Uh-huh. So you say. Some ways, you ain't that much older'n John Robert."

"Don't guess you and ole J.R. could get down for the show this weekend. I could come and get you."

The operator interrupted again.

When the last nickel clinked, Lee spoke. "I don't know."

Her pause lasted too long. Guthrie gnawed a lip.

80

"Sally and Ruben are coming this weekend. I might get away. Do you remember Sue Pierce?"

"Who?"

"No, you wouldn't. We met later in Houston. Anyway, her husband was killed in Vietnam four months ago. After I left Lane, she called and asked me to come for a visit. She lives there in Abilene."

"That'd be great."

"I'll see if I can work it out. If so, I'll see you there. If I don't make it, call me next week. Guthrie, thanks."

What should he say? So long, bye? I love you? "See you later." Thanks, yeah, thanks for loving ice cream, chocolate pie, and a downhill trail. He jumped from the booth hollering at the top of his voice. He sailed his hat skyward.

Below the hill, twenty mounted men riding palominos practiced intricate maneuvers in the arena. Heads turned his way. From the bandstand, musicians tested instruments and sent a disjointed shivaree up the slope to accompany his cavorting.

Guthrie picked up his hat then remembered his change. He floated back and retrieved it. She cared for him. Bring on the broncs! Saddle 'em backwards! He could handle it. She really cared.

Whoa! He'd have to remember to caution Flint to lie about his black eye. It'd be easy. The bull-riding profession created on-the-job black eyes and smashed noses. One way or another, he would convince her, that not only he, but also all his friends were the most passive beings south of the Canadian.

At the drawing, he told Flint of his talk with Lee and promised to make Wounded Knee look like a tea party if the bull rider caused her to learn of the rumble with the trucker. His pard acted hurt that anyone might think it possible he would dally with the truth. Only for his Texas friend and the possibility of filling out the fourth slot on a double date would he consider hobbling his tongue.

Later, Flint queued with the bull riders to draw for the animals he would ride. Guthrie stood in the saddle-bronc line. The show ran four nights, Thursday through Sunday. The one-hundred-sixty-dollar entry fee entitled each rider a mount for every performance. High-point-day-money paid seven hundred fifty dollars, and best over-all average for all four nights paid three thousand five hundred.

Guthrie received a large number sixteen to wear on back of his shirt and drew four slips identifying his mounts. Two of the horses were excellent performers. The other two, unknowns. Overall, a decent draw. Pretty durned good, actually.

As always, a few words with Lee buoyed his whole day. She beat a summer shower.

The presence of Albert Pearson from Cody, Wyoming meant world-class competition, but he'd expected that. Albert finished third in the standings last year. Another finalist, Hank Westerman visited with Guthrie before the drawing. Hank's attendance came as no surprise since he lived only twenty miles down the road.

Four pens were allotted to saddle broncs, one for each night's show. Straddling the top pipe of the Thursday night performer's corral, Guthrie spotted the iron gray, Salt and Pepper. Happy to draw the big gelding, he smiled upon seeing him slicked out and sporting a new coat. He'd taken second on him in Wichita last year.

The horse gave an honest ride, jumped high, and didn't stiffen too bad when he came down. He did have a tendency to lazy-up and crow hop some, but if you kept raking him, he'd earn a decent score. He wasn't an A-type, dominating animal, but ranged somewhere in the middle of the pecking order. The bronc generally bucked to the left, and never gave up. Those who knew him well had an edge. He telegraphed his cutbacks by lowering his ears.

Looking at Pepper's condition, contentment settled over Guthrie. The talk with Lee went well, he had saved his poke last night, and he had at least two excellent draws. A good feeling settled in about the show. A little tightness would take hold an hour or so before he came out of the chute, but when the gate opened and Pepper came out of his crouch, the two would wake the crowd. That moment of being atop all that power, knowing the animal's next move before it happened, made it all worth while. That was living. It'd be worth it without the prize.

Flint approached with a couple of bull riders. The purple around his eye had darkened, but not his smile. "You boys know old Guthrie, don't you?" Both cowboys nodded. "Don't rile him. He's about half-dangerous. Somebody said he built a reputation as the 'bandana bandido'." He laughed. "How'd you draw?"

"Pretty good, I think. Got a date with old Salt and Pepper Thursday night. How about you?"

"Good, start off with Butler's number sixty-two. Ought to get my fee back with him. I don't know about the next three. These boys gonna show 'em to me now, gimme some schooling on their little quirks.

"Say, wasn't that ole biddy in there wearing them FPF specs a grouch?"

Guthrie recalled the clerk Flint referred to. "Remember the lady you're talking about, but what'd you call her glasses?"

"FPF specs. You know. You saw 'em. Sit way out on your nose and look like the top half's been sawed off. You look over 'em and see everything normal. I think the lenses magnify about a hunnerd-power. You look straight down and, boy it's all right there, bigger'n life."

"Pard, I know the glasses, but what's the FPF for?"

Flint looked all directions, put his hand to the side of his mouth and exaggerated the whisper. "Frosty Pecker Finders! Up home, when winter sets in and it gets snow-writing time out back of the barn, lots of the boys have trouble finding their "frosties" in that cold wind. Lot of 'em start to carry FPF specs right after the first cold snap. Course, I don't have no need for 'em." He put his arm on one of his companions' shoulders and walked away, bent forward laughing.

Guthrie climbed from the fence chuckling. His mind conjured up pictures of shivering Yankees fighting layers of clothing then giving up in despair and fumbling desperately for eyeglasses.

84

10

Thursday evening near seven p.m., the day's heat slipped down to bearable. Guthrie leaned against a gate near the chute area. He feigned indifference to the crowd. In reality, this scene pumped him up. Grown-ups corralled rowdy kids, dodged cotton candy, and filed into the stands.

Some had the appearance of being—and in reality were—perfectly capable of crawling over the arena fence and entering the competition. Others, heavy with Air Force uniforms and even interspersed with some speaking foreign languages, craned their necks to take in the sights. Tourists, identifiable by flour-white or beet-red complexions, virgin cowboy hats, and new jeans, sprinkled the crowd. "Howdy" and "good to see yawl" drowned out "hello" and "good evening" in this bunch. Flint whittled nearby.

Wes Hodges' familiar voice rolled over the crowd noise. "A big ole Texas good evening Cowboys and Cowgirls. My name's Wes Hodges, and I thank y'all for making room for me to share tonight's fun. Welcome to Abilene and the West Texas Fair. We gonna have us a rodeo."

The band exploded into a drum-roll, and two mounted, flag bearers raced in opposite directions, around the periphery of the arena. The Stars and Stripes waved over a white clad cowgirl on a midnight black, and Texas' Lone Star streaked past above a lady dressed

85

in blue riding a sorrel. The flag bearers brought their animals to a skidding, side-by-side halt in the middle of the arena. A blond in a glittering evening dress stepped forward to lead her half of the Grande Entry and seduced the crowd with a shaky rendition of the Star Spangled Banner.

Barrel racing gave way to cutting competition, and by that time, the lights to the open-sky arena illuminated the action. Calf roping, heading and heeling, then steer wrestling followed. Loafing contestants, including Guthrie, cleared the arena when Wes announced the bucking events would follow.

The first riding event was billed as the "Wild Mare Race". Wild was apt, but race seemed a misnomer. Five mares free, but for halters and lead ropes, burst from the chutes. Each were trailed by teams of cowboys either clinging to the ropes with both hands and dragging belly to the ground or stretched out running with block long steps. Two men clung stubbornly to tail holds.

Planned to provide comedy with action, the event coupled with Wes's "Clem D Diddle Hopper's" narrative brought the crowd to its feet. While fun for the audience, the race gave contestants an opportunity for a one-way ticket to an orthopedic ward.

Five men carried saddles and ran, fighting the soft dirt to stay with the action. The purpose of the mayhem was to fight the horses into submission, saddle them, then get one man mounted. To win, that lucky cowboy's simple task was to stay aboard an unbroken, unbridled animal while beating his opponents to the far end of the arena, past a line, then back to the starting point.

Laughter interspersed Wes' amplified voice. "Makes assisted living look better all the time. Don't it? Tell you, them pawing, biting, kicking sons of bucks make a feller want to change occupations, maybe sell shoes. What they got going out there is sort of mindful of lacing a girdle to a mountain lion and marching him through a fourth of July parade. Hey, lookee there! I'll swun—I believe that ole boy's gonna make it."

After the winner crossed the finish line, Guthrie made his way to his tack stashed in an empty stall behind the chutes. His saddle shared the space with others. Their hornless pommels and deep seats marked them as belonging to bronc riders. Assorted rigging hung on the fences.

Earlier, he'd treated his equipment with saddle soap then rubbed both saddle and chaps with a cloth dampened with Neat's Foot Oil. He checked the girth and stirrup leathers then examined the halter rope that would serve as his single rein.

He'd limber up while the bareback boys did their number out in the arena. His gear attended to, all that remained was fifteen minutes of stretching and loosening. Flint held Guthrie's pocketknife and billfold. After some knee bends and thirty push-ups, he set his saddle on a blanket and straddled it. Whistling as he worked, he toed his boots into the ox-bow stirrups and bent forward over the pommel to touch his toes. Next, he bent his legs behind the saddle's cantle still keeping his boots in the stirrups.

The fact that he made a living at this was almost too sweet to be real. Money went the other direction in the only places he could think of that beat this for a good time. Seemed he fit here. Jesse had seen to it that as a child, bad or spoiled horses were off limits to his sprout. Consequently, Guthrie grew up thinking he could ride anything. In those early years, the old man earned 'side money' by keeping a few green ones around and breaking them for others.

Somewhere in the early grades, Guthrie began to sneak bareback rides on whatever Jesse had penned, but by then, being thrown just added to the excitement. He knew kids who jumped off the barn just to see if they could fly. At least, he gained an edge on them. Learned aerodynamics early. He had no memory of ever experiencing fear around a horse. Pain, yeah. Fear, no.

"You got old Pepper, don't you, Guthrie?"

He knew the man's face, but couldn't put a name on it.

"Uh-huh, how you doing?"

"Tolerable, you know he's pretty much a lefty."

"Yep, thanks."

The man took his rigging. "You're up third now."

A few minutes later Guthrie crouched above the gray as chute-men first tightened the cinch then the bucking strap. He watched as Pepper's ears twitched then lowered. He measured the heavy rein and marked the hold he wanted with a strand of mane. The horse twisted his neck, turned his head, and his eye widened. He tensed, stepped nervously back and forth. The noise of the crowd lulled. Wes' voice carried across the arena and echoed from the half roof over the seats.

"Ladies and Gents, the judges gave Mr. Patterson a seventy-seven on that last ride, and that puts him in the lead for today's standings. Let me direct your attention now to chute number four. A young Panhandle cowboy and my friend, Guthrie Sawyer is getting set to come out on an old gray named Salt and Pepper. Folks, this cowboy ranked 17th in the world last year and did it on fewer rides than any other bronc rider in the top thirty. His mammy and daddy named him after the County Seat of King County, and if you ain't been there, that's cow country. Say when, Guthrie, boy."

His elbows rested on the chute's top railing, supporting most of his weight. Pepper straightened, raised his ears, and Guthrie relaxed his arms. His weight settled in the saddle. He pulled his right rein hard toward his chest and moved his spurs forward in front of the horse's shoulder. He ducked his chin, leaned slightly backward, then hollered out of the side of his mouth.

"Turn him loose."

Flying insects fluttered crazily around the overhead lights. Pepper went airborn, ate some of the distance toward the dirt and the bugs, kicked, and, at the top of his journey, gathered his legs for a stiff-legged landing. Guthrie raked the horse's neck and shoulders with the spurs, wanting desperately to get his legs pointing downward before they bottomed out. A bruised tailbone the first night of a show didn't bode well for either pocketbook or standings. He got his feet toward the ground, took most of the shock from the stirrups with his knees, and waved his left arm over Pepper's tail for balance.

Salt and Pepper did his thing. Guthrie's chaps flapped in the wind as he rocked easily, raking with his spurs in rhythm with the horse's movement. Pepper made a gradual turn left. The blur of color in the stands separated into faces. The gray turned more sharply, and the pickup men headed his way.

The buzzer sounded, and a moment later, Guthrie sat on the rumble seat of the pickup man's sorrel. He held his legs up until they cleared Pepper's kicking perimeter then dropped to the ground and took three quick steps to conquer momentum. His hats-off, sweeping bow to the crowd dusted the ground before he strode quickly toward the chutes.

"Folks, you just saw a bronc peeler make a good bucker look great and earn a seventy-nine while doing it. Give him a good hand. He's likely earned a payday tonight, but with four more riders to go, there's always a chance he'll have to put our applause in the bank."

A few steps and a couple of back slaps later, the pickup man handed Guthrie's saddle to him. He went to Flint, got his own belongings, and took those Flint didn't want to be bothered with while working. Bull riding was the final event. Guthrie dropped off his saddle in the stall, and on his way back to the arena, spoke to one of the clowns. "Howdy, Walsh."

The comic's wink reflected from his make-up mirror.

Flint's ride, number sixty-two, was an Angus-Charolais crossbreed and a muley. He bucked in a

90

tight circle to the right, came out of that, then lost his rear footing. His butt dragged dirt. Collecting himself, he spun tightly to the left.

The Dakotan made it look easy, windmilling his free arm at the proper moment and shifting his weight and legs just right with the turns. He stepped off easy immediately after the buzzer and gained the fence two steps ahead of number Sixty-two.

Walsh ran behind and to one side of the bull, doing his best to be close in the event Flint needed him. His hand rested on the point of the bull's hip, just behind the flank. Flint scrambled up the fence. Sixty-two suddenly planted all four hooves, twisted, and lunged. His hornless forehead butted hard against the clown's hip. It wasn't a solid blow, but two thousand pounds didn't require solid to hurt.

Walsh fell, rolled, and scrambled trying to get to his feet. The second clown ran between Sixty-two and the limping Walsh, and with the grace of a matador, captured the bull's attention then led him in a race to the nearest fence. The clown won and from the top of the fence thumbed his nose at the animal. Flint and another bull rider helped Walsh to an empty chute.

Moments later, the jester made a stiff-legged return to the arena, his upturned smile now painted downward. He bowed to the crowd and swapped places with a third clown. His new job was mole duty inside a barrel near the middle of the arena.

Friday night, neither Guthrie nor Flint broke from the pack. Guthrie lost a stirrup the second jump out of the chute, almost fell, but regained his balance and made the buzzer. He scored a sixty-three on what he believed to be a sixty-ride. Flint marked a sixty-five on a less than average bull.

11

"Think she'll show?" It was Saturday evening, shortly before grand entry time, and Flint squatted beside Guthrie chewing a stick.

Guthrie sat in an aluminum lawn chair near the entrance gate. "Who knows? She sounded serious when we talked, but maybe she'uz just trying to be nice."

Would she come? Guthrie's sharp eyes screened every female entering the lot. By the time their car doors shut, he sorted them either no or possibly. The latter category got further study.

The crowd thickened, the traffic overwhelmed his roving eye, and an emptiness spread upward from somewhere within. Had he detected pity in her voice? Perhaps sympathy was a better word. It figured. A woman might drive a hundred and fifty miles to see someone she admired, but an object of sympathy, no.

He stretched higher in the chair. Midway across the rapidly filling parking area, two women entered the stream of pedestrians moving toward the ticket office. The one in front strode purposefully, occasionally rising to tiptoes, looking in all directions. For Guthrie, the crowd blurred to obscurity, and she walked alone, erect. Soft strands of her brown hair stirred in the breeze. She wore jeans, boots, and a green shirt. Even at a hundred yards, she stood out like a paint pony on a dark night.

He forced himself to notice the attractive blond beside Lee. She, too, was an eyeful. She hurried to maintain Lee's pace, occasionally taking short, dainty, trotting steps.

Guthrie stood, leaned his chair against the entrance fence and pulled the two courtesy passes he'd mooched from Wes. He moved toward the girls.

Flint was almost in his ear. "Which one? Which 'un is it?"

"Get off me, will you? Over there, the blond must be Sue." Guthrie nodded at the girls just as Lee spotted him. She smiled and waved.

Once introduced, Flint wasted no time. He quickly explained to Sue that the two of them had the heavy burden of seeing to it that Guthrie and Lee stayed properly chaperoned throughout the next thirty or so hours. With her help, he'd make certain an atmosphere of puritan behavior prevailed. Least he forget, the rogue appointed Sue to help him keep Lee and Guthrie acutely aware that only clean wholesome fun would be allowed—and that in limited doses.

The amused twinkle in Sue's eye revealed the facade of modest restraint she attempted with the dark and handsome, self-proclaimed "bull-riding king of the Dakotas". By the time they'd used the free passes through the gate, Flint had Sue chattering and laughing like a schoolgirl.

Contrarily, Guthrie struggled, searching for small talk. "John Robert's not with you?"

"No, he wanted to stay and play with his cousin. There's only a year's difference in their ages."

"Sally's boy?"

"Girl."

"Oh. How was the drive down?"

"Good. No problem. You ride tonight?"

"In a couple of hours."

She put her hand in his then waved her other at the fast-filling grandstands. "This is fun. I haven't been to a rodeo in years."

"Well, little lady, we gonna see to it you have a good time. There's a dance on the tennis courts afterwards." Guthrie offered his best Hollywood impersonation of The Duke, substituting D's for T's in little, but it fell flat. Finding their seats broke the ice, then he bought cokes, and the third night of Abilene's rodeo got underway.

Lee's father had been one of Ira Walker's ranch foremen for many years. They moved to town when she and Sally were in high school, but her dad continued to see after the ranch until his death. She'd grown up helping men do many of the rodeo events. At one time, she could hold her own at cowboy work.

Today's performers, however, had added a new twist. Lee immediately spotted the right-handed ropers dismounting from the off side to prevent the necessity of ducking under their ropes on the way to their catch. When Wes announced a roping time of nine point two

94

seconds, she looked at Guthrie appreciatively. "That's taking it down to a science, huh?"

He and Flint remained in the stands with the girls through the roping and the steer wrestling. The bull rider bought barbecue sandwiches, but Guthrie passed. A few minutes later, he and the Dakotan made their way to the chutes.

Guthrie's draw for the night, Teacup, passed as a black during the winter, but the sun bleached him to a dark brown during the summer. Less predictable than his color, he was a handful. The horse killed Bill Tinsly's hopes for a world championship in Dallas two years ago. Bill got airborn the second jump out of the chute, and though his championship slipped away, getting his life back netted a draw the way he told it. The horse might have a gentle, lady's name, but he never played the part.

In the last two days, Guthrie had learned all he could about the old outlaw and figured he'd pegged him as good as possible. They'd be breaking out of a right handed chute tonight, so chances were the bronc would go up immediately, give that twisting mid-air kick, and come in stiff. Five to three he'd cut left, back right, and go high with every move.

Guthrie knew if he could stay with him through those first two cuts, he'd have a good chance of marking well. Still, the hoss made it hard to keep your heels in front of those shoulders coming out of the chute.

Wes delivered his Saturday night performance to a standing room crowd. By the time Guthrie's turn arrived, he'd pitched his Red Skelton scene during the wild mare race and used a Dean Martin "trip to da couch" describing a dethroned bare-back rider. Guthrie spit out his kitchen match, marked the rein length, and wondered at the amount of ham in the man.

Superstition demanded the red shirt for tonight's dark horse. Economy accounted for the old, green, batwing chaps. Unabashed vanity added to his confidence. But pretty or not, he still had ten eternal seconds to survive on a hope-killing mountain of horseflesh.

"Folks, over in chute number five, we got a blue-blooded, gut-busting, old bronc with the unlikely handle of—are you ready? Teacup! Now, he ain't been rode since Charlie Rainface did it up in Idaho a year ago. If there's another rawhider up to the chore, it's that young cowboy crawling aboard down there right now. Hold your hats, folks. Here comes Guthrie Sawyer outta chute-number five on Teacup!"

Guthrie got lucky. The gelding gathered himself and cooperated. He hollered the gate open just as Wes closed his build-up. The crowd roared, as the horse bid to earn astronaut status. The open heavens came closer. Wind whistled in Guthrie's ears, and every nerve tingled with anticipation.

The juices flowed, and he rode the crest. This was one of the few things in life that merged his mind and body into a common, self-consuming goal. Let her rip, old pony. He had a Saturday-night gal to show what a real cowboy looked like. Before this night ended, he'd make her fantasy of wealthy bankers and rich cat-

96

tlemen look like yesterday's beans.

An instant before contacting dirt, Teacup converted to rigid stone. Guthrie's fist holding the rein drove into his nose. He tasted blood. The gelding dropped his head, and Guthrie's teeth rattled. His vision blurred, but he still straddled the leather between pommel and cantle, and he had pressure on both stirrups. His hat was missing. Maybe it had fallen or, perhaps, rested somewhere beneath his chin with his head sticking out the crown. He'd ridden through lots of landings, but nothing as jarring as that.

Again the bronc's head dropped from sight. He spun then leaped high, twisting himself almost upside down. Guthrie sat tight, leaning back and forth in cadence with every move and raking his spurs as far as his legs would reach. A final turn and Guthrie rocked forward, licked blood from his lips, waved his free arm, and hollered at the top of his voice.

The buzzer sounded. He waved off the pickup men, caught Teacup at the top of a leap, and pushed off with his feet and legs. The horse dropped from beneath him, and Guthrie went up and to the side. He came down standing then bowed, waved at the crowd, and looked for his hat. He wiped his bloodied nose and kicked dirt at the horse as it ran past.

"Give that cowboy a nice hand, folks. Look-a-there, eighty-four, and that puts old Guthrie in the lead through three rides."

Flint patted Guthrie's shoulder, handed him the missing hat, and waved at their dates while pointing at

Guthrie. A few minutes later, not to be outdone, Flint put the crowd on their feet with a bull that did everything right, but couldn't match his rider. Twice, before the buzzer sounded, the animal's head arched up then back, inches from Flint's face. Riding with his hat in his free hand, the Dakotan fanned the brute's face with the black Stetson.

In a spin after the buzzer, Flint relaxed and allowed momentum to carry him free of the animal. He hit the ground running and didn't stop until he topped a chute. He shook his fist at Guthrie, tipped his hat to Sue, and mouthed the words "seven hundred and fifty dollars". He scored a seventy-nine, took the three-day lead and day money.

The last bull cleared the arena. Walsh, still limping from Thursday night's encounter with the smoke-colored Angus, stood to the side while the other clowns rolled their barrel to the alley. The crowd milled toward the exit.

12

Earlier, Guthrie parked the station wagon near the tennis courts so they'd have the beer cooler close at hand. Arriving there, he unfolded his two patio chairs for Flint and Sue, and he and Lee sat in the open rear door of the Chevy.

"What happened to your eye?" Sue studied Flint's discolored cheek.

"A bull the other night. He came up about the time I

went forward. Horn is tougher'n my tender face." Flint raised an eyebrow at Guthrie then managed an expression of Saturday matinee courage for the ladies. His look told them to circle the wagons and not worry about the Indians. Old Flint would defend them, but save the last bullet, just in case some of the horde got through and took them hostage. The man showboated more than Wes.

"Aren't you ever afraid? Those monsters are horrible." Sue sounded sincere, charmed, and clearly interested in Flint Payne.

"Bulls? Aw, they ain't too bad. Inside that arena, things are pretty safe. It's the getting back and forth bothers me. My tender young friend there and I rode in Madison Square Garden about four years ago. Now, that was scary!"

Guthrie caught Lee's eye and motioned toward the dancers. He followed her to the slick concrete slab, his hands on her waist.

She turned, smiled, gave him her right hand, then fit perfectly in his arms. "Your friend is fun. I believe he's making a hit with Sue."

He nodded. "She's nice."

The night cooled, stars dotted the darkness, and the moon drifted overhead. Guthrie couldn't remember being happier. Still, the thought of what might be with this woman filled him with misery, longing. Once, a world away in Vietnam, and Lee married in Houston, he'd all but given up on any chance for the good life. Now, here he frolicked, her in his arms, riding the

99

swells of success in his craft. Everything seemed doable. Maybe, John Robert understood. Perhaps, the impossible was there for the taking.

Several dances and two beers later, Flint waited in the men's room for him to step aside so the bull rider could reach a paper towel.

"Seems you two are hitting it off pretty good." Guthrie said.

"Yeah, I like her."

"Flint, one thing, she lost her husband four months ago. Na'am."

"You trying to say something?"

"No, nope, I've said it. You know I'd trust you with my sister."

"I'll be gentle, Pard." Flint paused. "By the way what does your sister look like?"

Guthrie laughed. They joined the girls en route from the ladies' restroom and returned to the station wagon. He opened another round of long necks then lay on his back in the rear of the Chevy propped on an elbow. He studied Lee's face.

She leaned her back against his bedroll with her socked feet not far from his head. The crowd had thinned. Only a few couples moved lazily to the soft music. He and Lee listened to their friends' conversation.

Sue followed up an earlier remark from Flint. "You have some college then?"

"Yeah, when I returned from Na'am, I went to South Dakota A & E for fifteen months."

"What did you major in?"

"Animal Husbandry, the wrong thing. I might've got a degree if I'd majored in accounting, brain surgery, or whatever."

"That surprises me, Flint. I'd have thought you'd like that. You know, the animal thing and all."

"Me, too, and I do like 'em okay, but I just don't like getting that intimate with the dern things." Flint bummed a ready-roll from Guthrie. "What did me in was that last course." He sounded reluctant to talk about it.

"What course?" Lee asked.

"They called it 'Optimizing Genetics for Dairy Purposes'. Had a lab. I got paired up with a pre-vet gal, and it became our chore to collect bull semen for artificial insemination." Flint shook his head and chuckled.

"I think, maybe, there's some of this I don't need to know." Sue's voice belied her words. She looked toward the Chevy.

After a moment's silence, Flint added, "You're probably right."

Guthrie'd not heard the story before, but knew Flint was just warming up. He leaned toward Lee and whispered. "No telling where he's going with this. Want me to put a damper on him?"

Lee straightened slightly. "No, it's okay. We put 'em together."

"We could dance."

"Might as well see this conversation through. B'sides, it might be fun. Sue can take care of herself."

101

This time Sue broke the silence. "I understand over fifty percent of the dairy industry's cows were bred that way last year. But this is your story, Flint."

"How'd you know that?"

"My little sister, Beth, recently started work as a veterinarian in a large animal hospital. Mostly dairy stuff. During her college days, and even now, I'm her listening post. Mom and Dad think it's too gross to talk about. They still try to convince us the cows just walk around in the pasture until they find a calf." Sue chuckled.

"Really? Well, it's the cutting edge of veterinarian medicine. One of these days, in about fifty years, they'll find a good, bucking bull. When they do, they'll clone that devil." Flint paused. "And they'll probably put out a couple of hundred Flint Payne's while they're at it. Fact is though, if I got a choice, I'd rather come back as one of them pampered studs."

"No, Flint, you'll be a marker bull." Sue's voice carried the same seriousness as his.

"A what?"

"It was the last project Beth worked on in college." Sue kicked Flint's chair lightly with the toe of her shoe. "But go on, this is your story, get it over with."

In spite of the dimness of the moonlight, Guthrie could tell she smiled, but he remained uneasy. Seemed the story moved okay, though. He lit a Viceroy for Lee then his own. "Hey, yawl be careful. These two innocents you're supposed to be chaperoning are hearing all that."

102

"Don't worry. We're keeping it clean just for you two. Well, you put that old bull up in a squeeze chute and clamp him in where he can't move. One person handles the collection tube and the other one slicks up a plastic sleeve, puts it over his hand and arm, and goes to work at Mr. Bull's rear through all that nasty. A ways up there, you find the nerves that make him fall in love with that tube. You can imagine the rest."

Flint paused and tried to gauge his remaining beer by holding the bottle between his eye and the moon. He continued. "Well, we—the girl and I—were expected to rotate these jobs. I was embarrassed to death and so was she. To make matters worse, the teacher was a she, too. That poor girl! The old lady'd say, 'Now, hold the tube snuggly against his penis, dear.' Of course, that little ole gal'd drop the damn thing every time. Meanwhile, I'm back there in all that mess. I'll tell you!"

Sue made a soft strangling noise in her throat, coughed, and put a tissue to her mouth. The moon out-lined Lee's head, cocked at an angle. This all seemed redneck to Guthrie, but maybe he was the one out of step. He searched for sanitized street words suitable to convert this cow-lot conversation to coat and tie chit-chat. Sue's mom and dad's thinking had his vote. Yet, he guessed calves weren't Easter eggs. Flint had a way of making ugly look good and serious turn funny. Things still seemed innocent enough.

Sue acted interested, not offended. "Flint, I can tell you're a man of many talents. What about Eskimos? Do the men and women really rub noses in greeting?"

He laughed. "I don't think so. If them nerves ever migrate to sinuses, Rudolph's gonna have lots of company. You're joshing about that marker-bull thing, right? That's a new one on me."

"Beth says the biggest trouble they have with AI is catching the timing of the cow's ovulation correctly. You know it's quite short. In a natural setting, the bulls check it effectively, but the vets have been unable to duplicate that economically. The solution seems to be marker bulls."

"Uh, huh, and what's that?" Obviously, the Dakotan remained wary.

"They take a cheap bull, surgically divert his plumbing so his aim is off, fasten a bag of dye under his belly, then daily inseminate each cow that comes in from the pasture with a dye mark on her back." Sue leaned back like there was nothing to it.

"Ouch! You're lying to me."

"No, I'm not. Check it out with a vet. Even reincarnated, you'll always have a home, Flint."

Lee's snicker proved contagious. It spread to Sue then the bull rider. Relieved, Guthrie joined them in laughter. Lee clicked on a flashlight and wrinkled her nose. He doubled up then fought for breath. The humor of the possibilities brought to mind by the sheer stupidity of their imagination was overpowering. Talk about conversations going downhill.

The band quieted. Members cased instruments, packed sound equipment, then departed in a van. A middle-age couple, one of two pairs staying through the final dance, walked to an electric switch box mounted on a pole near the station wagon.

"Gonna put you folks in the dark." The man followed his promise with action.

"No problem. Goodnight." Guthrie waved.

Sue stood. "Flint's gonna drive me home. I promised the sitter twelve-thirty."

"That's okay. I'll tear myself away from this cowboy, and we'll both go." The lack of enthusiasm in Lee's voice leaked through.

"No, Lee, it's fine. Really. You guys got some years to catch up on. B'sides, I got a couple of moves I wanta try out on this lady." The quickness and sincerity of Flint's response settled the issue.

Guthrie stood. "Want me to drive yawl over to the truck?"

"No, we'll walk." Flint took Sue's hand.

"Don't wait up. I'll see you in the morning." Lee moved to Sue's vacated chair.

Guthrie took the other seat. He lit two cigarettes and handed one to Lee. "She's got a little one, huh?"

"A precious baby girl, two."

Sue's laughter drifted across the quieted grounds, and a moment later, twin beams of light probed the darkness in a sweeping arc.

"Being a parent, ain't it awful scary?"

"Oh, it has its ups and downs. Sort of like riding a bucking horse, I guess." Lee chuckled then turned serious. "You'd be good at it."

"Me? Naw, I don't think so."

105

"Afraid it'd slow you down too much?"

"Naw, I'd welcome a little two-step once in a while. A chance to let the moss grow a little. Seems I'm the only one hooked to a singletree. Thing is, I ain't real sure I'm ready to be patterned after by some little tyke who thinks I hung the moon."

"For what it's worth, I think you'd make a great pattern. But you mentioned scary. I'll tell you about scary. It's holding that little darling for the first time and seeing that precious, but twisted foot. The knowledge of all the hurt he's going to suffer growing up engulfs you. It's scary, all right. I was prepared for diapers and midnight feedings, not tragedy."

"Seems to me, the boy got a lucky break when God paired him with you."

Lee turned, tilted her head, maybe to take advantage of the stingy moonlight. "Did you really count those days since we'd parted?"

"What do you think? You think old John Robert told me who he was, and I just started figuring up days?"

"That's exactly what I think."

Damn her! How'd she always get him started lying? Of course it'd been a quick calculation, but now she'd boxed him in. He had to see it through. "All those years, every morning, the first thing after I rubbed my eyes, it hit me—two years, four, five years and six days since Lee broke my heart." A touch of humor colored his voice.

"You lying dog."

The laughter merged. "Well, maybe I missed a day or

106

two, but it's no lie when I tell you it hurt." How could he get her from that chair to the back of the station wagon?

"I'm here now."

He stood. Sometimes, just taking the rein and leading them right in worked best. But, what if she balked? He moved in front of her and took her hands, helped her to her feet.

She came into his arms like a rising tide. Merged every contour of her body against his and filled his arms. Her eyes reflected faint light and a soft smile curved her lips. Who did the leading here? Who gave a damn?

The kiss started slow and gentle, sort of a nice-to-meet'cha kind of a thing, but it took off from there like a rocket. Her lips parted, firm, giving one moment, demanding the next. Their tongues touched, and he went nuts. Her breasts, her hips pressed against him, yet, for his purposes, she seemed leagues away.

He ran his fingers through her hair then tensed with desire. His other hand pulled her tighter, kneaded the firm flesh beneath her hip pockets. He broke off the kiss, rocked gently, still hugging and breathing heavily. Moments later, she stepped away.

Guthrie moved to the station wagon, reached for the sleeping bag. "Just a minute." He unrolled the bag, unzipped it into a full blanket and spread it in the open space of the Chevy. She climbed in beside him.

Years ago, she was the first girl he'd ever kissed, well, the first that really counted. She'd taught him the art of foreplay. She, also, thwarted his every attempt at a more advanced course of study. He'd had to learn from others how to finish this rite.

Tonight was different. Discarded clothing flew in all directions, and in an explosion of panther-energy, he sensed being totally absorbed.

Bathed in moonlight and sweat and boiling with his love, she raged like thunder with desire and ancient needs. With one final scintillating burst of phantom lightning, his body convulsed, then Lee gasped. He collapsed into her arms. Exhausted, content, and silent, he dried in the arid desert air.

Later, he stirred, dressed, then sat on the vehicle's lowered rear hatch and pulled on his boots. He walked a ways from the fifty-seven, giving Lee a moment. He eyed the darkness along the ground wondering if rattlers came this close to town. He'd die a happy man if they did.

13

Lee dozed beside Guthrie, her head on his chest. Something within pushed sleep aside, left him restless as a fence-walker in a strange corral. His connection with Lee was unlike others he'd known. It had always been so, and being with her fueled the fire. This relationship had the scent of permanence. He could be penned, snubbed, and saddled for life here. That meant big-time changes.

Rodeo, as good as he'd become, still lacked consistency as a source of income. Even without the money factor—and he wasn't sure he could beat those odds—being on the road so much was no good for a family man. He should have stayed at Tech. He'd had no trouble with the grades, and now he'd be in residency somewhere with a bright future ahead as Doctor Sawbones Sawyer.

It wasn't the first time he'd regretted dropping out of premed. Maybe that explained resenting his mom's harping on it so. The smell of jungle rot and death in Vietnam had quickly convinced him of his penchant for big time stupid. Boredom had been the big thing, that, and a sense of guilt and frustration over spending money he didn't think his folks could afford.

A gray cloud drift under the moon, and he recalled Jesse retreating behind a wall of silence every time he tried to talk to him about the cost of college. His stock answer was, "It's Cora's money."

There was no question, but that her salary dominated. Jesse was proud. Making less than his wife probably tore his guts out, still. . . .

He had to get a grip. He was getting way ahead of himself here. After all, Lee probably placed little importance on the night's events. A kiss, a fling in the moonlight, he'd been down the road enough to know how little that meant these days. Oh, man! That arm of his Lee lay on went to sleep eons ago. Wiggling his fingers only managed to intensify the hunger of the ants that fed on the decomposing limb.

Lee opened her eyes, smiled, and kissed his neck. "Take me home."

"You're there."

She raised, and looked out the window, then shook her head. She scanned his face. Her expression held no tease. "I was such a fool."

"What?"

"Eight years ago, I was such a fool. You better take me to Sue's."

Guthrie pulled his boots on, windmilled his numb arm, then held his hand protectively over Lee's head as she crawled from the back of the station wagon. En route to Sue's, he turned on the radio and cringed at the squeaks and rattles contributed by the old Chevy.

Lee seemed not to notice, leaning lightly against him. "You like what you do, don't you?"

"Yeah, I guess so."

"How'd Cora and Jesse take it when you gave up premed for war?"

"You know about that?"

"I didn't count every day, but I kept up."

"It was hard for them. Way they acted, you'd think I did it for spite."

Lee smiled. "They got a sickness."

"Huh? What's that?"

"It's called parenthood. B'sides, Cora always bragged you were going to be a doctor. What is it, Guthrie, the excitement?"

"What do you mean? Vietnam or Rodeo?"

"Rodeo. I can understand you wanting no special favors during the war, or on the other hand, if you'd gone to Canada, but rodeo. What draws you? Is it the excitement?"

"Maybe. I don't think so, though. Have to admit I've thought about it a time or two. The excitement and awe of the crowd is it for a lot of the boys, and I have to admit I like that feeling of being so dog gone alive. When that ole pony gathers himself and you catch his rhythm and all, I just think everybody likes to do something good enough to get other's attention.

"Some of the men feed on the applause. They'd kill for it, wal, almost. Somehow, though, I think with me it's more getting a kick out of helping folks have a good time. You see 'em come in tired of fussing at the kids or each other. In the cities, they generally look a little bored. The first thing you know, you look back at those same faces, and they're all laughing or looking in disbelief at something going on out in the arena. That's what puts me into gear. I could be a clown or an announcer. It's just that I do this better, for now."

"You do put on a show. I'd say you and Flint sort of feed off each other."

"Come to think of it, we do sort of bring the other 'n luck."

Upon arrival at Sue's porch, she rested her head on his shoulder, and he sensed the sensation God must have experienced on the seventh day. The world was complete. His work had been good.

For the first time since bareback horses and wooden guns, he called the play. He kissed her—a warm kiss, a stirring of embers, and a joining to wash away wasted years. He leaned, held the screen ajar. Inside the door, she smiled, and followed its ever-narrowing opening until it shut in his face.

14

"Wake up!"

"What, huh? Guthrie blinked, rubbed his eyes, and kicked at Flint.

The bull rider had a foothold and jerked Guthrie's leg. He dodged the other foot and released the one he held. "Get up. We're going to church."

"Have you lost your ever-loving-mind?"

"That's it, that's the one I lost last night. Maybe, I'll find it in church. If not, it still occurs to me, my soul is long overdue a good cleansing."

"What time is it?" Guthrie raised to a sitting position.

"Fifteen years after six. You on a schedule?"

"You go save your soul. I'm going back to sleep." He flopped on the soft sleeping bag.

"Get up, Pard. I need you to take care of Lee while Sue and I wash away my sins. You got a white shirt?"

"Something tells me you two get together, there ain't enough soap in town." Hopelessly awake, he worked his way to the back of the Chevy and pulled the last ready-roll from the pack. "I didn't know you were so religious, anyway."

"Well, I am. Anyway, that ole boy may be right."

"What old boy?"

"That 'un who said, the only chance a cowboy has of

112

avoiding hell is for the Lord to grade on the curve. I don't want to be the worst wearing spurs and hollering giddy-up."

A few hours later, choking on a borrowed tie—and Flint wearing a New Mexico roper's white shirt—he, along with his sanctimonious convert, joined the women at the First Methodist Church. After the service, Sue's restaurant suggestion proved a success. Flint won over her little girl with the pheasant feather from his hatband then protected her from a too-friendly goose at the park's pond. An hour in the sun did the child in, and they separated until the evening show.

Guthrie managed a better than average ride on a horse named Amigo. The pickup men snatched him clean, and he maintained his lead. He won the average by two points over Albert Pearson. Flint gazed at a dark shouldered bull and barely nodded as he returned Guthrie's billfold accompanied by his own. Lee brushed off the bench beside her as Guthrie joined the two women before the Dakotan's ride. Sue sat on the other side of Lee.

Flint's bull, a big Brahma mix-breed, had been given a name and docked horns. The cowboys who named the brute didn't waste mental energy. Stingy with words, they just called him Blue. Those who clipped the horns acted more generous. They left about twelve inches.

The Brahma came out spinning, twisting, and kicking high. He brought an emphatic "can't make up his mind" from Wes by reversing his spin, but Flint stayed with him. The sheared horns whipped past, inches in front of the Dakotan's face. The crowd gasped with relief then again with stark fear as the buzzer sounded, and it became obvious the cowboy with the black hat had gotten his hand entangled in the bull rope.

Clowns raced toward the pair. The crowd rose to its feet. Sue grabbed her mouth. Guthrie fought his way to the aisle.

Flint tugged desperately at the wrap around his gloved hand that held him to the bull's back. The animal's movements jerked the rider's lithe body like a dog shaking a snake, but he stayed atop and centered on the broad back. The hand came free, and Flint swung a leg high to let momentum carry him to safety. The crowd screamed then sighed in relief. Guthrie was halfway down the aisle.

The bull's rump whipsawed and a hoof came down on back of the Dakotan's heel just as he hit the ground. Flint fell. Eighteen hundred pounds of infuriated monster turned on the helpless rider. He pushed with his hands and kicked at the Brahma with his feet.

One horn dug into the dirt inches from his chest. The other pounded into his stomach. The animal gored and twisted with his blood-drenched head, and Flint came free. He beat the bull's nose with his fists then grabbed a horn with each hand. His head fell back, the black hat still firmly tugged down to his ears. The enraged Brahma threw Flint's body high in the air.

Guthrie hurdled box seats. He gauged his leap so his left boot hit the top of the arena fence. He sank into the soft dirt, stumbled, then fell to his hands and knees.

Flint's body made a sick sound as it hit near him.

Behind the downed body, one clown desperately groped for a horn of the animal. The other bullfighter clung with a death grip to its tail. Walsh limped and half-ran from his barrel toward the melee.

Guthrie crawled on his hands and knees, struggling to rise. Sick with despair, he lurched to his feet. Only a short distance separated the bull from the motionless form of Flint. Continuing his charge, Blue raised his head. It was covered with blood—Flint's blood. The clown holding the horn lost his grip and fell.

Guthrie sprang at the bull, aware only of his hate for the brute and a stench that caused him to gag. The beast lowered his head and reached the rider first. He gored the now limp body.

All breath left Guthrie as he draped across the animal's neck. His left hand tugged at a horn, and he gouged with his thumb at the pig-like eye. Then came a loud crunching sound, pain more intense than life crashed inside his chest. Something smashed into his head, and the distant lights flashed crazily. He sensed himself again in the air. Quiet replaced real. Later, sirens, voices, and, again light drifted back. It became intensely cold.

The object appeared to be a clock, a big round clock. It hung on a white wall and had only one hand. Why would anyone have a one-handed clock? Maybe he was at the space center. They might even have a left-handed clock. Use it for count down. He didn't want to be at NASA. The farther from Houston he could stay, the better.

Clean sheets. An IV in his right arm. Funny, he didn't remember a car wreck. Where'd he been going? Man, it smelled nice here. Medicinal, but nice. Slowly, a piece at a time, his memory returned. His brain rationed him only what he could tolerate. Flint had to be dead. Yeah, and he'd been hurt. Maybe he was dead. That must be it.

Was this a holding pen? Was he waiting to be sorted and put with another bunch? There must be some serious dope in that IV. He really could care less about any of it.

"Guthrie? Are you awake?"

Who was that? "Lee? Oh, my God, Lee." A wave of memory washed over him. He burst into sobs, quiet sobs that tore at his heart, pulled at sore chest muscles, and screamed through pain in his head. Tears ran down the sides of his face. "What . . . what day?"

"Monday morning. It's three-fifteen. Oh, thank God, my darling. My crazy, crazy darling." Her watery figure stood over him.

His sobbing stopped, but the tears continued. "He's gone, isn't he?"

"Yes, darling. I'm so sorry."

Guthrie now understood Sammy's struggle with words. "There was a moment there, that son . . . had his horn in him, and he knew it was over. Still he fought him."

"I know, I know."

Guthrie dozed, jerked, and awoke. He located the clock's other hand. It made it read ten after five.

x

116

Someone grasped Lee's arm above the elbow, then a man in a white smock stood in her place.

"Mr. Sawyer, how do you feel?"

"Not too bad. What's wrong with me?"

"For starters, a concussion, bruised ribs and two bones broken in your left hand, but we'll get you fixed up. You'll be good as new in a few days. That is, if you stay away from rodeos." The doctor shined a light in Guthrie's eyes, muttered "good, good," then walked out.

The next time, Guthrie awoke to Lee's heavy breathing. She curled in a chair with her arms wrapped around her knees. A spread covered her. She stirred, blinked, looked at the clock, and stood. "Guthrie, I've got to call Mom and tell her why I'm going to be late. Would you like for me to call Cora and Jesse?"

"No, guess not. I'll call in a day or so. Tell Evelyn not to mention this for a few days."

"Guthrie, I'm not telling her any such thing. You know this will make the papers."

"Okay, if you don't mind, call them. Just say I've got a couple of little bones broke in my hand." Lee stood with her fists on her hips. For the first time, he could picture her in a classroom.

"You're not even going home to recuperate, are you?"

"Don't see no need."

Lee bit her lower lip. "I'll be leaving before noon. Anything I can do for you before I go?"

"No. Tell John Robert, hey."

15

The doctor removed the bandage from Guthrie's head Tuesday morning and signed his release. He stuck out his hand. "I patch a lot of banged up cowboys, but not many who did what I understand you did. You take care."

"Thanks, Doc." His image from the mirror revealed enough nasty to turn a strong stomach. He wondered if he could wear a hat, then where his might be. Last he'd seen of it, he was trying to wrap it around a bull's face.

Guthrie caught a cab to the rodeo grounds. The old station wagon looked lonely in the parking lot. He paid the cabby and realized he still carried Flint's wallet. The billfold held five hundred dollars and a card giving the South Dakota address of a brother, Rex.

Contrary to the doctor's instructions, he'd drive to a post office and mail everything, plus send word to Rex on how to contact the Abilene rodeo officials. It might be Flint's estate had money coming from the average. He couldn't remember hearing the bull rider's final score.

A note flapped on the office door saying uncollected prize money could be picked up at the city secretary's office. He had thirty-five hundred dollars there, so he'd get that then mail Flint's stuff.

Guthrie wiped sweat walking toward the station wagon. He wobbled slightly. That doctor may not have been such an old maid after all. He'd been pretty emphatic about no driving or physical activity. Boy, that elastic bandage around his chest was tight. Sort of made you suck up your milk and breathe short.

He probably should head for Saddle Horn and rest a few days, but if his mom saw him like this, she'd get back on that high horse about premed. He must have heard it a thousand times. "The money's there, every penny, all you'll need, enough to go right on through your doctorate."

Naw, to hell with it, he might have to sell popcorn when he got there, but Saturday's rodeo in San Angelo was the place for him. Something hung on the station wagon's radio aerial. A few steps closer and his eyes focused enough to recognize his hat on the antenna. Some of the boys must have put it there after his wreck before they pulled out.

Sunday night's events washed back at him and for a moment, with what looked like Flint's truck kicking up dust toward him. Was he seeing things? The pickup pulled to a stop beside him. It was Flint's.

"You Guthrie?" The kid crawling out looked under twenty.

"Uh, huh."

The boy stuck out his hand. "I'm Jackie Payne. They said at the hospital, you'd just left."

"That's right. He told me they'uz three of you. You must be the little one." Guthrie gripped the swarthy youngster's hand. "I'm glad to meet yuh."

"They told us what you did. I wanted to find you before I headed north."

119

"Who? Told you what?"

"A fellow named Wes Hodges called first." A muscle rippled in Jackie's jaw. He conquered the mist in his eyes and locked them straight on with Guthrie's. "After he told us about Flint, seemed like we all wanted to know more. Rex called back, and that's when he told us about you and how you fought that bull."

"I'uz too little and too late. Your brother was my best friend, and I couldn't help him." Guthrie fought his own mist. "Rodeo ain't gonna be the same without Flint Payne." He dug in his pockets. "Here, here's some stuff of his." He handed Jackie the money-filled wallet and a pocketknife.

"Thanks, I didn't know about this. It ain't why I looked you up. Just wanted you to know we appreciate you, and we're glad you're not bad hurt."

"You heading back with the truck?"

"Yeah, Rex is flying back with the . . . the . . . casket. Should get in sometime in the morning." Jackie thumbed the corners of folding money. "You need any of this? He'd want you to have it."

Guthrie shook his head, put a hand on Jackie's shoulder. "You pull over and sleep some. Your folks lost enough. Know this is hard for them, but tell 'em to be proud. Men like their boy don't come along often. They're like fireflies. He did for grown-ups what lightning bugs do for kids." Guthrie choked. "I'll miss him."

Wes Hodges worked the San Angelo crowd and, now, did the same in El Paso. "Ladies and gents, working

120

hurt is part of cowboying. Whether it's on the ranch or in the arena, pain's generally taken as a part of the job. It's paid no mind. In spite of that, old Guthrie Sawyer, down there in chute number three has to be tallied among the toughest cowboys to ever pull on a pair a chaps."

The chestnut flinched then tensed as Guthrie's weight settled onto the saddle. The animal erupted straight up from the chute, pawing, falling backward and slinging his body.

"Watch out, Guthrie!" Real concern, not showmanship filled the amplified voice.

Strong arms pulled Guthrie up and away. Flames of pain licked his sore ribs.

A chute man near the horse's head half-fell and half-jumped to the ground. He slung his hand and hollered. His oaths cast doubts on the mount's ancestry back to the Conquistadors.

The horse slid away down into the chute. Thank God for those hands pulling him to safety. The top rail rubbed Guthrie's rump. His feet found footing. The bronc stood, and Guthrie again worked himself into position to mount the outlaw.

"Close call! I was talking tough. Two weeks ago this cowboy fought a bull off a dying friend in Abilene and came out a little squashed. Last weekend, he rode three nights in San Angelo. If you've ever had busted or bruised ribs, you know nothing hurts worse. Well, he had 'em. For icing, he rode with broken bones in his hand and a concussion.

121

"With one arm wrapped to his chest, he worked them bronc's like a three-legged dog in a rabbit hunt. Must have had more tape on him than those Egyptian mummies. He's healthy tonight, though. Riding with only a broken hand and a little dizziness. A round of applause for Guthrie Sawyer on Reject."

The gate swung open, and Wes' words faded into crowd noise. Reject didn't buck. He ran. Guthrie raked him with the spurs, but got no response. By the third step, he knew this gelding danced to the wrong music. Something wasn't right. He normally gave a good ride, bucking to the left. Not tonight, he wasn't going to buck, or turn, and he might not stop until next week. Whatever ghosts raced through its ignorant brain, this horse spelled trouble.

Guthrie quit spurring, put his sore hand with the other one, and tried to turn the crazed animal. True to the old-time, bronc-rider's code of never spoiling a horse by surrendering to bad behavior, Guthrie dismissed any idea of jumping. The time to bail off came and went. They passed the pickup men near mid-arena. The fence at the far end loomed.

The crowd noise stopped. The roar of the horse's breath replaced all sound. The animal looked neither left nor right. They neared the oval-arena fence at an angle. They'd hit a glancing blow on Reject's nigh shoulder. In their path, behind the fence, people in box seats rose.

There'd be no turning or leaping, this snake wasn't even seeing. Guthrie shifted his weight to the right

122

stirrup and lifted his left leg just prior to impact.

Reject should bounce, probably regain his balance, and there'd be a pickup man on the way back down the arena. The thought flashed in his mind, its comfort momentary. The horse's body hit, then it all became jumbled, but the big thing was, he didn't bounce. They went through.

Steel pipe and wire mesh fence went with them. Reject ended on top. People screamed. Now the chestnut bounced, up and down, above Guthrie. Pain, God, how he hated it. He'd hurt so damn much.

Each time the horse went up, his feet slipped from beneath him, and he came down, stopping inches from Guthrie's face. Wedged between fragmented, steel-seat supports on either side, he avoided much of the animal's weight.

Again, Reject fell sideways, screamed a fear-laden cry, far more shrilly than the humans around him. He thrashed and blotted out the light. The chestnut twisted again. His hooves slipped on wet concrete, slammed against the pinned cowboy.

Fear choked him. He wallowed in slime, viewed folds of the horse's wrinkled skin near the girth and beneath its forelegs. Then came the pattern of swirled hair gathering to the gelding's naval. All the wrong side of things—things a rider hopes never to see—panned before him. He drifted away from his pain, quit fighting the shadows, and wrapped himself in darkness.

Winter winds blew across his body, and foul odors from the floor's slime wafted away.

123

Guthrie didn't know how long he drifted, but the person behind that curtain had big-time trouble breathing. Whoever, they sounded like they were hooked to a windmill. Pull, push, breath in, breath out. Guthrie shivered. They'd put him back in those refrigerated pens again. Maybe, it was a hospital or perhaps a funeral home. Set up another drink, bartender, this ain't like last time. Hurts too much. Those clouds up there moved. No, shadows. It was shadows.

Someone peered at him. "Hey, boy. How you doing?"

"Sammy?"

"Who? Sammy? No, Guthrie, it's me, Jesse. Sammy ain't here. I 'un get him, though, if you want. Take a couple of days, but I 'un go now. You're in a hospital, remember?"

"Uh, yeah. Had a wreck, didn't I?" One arm wouldn't move so he lifted the other to his head and found it bandaged.

"Yeah, you got caught up in a runaway. Should have bailed out." Jesse seemed to talk from a well.

"Now you tell me. It's El Paso, right?"

"Uh huh, you're in what's called ICU. I better go get Cora. She's been near crazy." Jesse began to fade away.

"Jesse, how long yawl been here?"

"Since day before yesterday. I'll see you again in a bit. I'm going to tell Cora."

He must be serious hurt if Jesse came. If they'd been here over a full day, he'd been out of it no telling how long.

His mother appeared almost instantly. Dark rings

124

sagged beneath her eyes. Her lips were set, stiff, and stern. Her expression softened. Her eyes moistened, no tears, but honest to goodness mist shone there. She leaned and kissed his forehead. "How you feel, Son?"

"How long since you slept?"

"I don't need much sleep. How you feel?"

Guthrie tried not to make a face. "Pretty good. How yawl?"

"We're okay. Erilee called awhile ago. Jesse's calling her back now. I told him to when he came out and told me."

"Told you what?"

"That you come to."

"Mom, how long was I out?"

"This is Wednesday. It happened Saturday night."

"What all's wrong."

"That concussion thing is the worst. The doctor wouldn't say much. You aggravated all those old injuries and added a dislocated shoulder. Do you hurt?"

"Not too bad. Guess Erilee's pretty worried."

"She'd probably be here, but her mother's having a bad week."

The second day of consciousness, Guthrie's sight cleared. At noon, Jesse and his mom stopped by on their way home. Cora exacted a promise he would come straight to Saddle Horn upon his release. He walked to the elevator with them. Jesse held the brim of his hat in both hands, and his mom wiggled her fingers at him through the elevator's last opening.

Shortly after breakfast the next day, a young man

delivered an arrangement of cut flowers. The note read, "I can't leave Mom right now, but think of you every day. So glad you're better. With all my love, Erilee."

He held the container, bringing his nose close to daisies, gladiolus, and others he couldn't name. The blossoms' faint aroma brought a sense of loneliness, a longing for Lee. He looked at the petals, thought of her smile, the way she wrinkled her nose. He sat on the edge of the bed, wanting to call. With a sigh, he picked up the phone and dialed. At least he could hear her voice.

Her mother answered. "Guthrie, I'm sorry, she's not here. Lane called last night, and she left with Ira's pilot for Houston about daylight. Is everything all right with you?"

"I'm fine, Evelyn. How are you doing?"

"Better, today. She'll be glad you called."

"She is coming back?"

"Of course. You want me to take a message?"

"No, everything's fine. I'll talk to her later."

She'd lied to him, big-time. She could leave her mom for old Lane. All he had to do was pick up the phone, and she was off to Houston, but Guthrie Sawyer, ooh, no. She was with that Lane Walker right now. Guthrie's heart pounded, his temple throbbed, and he suddenly wanted to lie down. He eased his head to the pillow and stared at the ceiling.

16

Guthrie lay on the bed, his eyes closed. Across his mind, blurred images of the oval of horse's hooves thrashed before his eyes. Seemingly, each movement attempted to brand his nose and forehead with the v-shaped frog imprint so visible in the hoof's sole. Someone knocked on the door. He roused.

"Come in."

A thin-faced, little man wearing glasses peeked around the door then approached Guthrie's bed with short rapid steps. "Mr. Sawyer, good. I didn't want to wake you. Thought you might be sleeping. I'm Leon Irvin."

"That's okay, I'm about caught up on rest." They shook hands. "Have a seat."

Leon pulled the chair closer to the bed. "Pretty flowers."

Guthrie nodded, pushed the button that raised his head. Probably a preacher ran through his mind.

"Mr. Sawyer, I'm the City Attorney for El Paso."

"Just call me Guthrie. In other words, you're a lawyer?"

"Yes, that's right. The city manager called, and we were discussing how much the rodeo does for the community, how proud we are to have it. Well, Mr. Monroe thought I might come by and see how you were getting along. That was a mighty bad spill you took."

Guthrie shook a cigarette partially out of a package. "Want a smoke?" Leon shook his head. "Mr. Monroe

127

would be the city manager?"

"Why, yes, he is. I didn't make that very clear, did I?"

"No, no, you did all right. It's just my head. It's still sort of idling."

Leon smiled. "Guthrie, like I said, we're proud of the rodeo and especially you boys that come in and voluntarily take those risks and all. Actually, Guthrie," Leon leaned and lowered his voice, "the city does quite well with increased business when you all are in town."

Guthrie reached for the lighter Jesse'd placed on the bed stand. "I understand. We try to put on a good show."

"Yes, and that you do. Guthrie, I'll just come right out with it. The city wants to pay your part of the hospital costs. You understand, show our appreciation."

"Why, that's mighty big of you, Leon. I gotta say, It's pretty unusual, too."

"It is unusual, but we're a Western town and proud of our heritage." Leon beamed. "We just like to do what's right."

"I appreciate this."

"Good, good!" Leon fumbled with the latch on a briefcase. "There're a couple of papers here, just routine stuff. It'll help move everything through the hospital's accounting department." Leon pulled a pen from his pocket. He stood, leaned over the bed, supporting the papers with a note pad. "If you'll sign both right here, we'll take care of everything. Won't cost you a cent."

Nervous as a sinner in Church with a weak bladder, this guy appeared to prefer other places a little too much. Guthrie took the pen. This luck he'd not expected. He had a policy through the association, but still, this bill would have hit him hard. He read the word release at the top of the form.

Whoa! Something wasn't right here. No wonder Leon hurried. The lawyer dealt from a crooked deck. At least the trucker in Abilene had been good at it. The little shrimp. "Who am I releasing from what?"

"Don't pay any attention to that, Mr. Sawyer. It's like I said, just paper work to show we're authorized to settle your account." The attorney adjusted his glasses, pointed at the signature blank.

"Leave them here. I'll study them. Maybe sign. If so, you can pick them up tomorrow."

Leon gathered the papers, backed toward the door. "No, no, that's okay, Mr. Sawyer. I see you have some reservations about all this. I'll contact you later." He disappeared around the door.

Guthrie puzzled over the meaning of the lawyer's visit. The man's behavior tugged at his mind most of the afternoon. Shortly after supper, Wes Hodges called from Hobbs, New Mexico. The announcer arrived there earlier in the week to do the Old Settler's Reunion and Rodeo. Guthrie assured him he'd be back on the circuit in a few weeks then mentioned the lawyer's visit.

"Guthrie, don't you sign no release. You hear me? That box you landed in belonged to the Radcliffs. You know who that is?"

"Yeah, they own the Seven-Y-A spread, don't they?"

"That and about half of Chicago. Anyway, they put a

129

bevy of lawyers on that wreck of yours. Seems like, their grandbaby was hurt bad. Guthrie, word I got is, some of that new fence wasn't welded, just tacked. Right where you hit was the only place like that, but somebody screwed up. Were I you, I'd get me a good lawyer, maybe sign on with that Y-A bunch. This could be your ticket."

"Wes, thanks. You catching a cold?"

"No, just a frog in my throat. Thinking about having it seen about though. See ya."

"Thanks for calling." Guthrie slowly cradled the receiver. So that was it. No wonder Leon pissed on his leg so, trying to butter him up.

A white cloud drifted slowly in the late afternoon sky. Wispy bits of vapor separated, disappeared, and changed the shape of the original image. First it had been a panther then the long tail became a striking leg and a hoof developed. He trembled. God, what was going on? It was only a cloud, an image in the sky. He wiped sweat from his forehead, forced his view back to the room.

His mind failed to focus. Lawyers, hospital bills, he wondered what his stay would cost. Lee and Lane were together. Was she going back to that gutless slab of high-toned garbage? Hospital bills—John Robert—the boy's face appeared then his back, hobbling toward a hurdle. John Robert turned, and the mental image of all that determination and courage from the boy's face bathed Guthrie with a sensation of well being that startled him.

Excited, the picture remained. John Robert, Flap, had the answers. Maybe the boy had just hit a nerve, perhaps, a want-to-be-a-dad nerve. Whatever, he would help the boy. To hell with Lane, to hell with Lee! They were going to be or do whatever they decided, but that boy deserved his chance. Maybe this wreck was the ticket.

He picked up the phone and dialed Saddle Horn, Evelyn's number. "Hello, Mrs. Kramp? This is Guthrie Sawyer. Do you have a number in Houston that'll reach Lee?"

Evelyn informed him Lee had returned home and put her on the line.

"Guthrie, dear, how are you?"

"Fine. How was Houston?"

"How was it? Oh, just peachy! You should have been there."

"For a daddy who's cut him off, sounds like Ira's taking pretty good care of little Lane, bless his heart."

"Guthrie, what's eating you?"

"Nothing, I'm sorry. Guess I'm outta line. It's just the idea of you and Lane together."

"There were papers to sign. Nothing's changed there. Cora said you were coming home for awhile. When will I see you?"

"About a week. How's old J. R.?"

"He's fine."

"Lady across the hall says her grandson, who lives down at Pasadena, has a bad hand. Said he's born with it. I told her about John Robert, and she had a million questions." Guthrie held a pen and paper.

"Give her Dr. Casey's name. Dr. A. D. Casey, over at Gulf Coast General."

"Thanks, I'll tell her." He quickly wrote the names.

"Guthrie, I'm so anxious to see you. I haven't been able to get Flint out of my mind. He was so full of life. I talked to Sue last week. It hit her awful hard, and now this happens to you."

"Yeah, same here about Flint. Did I tell you about talking to his brother?"

"Uh-huh, last week."

"Seemed like a nice kid. And speaking of missing somebody, my old sore head won't think of nobody but you."

"Just make sure it stays that way."

"So long, sweetheart."

Guthrie hung up the phone then sat on the edge of the bed looking at the attorney's business card and thinking of Erilee. Maybe she told it straight. Certainly there would be legal affairs to take care of in a divorce. Down deep the old hurt still smoldered, but he didn't have to act like some jealous kid.

He dialed the city attorney's number. Leon agreed to drop by at nine, tomorrow morning.

An elastic bandage wrapped a metal splint fitted partially around Guthrie's left hand. A sling around his neck supported his dislocated left shoulder. Otherwise, his body was now free of all hospital harness. Saturday morning he enjoyed the luxury of a shower. He shaved, put on Levi's, and felt whole again. A nurse helped him thread his arm into the sleeve of Jesse's robe. His mom mentioned that it had only been worn once. His dad mumbled something about it being drafty from the bottom up and indicated Guthrie should keep it.

A cleaning lady worked on the room when Leon arrived. Guthrie pushed back his breakfast tray and nodded for the lawyer to follow him. "We'll go down here and let her finish up. Want some coffee, Mr. Irvin?"

The waiting room beyond the phone was small, quiet, and unoccupied. Guthrie took a seat and the lawyer sat opposite him with a coffee table between.

Leon set his briefcase to one side, blew his coffee, and smiled. "Now, what's on your mind, Mr. Sawyer?"

"Some folks said it looks like the welder may have missed a section in that arena fence."

"I'm not aware of that."

"I suggest you check it out. Here's the deal, Leon. I've got an eight-year old friend—write this down— John Robert Walker. J. R. has a birth defect, a tendon or some such thing going to his heel. It's been examined and the medical details are known to a specialist in Houston." Guthrie nodded at the lawyer's writing pad. "His name is Doctor A. D. Casey at Gulf Coast General. He can probably give you a good idea what corrective surgery and follow-up visits should cost.

"I want you to get the signature of everyone necessary on a document to Dr. Casey and the hospital down there saying how anxious the City of El Paso is to pay

133

one hundred percent of that boy's expense for the procedure.

"Also, I want this all taken care of before school starts. The boy's grandmother is ill, and it'll be more difficult later. Now, you get that paper here along with the clause about covering my expenses, and we'll call things square. Bring me the papers properly signed, and I'll give you your release. How's that sound?"

"Well I don't know, Mr. Sawyer. I don't see any connection between your accident, one which you signed a prior association release on, and a boy's birth defect." Leon rolled his pen between his fingers.

"Leon, I'm not gonna fuss with you. We both know faulty facilities void any release. You keep talking, and when you leave here, my next call will be to the Radcliff's lawyer to talk about all this pain and mental anguish that's pestering me. There's also a matter of lost purses I've not even mentioned.

"Once again, I suggest you take what you got and run." Guthrie lit a Viceroy and watched the creases on Leon's forehead protrude as his face reddened. The champion of justice wrote furiously.

"Another thing, Mr. Irvin, I'm doing this anonymously. No one but you and I, and the necessary city officials, are to know I'm involved. Not the boy, his family, no one. Can you handle all this, or do you need me to get you some help?"

"I've got it, Mr. Sawyer. There's no need for others."

"Just tell the mother an anonymous benefactor wanted to do this for John Robert."

• • •

The orderly stepped between Erilee and John Robert's gurney. "Surgery waiting room is there to your left, Mrs. Walker. A doctor will be out to talk to you as soon as they have information."

Swinging doors closed behind her son, separating them. An ocean of fear, tears, hysteria cried to be unleashed. She fought back the urge to give in to the emotions and curl crying on the floor. Instead, she walked unseeingly through the waiting room to east-facing windows. She'd wanted so to kiss that brave forehead one more time. He was giddy with medication, unafraid. What would happen to his spirit if this didn't work?

It had all come about so fast. The call last week from Dr. Casey's appointment clerk explaining the benefactor, then two days later the doctor's assistant phoned. Lane's dad had to be the person making this miracle possible.

It was Ira's way of saving face, not backing down from his vow that Lane had to make his own way, support his own family after flunking out of college. The old miser defined hateful and stingy, but thank goodness for this. Still, how anyone could totally ignore a grandson like Ira did amazed her. No wonder Lane was so screwed up. He had no one to learn from. This was one of Ira's few decent acts, and it shamed him. Sad, worst of all, it typified her son's paternal family.

Outside the hospital window, early traffic on I-45 thickened, light clouds drifted in from the gulf. Why couldn't the sun be shining? She silently mouthed the words "Our Father which art—" She finished the fourth verse of The Lord's Prayer and turned from the window more at ease. She poured herself coffee, smiled at the middle-aged lady sitting across from the couch, then picked up a magazine and absently flipped its well-worn pages.

Her thoughts drifted to Guthrie, how alone he looked after tousling J. R.'s hair and waving bye at the Lubbock airport. He constantly amazed her. At times the oldest man in the Panhandle, then the next moment, the most fun loving kid in the world. She had no idea a man could be so sensitive, so uninhibited with some emotions while so protective of what must be scars from Jesse's escapades.

Guthrie'd been home from El Paso three weeks now and that steel blade of a body of his seemed healed. Still, he worried her. He was more restless, less confident, and slower to laugh. She knew he missed Flint and the rodeo, but he wouldn't talk. Hid his own needs, maybe too well. For her part, she just rattled on, mostly about how John Robert hung the moon.

Lord, she missed him. What kind of woman was she? Her only child a few feet away in that awful room, undergoing surgery, and she sat here thinking of Guthrie Sawyer's hard body, his gliding, cat-like movements, and the swagger to that flat-butted walk with the rippling buns. She could almost sense him beside her, listening to her stupid chatter.

Perhaps she shouldn't have discouraged his coming,

but she'd thought, for John Robert's sake, Lane had to be told about the surgery. She'd been afraid of what Guthrie might do if he and Lane got together. It'd be just like her ex to make some smart-mouth comment, and that would never work. As much as she longed for Guthrie's presence, she'd been right. Best those two were kept apart. She didn't know the historical basis for it, but bits and pieces of conversation taught youngsters growing up around Saddle Horn that you didn't mix whiskey and Indians or Sawyers and Walkers.

A teen-age girl listened as the middle-age woman spoke in low tones. The conversation concerned a car wreck and an injured young man. The girl listened attentively, but her sight remained fixed on something across the room.

Lee followed the line of vision. There he stood, straight, checking others in the waiting room. Guthrie's eyes met hers. A smile broke across his face. Quick steps brought him to her.

She stood, content in his arms. She lowered her head to his shoulder, squeezed him, and trembled. A tear ran down her face, disappeared against his shirt. "Tight, hold me, tight."

17

Dr. Casey exuded confidence and explained to Erilee that John Robert's surgery had gone well. He viewed the prognosis with guarded optimism. Shortly afterwards, Guthrie listened to the boy's end of a phone conversation with Lane. John Robert excitedly informed his mom that his dad would be by shortly after lunch the following day. A really big business deal prevented him coming sooner.

Guthrie caught a nine a.m. flight to Lubbock the next morning and drove on to Saddle Horn.

Three weeks later, he and Lee sat in the station wagon watching the boy negotiate the low steps of Evelyn's front porch. He still took the steps sideways, one at a time. Four days with a walking stick after the earlier crutches left him a little tentative.

"Where we going, Guthrie?" John Robert grunted while closing the car door with his mom hanging onto his belt.

"Lee's got sandwiches in that box, and the cooler's full of cold drinks. We're going to drop by Bud's then stop back by the rim of Wild Mule Canyon. We'll eat those sandwiches, your mom calls it a picnic, out at a place I know and watch God turn off the lamp down in those brakes."

John Robert chuckled, snorted through his nose, and gave his mother a knowing look. The glance seemed to say. "You sure picked a Lou-Lou."

On Main Street, Guthrie stopped short of the state highway intersection and allowed Sam to coast past, performing a U-turn in front of them. The musician rode his bicycle off the highway at a fast clip. His guitar was strapped to his back. He stopped, smiled broadly and leaned his bike against the side of the service station. Guthrie backed up and parked beside him.

"Sammy, this is Lee's boy, John Robert."

"Well bless my s . . . soul." Sam stuck his hand in the open window and shook the eager boy's hand.

"Used to, you could call me Flap, but I about quit."

" 'Bout q . . . quit what?"

"Flapping. I had a operation to quit flapping."

Sam rolled letters on his tongue an instant, looked at Lee. "Good. Where y . . . awl going?"

"Bud's, then the canyon."

"M . . . m . . . me, too." Sam slipped the guitar sling over his head, held the instrument in one hand, opened the tailgate and crawled in. He sat between Guthrie's bedroll and saddle in the station wagon's cargo space.

Guthrie looked at Lee. She smiled and shrugged her shoulders. He hooked his thumb at the sandwich box. "How many's in there?"

"Enough."

"Let . . . m . . . m . . . me off at overlook."

"Wherever you want, Sammy."

Lee's eyes questioned him. "Y'all been there together?"

"Lots of times." Guthrie took her hand. "That last year of school, after you left, he and I turned off the lights out there a bunch."

They dropped Sam off at the canyon's rim with his guitar and a cold soft drink. Guthrie walked to the rock ledge and helped Sam inspect for snakes.

The rocky lookout projected over a sheer drop-off of perhaps eighty feet. Before them, open space blanketed raw, washed land, and in the distance, the other side of the canyon formed the horizon. The sun dallied an hour high, while below, shadows formed a devil's lattice-work covering miles of canyon floor.

Strains of Sam's music probed the valley's depth, followed the cars departure, then faded behind them.

"Won't he get lonesome before we get back?" John Robert placed his face opposite the remains of a windshield-splattered butterfly and frowned.

"Not him. He and time are friendly." Guthrie rested his arm on the seatback. "There'll likely be deer and coyote, no telling what, coming out down there below him. He'll watch those fading shadows and play his music."

"Animals come in spite of the music?" Lee's disbelief showed.

"Sometimes, I think, because of it." Guthrie smiled.

John Robert turned in his seat. "I want to go back and wait with him."

"We'll see him again in a minute. I think Guthrie and Bud have something to show you."

"What! What's Bud got out there, Guthrie?"

"Never can tell. Might have an old sow with baby pigs or something."

"Humph!" The boy made a face then folded his arms and stared at the dash.

A few minutes down the highway, a cattle guard broke the barbed wire fences' rank. Worn parallel wheel tracks wound from the pavement through a pasture of short grass and low brush to the higher elevation occupied by Bud's place. Waist-high mesh wire mounted on posts and two-by-fours surrounded the ancient ranch house.

Bud's wife, Jean, surrendered her Stanford dormitory room years earlier and followed her new marine husband back to their Texas roots. She did not surrender her love of plants, hence the mesh wire. It protected flowerbeds and the surrounding lawn from inquisitive livestock.

The two-story house stood at attention. No frills adorned its straight and functional frame. Stoic and weathered, only a few areas of scaly paint varied its color from that of the seasoned mesquite roots scattered in the pasture. Fifty-year old lightning rods peaked at the roof corners and connected with twisted iron that followed ridgelines and eaves to an ultimate ground. The front faced Wild Mule Canyon, and to one side stood a barn more recently painted and larger than the residence.

Two tongue-lolling mutts greeted the station wagon, yards from the enclosure's gate. Their mixed features spoke to the fact that chance and convenience, not pedigree and prejudice controlled the circumstances of ancestral social life. Still, thick, shaggy coats and a knee-high size indicated a dominance of shepherd heritage.

Lee looked around. "Reckon anyone's here?"

"Don't know. If not, we'll just go in and wait."

"I'm not about to go in Jean's house uninvited. Don't they lock up?"

"Heard Bud say once, he'd never had a key in his

pocket." Guthrie braked the car, noted her raise an eyebrow.

John Robert pointed at the dogs. "They sure got long tongues. Why don't they bark?"

"Naw, he was serious, Honey. Said his daddy lost the house key years ago, and when he bought a new pickup or car, he left the things in the ignition. I believe him."

"Sounds a little dumb. He'll end up ripped-off one of these days." Lee looked toward the barn. "His pickup's over there."

"May sound dumb, but think of the relief of not having to run around locking things up all the time. Way he explains it, if anybody makes it this far out, and he's home, he'll invite them in. If he's gone, nobody would hear 'em break in anyway. Bud ain't dumb. The dumb one would be whoever tried to sneak in. Chances are that thirty-thirty in his gun rack's loaded."

"Okay, okay, I wasn't running Bud or Jean down. After Houston, it just seems strange."

Guthrie put his arm around her. "You just went and got citified. There he is. I bet Jean's in town."

Bud led a sorrel from behind the barn toward a stout snubbing-post in the center of the corral. He held the young horse's halter rope with one hand and carried a deep-seated saddle with the other. He hollered. "Yawl get out."

John Robert opened the door, crouched to his knees, and put his hand out to the two dogs. They sat on their haunches, panting, and appearing to smile.

Guthrie took Lee's hand and walked her to the corral

142

fence. "Bud, you know Lee. This is her son, John Robert."

The rancher finished tying the horse and stepped through a gate. He silently mouthed "Lee", smiled and winked at the youngster. "Yeah, I saw old John Robert two or three years back. He was up town one day with his daddy. How you doing, John? Guthrie tells me you had a operation."

"I did. Why don't them dogs bark?"

"Those dogs." Lee smiled at Bud. "Is Jean here?"

"She's after groceries." The cowman turned his attention back to John Robert. "I saw yawl coming halfway down to the highway and told them to be quiet."

"They know English?"

"No, I know dog."

The boy looked inquisitively at Guthrie.

"Don't get me in the middle. This is between you and him."

The kid looked at Bud. "You don't know dog."

"Just clap your hands and holler sic-em," he said.

John Robert did as instructed, and the dogs ran to the fence barking furiously at the tied horse. The horse braced his legs, rolled his eyes, and leaned backward, fighting the halter.

"Hush," Bud hollered, and the dogs quieted.

The boy showed new respect for his host.

"Sic-em is speak, and hush is quiet in dog."

"I may need you when school starts, Bud." Erilee laughed.

"Naw, you're a little after me or you'd remember, I

143

sorta draw the line at school. Me and it never did mix too good, but I'll bet you're able to hold a tight rein on 'em."

John Robert moved in front of his mother and faced Bud. "Mom said you and Guthrie had something to show me."

"That's right. I was talking to Jesse, you know—Guthrie's dad—about a problem I got. See that sorrel with the white sox there at the side of the barn?" Bud pointed at a blazed-face mare that grazed with a couple of other horses. "Well, she's been at the top of my string since I's a teenager. Don't generally work mares, but she's an exception."

The boy's gaze alternated from the mare to the rancher.

"John, she's the kind that always wants to be in front, be a leader. She's getting a little age on her, now. Oh, she still wants out front and gives me all she's got, but I want to ease off on her a little, get her off the ranch. Not working so hard.

"Well, Jesse heard me say something about it and offered the use of those lots of his, there just a few houses down from your grandmother's." Bud paused.

"This is where you come in, John. Jesse said, if I could find a kid somewhere who would see to Maude, feed her twice a day, and maybe ride her some. You know horses need a little exercise. Said, if we could just find someone to do that, I could leave her there at his place." From Bud's tone, he could as easily deal with a cattle buyer for the total of next year's calf crop.

144

"You think of anybody could maybe handle that?" He looked at John Robert then waited patiently.

The boy seemed to have forgotten the dogs. He swung his cane rapidly, taking a few quick steps toward the mare. Maude grazed with short shearing bites on close-cropped grass. Her muzzle worked rapidly, selecting and arranging bites, and her small fox-like ears moved back and forth. Half-dollar size blobs of white hair along her withers indicated healed, saddle scalds. Her tail swished, and she rolled the skin beneath the white spots, fighting flies.

John Robert pinned a don't-let-me-down look at his mother. "I could do that."

"It'd mean getting out of that bed at my first call every morning before school. You have to be sure. You're talking big time responsibility, but, yes, I think you're big enough to handle it, if you're sure."

"I am. Bud, how about me? I'll do you a good job."

"Good. It'd sure help me out."

John Robert shuffled to the fence as fast as the cane would permit and stood watching Maude. He hollered over his shoulder. "Thanks, Bud."

"I thank you, but tell Guthrie. He sorta got this thing rolling."

Guthrie stood a few feet behind the boy. John Robert turned and walked to him. He stuck his hand out to shake. "Thanks, Guthrie."

"You bet, J. R., but I just got them two started."

"It's your idea though, I bet'cha."

Guthrie pointed at Maude. "She's as good as they

come, boy. See how broad that forehead is and them big round doe eyes? That spells smarts. She's got high withers to make a saddle sit good and long curved pasterns for a soft ride and speed. Those straight legs put the finishing touches on her then you can add to that what Bud said about wanting to be where the action is. She's a keeper, all right."

John Robert hustled to his mom. "Ain't she pretty, Mom. See her big eyes. When can we bring her to town?"

"Two weeks. The doctor said you could do away with your walking stick then. Seems to me, you've a couple of pretty good friends, huh?"

John Robert crawled under the fence and limped close enough to pet Maude. The mutts marched to either side of him, watching the mare.

Guthrie nodded toward the corral. "Looks like that one's still a little rank."

"Uh-huh, it's his second time at that post. He's not taking too kindly to schooling.

"Hey, how about me going in and pulling some T-bones out of that deep freeze and putting them on the grill. Jean'll be back shortly. After we fill up, we'll sit around and gripe about the government."

"No, we got a picnic." Guthrie walked with Lee toward the car. "We left old Sam over there at the over-look. Better see to him. Sounds good though, we'll catch you another day."

"Anytime. Before you go, come tell me what you think of this colt's hoof. It abscessed about six months ago, but I think it's going to be okay."

Guthrie closed the gate behind them while Bud walked toward the sulking two-year old. The cowman soothed the colt with soft-spoken praise and flattery. He put one hand under the horse's neck, near the chest, and rubbed its shoulders with the other, repeating phrases like "that's a good boy" and "sure, you're just a pet". The horse fixed his eye on Guthrie and followed his progress toward the snubbing post.

Nearing the horse, a sense of uneasiness washed through Guthrie. The realization that he viewed this stringy two-year old as a threat gave him a cattle-prod jolt. Hair on the back of his neck tingled, fear chilled him, and stationary objects seemed to waver. Even the steady Bud swayed like wind-stirred wheat.

18

Guthrie blinked the low sun out of his eyes and accepted that he, not the world, swayed. He forced himself to move beside Bud just as his friend bent to pick up the horse's hoof. His attempt at nonchalance left him feeling about as useful as an egg-sucking dog.

The horse shied, moved away in a sudden reaction to some inner fright. Prevented from rearing by the short line, he attempted to paw with the foot Bud held. Guthrie leaped backward. Fear mocked him, and bile burned his throat. Never had he been so scared. In combat there was reason for his fear. This was strange, seemingly self-imposed, yet, uncontrollable. He stood and shivered from a chill. Sweat rolled down his forehead.

Bud retained his hold on the foot, hollered "whoa horse" and followed the animal's movement around the post. His parental tone surrendered to the fury of the moment and now held odious overtones. He glanced over his shoulder, holding the hoof with one hand and pointing at it's sole with the other.

"See that? Reckon I ought to—" The rancher glanced up and dropped the hoof. He straightened and put a hand on Guthrie's shoulder. "Here. What's the matter, Guth?"

"I, I don't know. Think I better sit down."

Lee held the gate, waiting. A look of concern covered her face. She took his arm, walked beside him. By the time they reached the station wagon, he sensed strength returning.

He sat in the passenger's seat. "Believe I'm gonna live."

"Honey, what is it? Your head?" Lee scanned his face. "You're white as a sheet."

"Maybe, that old stringy bronc just scared me to death."

"Humph! Fat chance of that. What's it been, only about a month since that concussion? You better take it a little easy, man. Times are too hard to have a stroke or something. Believe I'd stay out of this sun for another week or so." The cowman's voice was now filled with friendly concern.

Lee walked around the car. "I'll drive. Come on,

Johnny. Let's go see about Sam."

John Robert carried his cane and limped toward the car. He opened the back door and climbed in. "Two weeks, Bud."

"Okay, boy. See you then. Yawl come back."

"See you, Bud." Guthrie's mind swirled.

Lee drove slowly toward the cattle guard.

Guthrie lit a cigarette. She glanced over every few seconds. "I'm okay, Lee. Don't worry."

"Maybe we better take you home and come back for Sam."

"No, I'm all right, I tell you."

Lee threw both hands, palms up, inches above the steering wheel. "You don't nearly pass out and two minutes later be all right. You ought to see a doctor."

"I tell you, I'm okay."

"What happened? Did you pass out, Guthrie?"

"No, John Robert, I didn't pass out. Just had a little headache or something."

"Still hurting?" At least, she kept a hand on the steering wheel.

"No, my head doesn't hurt. Think it's mental or something. I'm tired of talking about it. How'd yawl like old Maude?"

"She's pretty." Lee turned onto the highway.

"Best I ever saw." John Robert quipped. "How old is she?"

"Her mouth says sixteen."

"Is that old?" John Robert thumped at a spot on the inside of the windshield. Outside, opposite his thumping, a grasshopper clung precariously, fighting the wind.

"About fifty in people years."

"Dog talk! People years, horse's mouth! I think you and Bud just like to show off." John Robert met his mother's gaze. "But, I'm sure glad you're friends of mine."

"You probably got us nailed pretty good." Guthrie gazed out the window. What happened was undeniable. That stringy, little pot-bellied two-year old scared the daylights out of him. Made him unable to function, conspicuous in his cowardice. This had to be tended to, fixed.

To work with animals, a person had to be free of fear, especially horses. They could sense it, maybe smell it, but it frightened them, made them do stupid, wild things. Put a scared kid on a plodding, plow horse, and the plug would turn into a crafty outlaw. Soon, it'd be looking for ways to rub the rider off, run away, or any number of things to cause hurt. Dogs, cats, even cattle seemed to have a sixth sense concerning fear, and anyone hosting it became their victim.

At the overlook, Sammy's music pulled Guthrie from his thoughts. He carried the picnic goodies and cold drinks over Lee's admonitions, noticing she wasted no time in getting hold of John Robert's hand for the short walk out on the rock. Posts abutted either side of an outcropping that ran next to the road. Access to the area where Sam sat was flat, unobstructed.

150

"Guthrie, when does the lamp go out?" John Robert asked.

"When the top of that sun buries itself out yonder behind the prairie, you turn back and look into those breaks. You'll see the light get dimmer and disappear by the second."

Sam ignored them, apparently intent on coaxing virgin notes. He seemed absorbed in his instrument's strings. Lee spread a tablecloth, and Guthrie made a second trip to the car for the chairs and his bedroll. John Robert crouched near Sammy on hands and knees and looked out over the sheer bluff. He raised a fist, when to the west, the sun kissed the prairies. The great void before them lay in shadows.

Blue dominated the canyon, its hues varying to purple, almost black, along the floor then rising to sharper earth shades near the ridge. They feasted on deviled-eggs, chips, and sandwiches while watching the ravines darken. Afterward, Guthrie and Sam smoked. Coyotes yelped in the distance. The sounds echoed from the depths then total quiet. Bullbats flapped with spurts of energy high overhead. The evening star stood guard over all.

Today happiness, because of those sharing the moment, filled this spot that often before hid his loneliness. Tonight, he felt akin to whatever leathery old settler first pinned the name of that most stubborn of draft animals to this spot.

John Robert swept his arm in a circle that encompassed the canyon. "Who owns this?"

"Well, Bud's wife's great-granddaddy settled it, her granddaddy fenced it, her daddy married it, and she and Bud's doing their best to hold onto it. To hear him tell it, the second two of her ancestors had it easier, but even the Indians and bad men didn't compare to what he puts up with today, dealing with the IRS and corporate packers." Guthrie sighed. "Yeah, old Jean and Bud's got the deed, but to tell the truth, all of us that come this way with enough time to see the lights come on or off have a little equity."

Sam stroked the strings with a flourish, pointed his pick at each one in the group then swept the canyon. "W . . . We just let B . . . Bud work it." He shut his eyes, sat erect, and swayed to the rhythm of his music.

"When did you first start coming here?" Lee refused his cigarette offer.

"Mom and Jesse used to bring me and Irene out here when we were little. Sometime or another, they stopped coming."

Lee took his hand. "Why don't you ever call him Dad or Pop or even the Old Man?"

"Don't know. Just doesn't come that easy."

Sam downed the last egg, mumbled something about snakes, and glanced at the closing darkness. He and John Robert made their way carefully to the car.

Lee's chair sat next to Guthrie's. Her shoulder touched his. "You've a good boy, there, Ma'am."

"And I've a good friend right here." She turned, faced him.

He kissed her, testing. He pulled her closer, remembered his other companions, then released her.

"We better go." Her eyes contradicted the statement.

"Yeah."

One of Saddle Horn's three street lights cast a dim glow as Guthrie parked under it and opened the back of the station wagon to load the sleeping Sam's bicycle into the cargo space. John Robert's head rested on the bedroll, Sam's on the hornless bucking saddle. He woke Sam and put him and the bicycle out at the shed behind Rita's. It sounded like the jukebox covered for Sam's absence.

A moment later, at Lee's mother's, Guthrie carried John Robert to the front door. She reached for her son and whispered she'd be right back. He moved to the front yard swing and smoked. She came out a few minutes later, took a seat in his lap, then explored his knees with her curled toes. The swing drifted back and forth. He ceased examining the clouds and moon overhead. Guthrie sensed time falling at their feet.

Who said you couldn't come home?

19

Days were the hardest. Alone with his uncertainties, Guthrie relived images of the arena wreck in El Paso, the shakes brought on by the young colt, and tried to fight the dirty feeling of cowardice that haunted him. Three weeks into the new school year meant Lee, Cora, and Flap, stayed busy. Time passed slowly. He helped Bud move stock to different pastures and found, to his surprise, even well trained cow horses gave him a sense of uneasiness.

Most nights he visited Lee and Flap, still he grew restless. Work established his identity, and at present he had none. Like a spoiled bronc, he found himself shying at his own shadow. He fought fear with sweat, consoling himself that by fighting this head thing, he'd get back into the groove soon. When he did, his body would be in shape.

Since the dizzy spell hit him, he'd only missed two days of roadwork. Now, he jogged on the wrong side of Main Street against a non-existent traffic flow. The absence of cars reassured him. Regardless of little activity, he preferred this side. It comforted him to face Saddle Horn's drivers instead of trusting their eyesight. It wasn't beyond the realm of possibility for some of those old-timers to holler "whoa" instead of hitting a brake pedal.

Guthrie took rapid, audible breaths. Finishing the return leg, with six and a half miles behind him, he lacked a half-mile being home. His route through town and down the highway past Rita's, measured exactly three and a half miles. In spite of his rapid breathing, another eight miles were doable if he slowed slightly, but he'd stay with his present pace and stop upon finishing the few blocks home.

His physical condition no longer kept him from the arena, but this other thing blocked his return. Some of the guys back from Na'am carried a similar load. There was a name for their deal, post-traumatic stress syndrome. It seemed for every war, they put a new handle on the same ailment. He'd seen movies where they called it shell shock in the First World War, then the battle rattles in World War Two. He'd heard Korean vets talk about guys going Asiatic. Put any name on seeing death too close and fear too often, and you tallied up to the same answer—ass deep in rattlesnakes.

Guthrie finished his shower before his mom got home from school. Later, he watched through the kitchen window as she extracted herself from the front seat of the Bel-Aire with a sack of groceries in one hand and school papers in the other. She thrust a hip at the car door, but only created enough momentum for it to close without latching. She backed into it again.

Humor then sadness worked at Guthrie. Age lapped at his mother, wore at the barriers of self-defense she erected, dimmed the light in her eyes, and dulled the glow and texture of her skin. He thought of Evelyn and opened the door, took the groceries.

"Anything else out there to bring in?"

"No, that's it."

"Mom, why don't you catch a nap? I'll go get burgers at the drive-in later." Guthrie raised his voice to make sure it followed her down the hall.

"You know I don't nap. No, I'm gonna make cornbread and put on some cabbage. We'll heat those beans." She took a deep breath. "Do think I'll change then watch TV a few minutes, though."

Guthrie walked to the porch. He leaned his back to the wall, slid down to a squat, and rolled a smoke.

Striking a match, he congratulated himself on having restrained the urge to light up since the one at noon. He inhaled deeply, experienced the light buzz he always noticed with the first drag after a few hours abstinence, and basked in the glow of the late September sun.

He mentally reviewed his lifestyle. The pattern had grown familiar over these last few years. It had started in the service and continued to the present. There would be long hours, sometimes days, of idleness, waiting, trying to stay ready, then short periods of intense action mixed with enough danger to both exhilarate and exhaust him.

The sound of a TV commercial drifted through the open window, joined with his mother's catnap breathing. She'd never admit it, but she broke her own most sacred commandment. Rest, in her mind, ranked near pampering, no matter the fatigue. Any form of caring for oneself took on ominous tones of self-indulgence. She was an enigma of contrast, embittered, yet loving, charitable to misfortune, yet resentful of success.

Was he more like her or Jesse? No, he wasn't like her. He was more like Jesse, without judgement of others, happy to look out for himself, but also enjoying other's success. He wished he understood her better. His first memories of her dripped with dependence and attachment. She made all the good things, and most of the bad, happen. She provided the laughs, the spankings, and the reprimands. Jesse restricted himself to "atta boy" or "Guthrie, don't". He heard her stir, turn off the TV, move to the kitchen.

He followed her to the small room and sat at the breakfast table. His mother handed him a glass of ice tea, poured another then set the pitcher nearby. The old Dodge pickup rattled to a stop in the front driveway, then Jesse hollered "hey" from the front of the house. His footsteps moved toward the bathroom.

A moment later, Cora's back was to him as she stood at the cabinet busily blending cornmeal into a buttermilk batter. She beat the mixture, and her spoon made sharp rapid clinks against the bowl. Her shoulders slumped. Gray seasoned the wisp of brown hair hanging beside her eyebrow.

Strangely, he remembered the security of clinging with tiny fists to her skirts, of standing between her knees when she sat, the comfort of her lap. His senses freshened memories nearly a quarter of a century old. He recalled his special bond with a young mother's body, spoiled only slightly by perfume. A subtle fragrance, rich of soaps, cooking-spices, baby powder, and her own identity, flowed from his past. How many rubbings of Vick's ointments had there been? How many warm, flannel, chest cloths?

He suddenly longed to hug her and tell her he was sorry for being such a hand-full. He leaned and plucked the cup towel from its rack. With a deft movement, he twirled the towel into a roll and popped the end near his mom's hip.

Cora flinched and whirled. Her eyes flashed. "Young man, have you forgotten what happened the last time you did that?"

157

He had forgotten, but now remembered how years ago she chased him out the screen door with the flyswatter into the startled Jesse's arms. She'd threatened her husband with several forms of death and a widower's loneliness if he failed to do her bidding with their unruly son. She suggested since he was too big for spanking, perhaps forced baptism would make a more lasting impression.

At fifteen, he'd made little showing against the stout Jesse and ended up doused in the metal horse tank that stood near the backyard fence. That the trough had long since disappeared reassured him.

"Mom, I don't know if I ever really said it, but I'm sorry about all the grief you've had, you know, losing Christina and all."

Jesse entered and sat opposite Guthrie. Cora didn't turn. She took a glass from the cabinet shelf, set it on the counter then removed an ice tray from the refrigerator. The tray's aluminum lever failed to pop the ice cubes free, so she ran water over the its bottom, worked the cubes free, then put a handful in Jesse's glass. He took it from her. Bending, she kissed Guthrie's forehead then opened a lower cabinet door and rattled metal pans.

Jesse filled the tea glass then caught Guthrie's eye. He shook his head too late to stop the next question.

"It was a summer flu, dysentery, wasn't it?"

His mom filled the skillet with cornbread mix, set it into the preheated oven, then with both hands on the cabinet top, stared out the window. "That first day, in

158

the morning, she had such a good time playing with the thread spools." Cora glanced at Jesse. "Remember? You strung them on a string. I was potty training her."

Jesse nodded and examined his hands.

"I was fixing dinner when she got quiet. She'd dirtied her little panties. I—" A sob interrupted his mother.

"It's okay, Mom. You've told me most of it before. You don't have to go over it again."

The softness of Cora's face gave way to fierce determination, almost anger, and she seemed involved in some form of masochistic struggle, a self-mutilation. Torn by her sorrow, he thought of stories concerning the first women of these plains. Strong, black-headed, swart women dressed in skins. They slashed their bodies to ribbons over grief for the dead. He wondered at the similarity of his mother's actions.

She turned. Her eyes moved left then right, reflected flashes of light. With her hands to her face and only a narrow opening to speak through, her whisper barely reached them. "I—I spanked her." She sat unexpectedly on Jesse's knees and groaned softly. He put his arms around her waist. His head rested on her back.

Guthrie wanted to run. Hell, so what else was new? Even his best motives found their way to the pile behind the barn.

His mother reached and touched him. In a moment, she regained partial control. "It's okay, Guthrie, you didn't bring this on. I'd talk about it twenty-four hours a day if anyone would listen. It's been going over and over in my mind for thirty years.

159

"I sat up with her all that night. The next day her fever was high and her skin so dry." Her eyes glazed with tears. "Old Doctor Aikens said we were losing her. Our only chance was the hospital in Lubbock. Jesse made it in an hour and twenty minutes." His mom took a deep breath. "She seemed some better about midnight. Around three in the morning, I—I fell asleep, just for a few minutes. I awoke and reached and touched her. She was cold." Cora stepped to the oven, absentmindedly checked the cornbread.

Guthrie squirmed then rose to his feet, understanding for the first time her connection between sin and sleep. He touched his mother's shoulder, stopped in front of the screen door and looked toward the small barn and pens surrounded by the three-acre pasture. Maude stood in the lot, ears up, facing home and Wild Mule Canyon.

He came back to his chair. "Jesse, Mom, I want yawl to take that money you always said was set aside for my medical schooling and, Jesse, I want you to take her to Galveston. Yeah, go to Galveston, and spend a week watching the waves come in."

"That water's dirty." His mother's voice was bitter.

"Then, I know. Jesse, yawl go to Salt Lake City. Sit there in the evenings and listen to that Mormon Choir."

"Guthrie, for Heaven's sake, school just started! Besides, you don't understand. That money had a purpose. We don't need to go anywhere."

He looked to his dad. Jesse met his eye. "I got nothing to say about that money."

"Well, damn—excuse me, Momma—Jesse, take her

160

to Vegas. See if you can beat that crap game out there. Get drunk, take in some shows, do something, just the two of you."

"I said, I got nothing to say about any of this." His dad stood and walked toward the front door.

Guthrie threw his arms in the air. "It's just that yawl used to have so much fun. You kidded each other and laughed. You'd leave Irene and me with Mr. and Mrs. Hefner and slip off on Saturday night to those dances over at New Hamburg. Now you droop around here, watch that electronic wasteland, and grow old."

"There's worse ways and ones to do it with." His mom patted him on the shoulder. "Go tell him to put the cork back in it and come on in and eat."

His mom sat at the table when he returned. Jesse followed him in and sat next to her. Guthrie pulled his chair back just as the phone rang. He turned, snatched the receiver from the base and snarled, "Hello."

"Guthrie?" The person at the other end coughed, cleared his throat then a series of coughs followed a moment's silence.

"Hello? Yes, this is Guthrie. Hello?"

"Mr. Sawyer?"

"Yes."

"This is Bernice Hodges in Amarillo. Sorry. A coughing seized Wes. He's got a terrible cold, been hoarse for a month."

"Yes, ma'am. He mentioned that when we talked last. Tell him I didn't mean to holler just now. I sometime forget there's real people on the other end of this thing."

"Guthrie, he said if you were still just recuperating and could do it, he needs help announcing the Santa Rosa Roundup. It starts Friday at Vernon. He thought you might take over the microphone about half the time, let him rest his voice some. He thinks you'd do well with it. What? Just a minute, Guthrie, he's trying to tell me something."

Sounds of silverware on plates issued from the kitchen. His iced tea glass formed condensation droplets, and he finger painted tepees. Thoughts of those earlier people inspired a small, stick-figure doll, then he rubbed his makeshift easel clean and dried his fingers on his trousers. According to Jesse's teachings, all that moisture might spell rain.

Her voice brought him back to the present. "He said you all would split the pot, and he'd sure appreciate it. Okay, Dear. He says it beats broncs. Can you do it for us, Guthrie? I'd appreciate it, too. Tell the truth, I'm sort of worried about him."

"Bernice, I'd be tickled. Where and when?"

"Said he'd see you at the office in Vernon Thursday evening at five-thirty. Thanks, Guthrie."

"Thank yawl. Tell him to take care." Guthrie hung up and turned to his folks. "Looks like I'm going to work."

"Who's Bernice?" his mother asked.

"Wes Hodge's wife. You know. The announcer?"

Jesse wiped at his face with a napkin. "You gonna help Wes?"

"Looks like."

His dad poked playfully at Cora's shoulder. "Next

thing we know, he'll be wearing white shirts and ties and speaking at the Lion's Club. You're wising up, boy. Never heard of a microphone kicking anybody."

"When you leave?" His mom passed the bread.

"Tomorrow."

Afterward, he walked down to Lee's Mother's. Evelyn's strength appeared to ebb daily. Lee sent Guthrie to the Dairy-Do for burgers and heated soup her mom. Later, she sat with him in the swing and watched John Robert practice starts for make believe races. The boy mimicked an announcement of the start of each race and mentioned himself as the Olympian to beat in each event. He jogged about without aid of a cane and with only a slight limp.

"He's doing well, isn't he?" He caught himself paying more attention to his grammar these days.

She nodded. "He's so proud of himself. It's a miracle, Guthrie. I see Momma and get so low, then here he comes bursting into the house and things sort of even up. I never thought I'd say it, but thank goodness for Ira Walker."

Guthrie looked at her. "What'd he do?"

"He had to be the one who did it. You know, the hospital benefactor."

"Oh, that. Yeah, guess so." Figures. He told her about Wes' call and the new role he'd play at Vernon.

"You said a few weeks ago that you thought you could be happy announcing. I'm glad, Guthrie. I think you'll be good. You're not going to ride, are you?"

"No. Matter of fact, think I'm losing my nerve. I may

never climb back into a saddle."

"Yeah, right. That'll be the day." She laughed.

He was serious; however she wouldn't hear it. Same with everyone. He started to explain, then decided to spare her. Tonight, he'd rather just sit beside this woman who stirred him so deeply. Reality could wait.

Shortly after noon the following day, he drove past Wild Mule Canyon and the overlook. Vernon and the Santa Rosa Roundup waited two hours down the road. What a day! Bright sky, a road stretching into the distance, and Erilee at home waiting. He squinted. In the distance, sunlight reflected from chrome, and an automobile hurtled toward him. Two occupants in a blazing-red, Corvette convertible zoomed past.

Lane Walker drove, and beside him rode his little sister Karen. Looked like Saddle Horn would be hosting both the Walker brats. Try as he might, he saw no silver lining on that cloud. He tried to remember what age Karen had been when he graduated. She'd not reached high school. He hoped for John Robert's sake that Lane visited his son—only his son. Somehow, the day just shed its brightness.

20

Ira Walker's massive ranch house sprawled more than a hundred yards north of the state highway and eight miles out on the road to Childress. A paved runway, punctuated with a windsock at one end, ran north and south in the flat east of the main buildings. A huge barn surrounded by corrals sat nearer the house on the opposite side. Between the house and barn, two smaller sibling-like buildings served as bunkhouse and cook shack. Across the roof of the red barn, painted inverted Vs connected to either end of a white strip, telling all arrivals they entered the headquarters of the Walker Sawhorse Ranch.

At the moment, Ira stood tall and straight, almost Patton-like, on the upstairs veranda. He watched the Corvette turn off the highway. Apprehension throttled all thought of congeniality. The idea of being in his son's presence created a roaring in his ears, a pounding in his temples. He'd never understood the boy. In all the years, Ira found no common ground.

Perhaps, he saw too much of himself in Lane, a part he'd rather deny. On the other hand, best he could tell, they differed in most everything. He didn't know, and at this point, had no plans to figure it out. It took all his energy trying to repair the consequences to worry about the cause.

Earlier, he'd dismissed Lane's failures as stages that would be outgrown, improved upon with maturity. He'd been wrong. Instead of improving, the mistakes grew more serious, the costs more expensive. Leaving gates open and foundering livestock soon progressed to drunken sprees and wrecked cars. Knocking-up that Kramp girl had been the last straw. After that crowning achievement, he spoke little with his son.

The boy's mother had spent a fortune trying to keep him in college and out of Houston jails. She added to the problem, making it easy for Lane to avoid the pain of his own errors. Sybil spoiled the kid. Ira pushed thoughts of Lane from his mind. Karen lit the lantern in his life.

The car followed the circular drive to the front of the house and pulled to a stop. His beautiful daughter waved. Sight of her happy face eased the pressure, brought momentary relief from the noise in his head. She possessed all the qualities her older brother lacked. Her coloring and features took more after Sybil, but she was Walker, top to bottom. Bright, proud, and self-confident, she mixed equally well with Houston's social elite and the homeliest wives of the poorest cowboys on the ranch. He turned and walked through the double doors.

Ira moved to his desk and plucked a cigar from a box. He dampened the dry outer tobacco with his tongue, took a partially straightened paper clip from the desk drawer, and poked a hole in the tasty end of the stogie. He leaned back in his chair while sucking the smoke to life from the flame of his lighter. From a painting across the room, his grandfather's piercing gray eyes followed his movements. The brim of a Stetson partially shaded the face in the lifelike portrait. The door to his study opened.

Lane had lost weight. He looked as uncomfortable as Ira felt. "Well, we're here."

"I see that. Want a cigar?" Ira raised the box.

Lane sat. He shook a cigarette from a pack and lit it without answering. "What's on your mind, Dad?"

"How was the drive?"

"Not too bad after we got out of traffic. It's a bitch till you get this side of Austin. You said we needed to talk." His son's eyes were cold, calculating, and identical to those in the painting.

Ira leaned across the desk, stuck his hand out. "Let's bury the hatchet."

Lane's grip ranged between firm and nonchalant. At that moment Karen bounced through the door and skipped happily across the room.

"Daddy, Lane, it's good to see you two acting civil to one another."

Ira stood, prepared to grasp Karen by either shoulder. She didn't slow for that, but came into his arms, hugged him, and kissed him on the cheek. He thought of her skinny-kid days when she'd jump and wrap her legs around his waist while mussing his hair. Now, her large brown eyes searched his face. "I'm glad you two are working it out."

She turned toward her mother standing in the doorway. "I've been working on Lane for the last three hundred miles, and he's promised to behave. What'd you do to make Daddy come around?"

Sybil's bearing was regal; her beautiful face an emotionless mask. Only the faintest inkling of a smile twisted at the corner of her lips. Her features softened while looking at her daughter, masked all that cold steel she carried inside.

Ira knew anger still boiled just beneath that poised exterior. Earlier, he'd tasted the lash of her sharp tongue, witnessed her resentment firsthand. She repre-

167

sented one of the few things in his world he could not manage, manipulate, or buy. Her beauty not only matched his good looks; her will equaled his strength and stubbornness. She understood power and control, and thanks to his father, her name appeared beside his on every document, title, and deed they owned.

The old man had put it in the will that his daughter-in-law would share equally in the estate. His way of ruling from the grave, keeping his son straight. Ira had fought the tight rein all his life. The elder Walker had little use for a mount that too easily broke gait or shifted direction.

When he raced to his bride-to-be's side and proposed marriage, he thought he'd found a range free of fences. Instead, it only turned out to be a bit with a harsher curb and a tighter rein.

Sybil lit a cigarette and stuffed the lighter into her skirt pocket. "Karen, you know I never interfere. Come, dear, let's have coffee by the pool. I want to hear about that new beau. What's his name? Raul?"

Ira watched the two women disappear below the top of the stairwell. Even in height and side by side, his wife's lighter colored hair sank from view at the same moment as Karen's.

He turned to Lane. "So, how's the car business?"

"Not too bad, but that sales manager is a real prick."

"Really? How's that?"

"You know how some people are. Give them a little authority, and it goes to their head. He thinks he's hot stuff."

"I'll level with you, Son. I'm thinking of buying that dealership. They're strapped for cash, you know, in a real bind. I know the location's good. What do you think? Can Buick stay competitive the next few years?"

He really couldn't care less about Lane's opinion. Too big a deal to rely on a playboy's whim. Chuck Windslow said buy, and Chuck knew the business. His interest with Lane was to see if the kid showed any sign of taking hold. Besides, he wanted to soften him up some, make him at least think there was something in this for him.

"I don't know, Dad. A lot of young people are moving away from big cars. If you're going to put money in that business, I'd look at the foreign makes. They're gonna be hard to beat the next few years."

"Poppy-cock! Americans like big cars. Gas is cheap and plentiful. Most men can't even wear a hat in those imports."

"Maybe, maybe not, but a lot of people say the days of sixty-cent gas may be coming to an end. Is this why you sent for me?"

"Partly. I wanted you to know what I had in mind. Down the road—if you want, of course—I'd want you running things."

"I could do that."

"Lane, have you got another woman?"

"What? What business is that of yours? Damn, Dad, I'm twenty-eight years old."

"Well, act like it then. I just asked you a question. One I'm still waiting on an answer to."

169

"No, I ain't got another woman. Other women, yes! Another woman, no."

"Good! Good! This thing between you and Erilee's been on my mind. It's dealing me misery. She's seeing that hippie kid of Jesse and Cora Sawyer's, you know."

"Guthrie? Hippie! Dad, that guy's about as far from a hippie as they get."

"Well, rodeo bum, whatever. And then there's your boy." The sound of the current in Ira's head rose again, and he sensed warmth flood his face. He stood then strode back and forth puffing the big cigar. "That kid needs a father. All boys do. Did you know you let somebody, some kind of charity deal, provide the money to get his foot fixed? Is that a kick in the ass, or what? Ira Walker's grandson a charity case!"

"What are you talking about? Erilee told me you did that."

"The hell she did. I didn't. Evelyn and Sybil talked on the phone. Whoever did it didn't want their name on it." Ira paused. "It makes sense, though, that she'd think it was me.

"The Walker name's been respected four generations in this Panhandle. We've held our heads high and commanded respect. Since that gal brought your kid back here without a daddy, I find myself dodging Saddle Horn like a coyote circling bad bait.

"You need to think about it, Lane. The main difference between fatherless and bastard is canceled paper. Hear me straight. This family ain't got room for a bastard grandkid. I want you to fix up that part of your life."

"Fix it up? What does that mean?"

"Get that woman and kid back. Be a husband and father. Get a grip. Them monthly sales meetings'll be a lot more fun when you're sitting at the head table signing bonus checks. Get my drift?"

"In other words, if I wanta be President and CEO of Academy Buick, I have to get Erilee back."

"That'd go a long way toward assuring me you're ready for the responsibility of a job like that."

Ira extended his right hand, shook with his son as he straightened from his chair. He slapped his left hand onto Lane's shoulder. "Don't take it so serious, boy, the fun's just starting. Nothing makes a man look as good to strange women as being married. Shows he's serious and wanted by others."

Lane shook his head and grinned ruefully. "Batching is getting a little old."

"Good, good. Let's have a drink, and I'll beat you in tennis." The roar in his head diminished. Sybil monopolized Karen somewhere downstairs, but he'd make an appearance long enough for Karen to update him a little.

21

Erilee squinted impatiently through the dust-covered windshield and turned the car toward home. Recently, the distance from school to her mother's had proved elastic, its length dependent on her own nervousness, which in turn, depended on her mother's condition.

Time between Evelyn's transfusions governed that, and three days had passed since the last one. This morning, her mom showed signs of weakening. Lee hurried.

Thank goodness for Fridays, even though this one proved a typical West Texas, fall day. Sand-laden wind increased throughout the morning, until the front passed, then the gale died, the temperature dropped, and the air cleared. Now, if she could just settle down and get her mind to do the same.

John Robert wouldn't shut up about his dad, and her mother and Guthrie wouldn't talk at all. Her fourteen first-grade students rattled constantly. She'd never seen so many runny noses and blank stares in her life.

And then there was little Ginnie Owen. How could a grown woman lose an argument to a six-year-old child? She could still see Ginnie's impish smile, the child's angelic expression as she looked up and said, "Miss Kramp, you're making me nervous."

Erilee ran her fingers over the side of her purse and assured herself of the presence of the four-day-old pack of cigarettes. Conceivably, she'd eat one of the damn things. It definitely was a multi-cigarette day.

Four Tylenol had only managed to slightly dull the ache between her temples. She removed her foot from the gas pedal then slipped off the high-heels. Her toes felt more like she'd been shoeing horses than teaching first grade. It seemed every little precious south of the Canadian had walked on her feet.

Even her conference period had offered challenges. Sitting in a bathroom stall and watching a river of water approach from an overflowing lavatory left much to be desired. Among the world's wonders, the sanctified privacy of her mother's clean and fresh-smelling bathroom ranked high. Perhaps she should have paid more attention to that college aptitude test that suggested a marketing career.

John Robert sulked in the seat beside her, rummaging through his backpack. She shouldn't have been so short with him. He'd asked for none of this, yet paid the highest price. Damn divorce! Still, right now, she just couldn't handle hearing about his argument with Sandy Norwood over whose daddy was richest.

There were too many demands on her, too many wanting a piece of her, looking to her for strength. Her mother was failing, John Robert's eyes blamed her for Lane not being around, and Guthrie was probably swapping lies with some barrel racer at this very moment.

She pulled to a stop beside her mother's front porch wondering what she'd find inside. She forced John Robert to wait—enter after her. Rays of refracted sunlight streaked through dust-laden air and cast an eerie glow across the shade-darkened bedroom. Flickering light from the TV did little to improve the dreariness. Her mother lay propped on a pillow watching vague figures dance in the electronic snow.

John Robert burst through the door and stopped beside his grandmother's bed. "Ma'am Maw, we saw a picture today about outer space and rockets and things, and guess what."

"My goodness, what?"

"It showed Houston Control out at NASA. Dad and I were there twice."

"Well, isn't that interesting? You've had a good day then, and you're going to like this. Your daddy called just a few minutes ago." She looked at Erilee. "He's at Ira and Sybil's, wants you to call him."

John Robert talked to his dad first then Erilee got on the phone and agreed Lane could come over after supper to visit. She hung up, fighting intense sadness. He was going to make a play for her, try to get her to take him back. Damn him. He used the boy. It was in his voice. She knew him too well. His comment of needing to see his son was out of character, a ruse. His timing was good. She'd give him that.

Lee cloaked herself in the luxury of her mom's bathroom, and for the first time since early morning, relaxed. Tears flowed soundlessly. Later, her mascara-streaked image stared back from the mirror like something from a pagan rendezvous.

The smokes proved helpful, and after washing her face, she moved to her room to change. She squirmed into jeans, fought the overpowering pull of the bed, then gave in and flopped on her back. With her bare feet raised overhead, she traced the outlines of the high heels while wiggling her toes.

John Robert passed her door, glanced in, and made an all too masculine face of disgust. "I'm going to feed Maude before Daddy gets here."

Lee stepped into loafers, went to the kitchen, and

poured tea. With a glass in either hand, she walked to her mother's room. She set one near the bed, the other on a coaster on the dresser. It took several tries to get the room's blinds evenly raised. Her son moved down the alley toward the Sawyer's barn. "He's so excited."

Her mother lifted her tea glass and traced shaky fingertip marks in its moisture. "It's right that he is. In spite of my catty remarks about Lane, I want you to know I'll never question your decisions about that marriage, either the ones past or those yet to be considered. I can't imagine what divorce is like for any of the three of you."

Erilee faced her mother, trying to hide her own concern. "Are you okay?"

"Just tired." Evelyn sipped the tea. Her sleeve hung below her elbow as she held the glass to her lips.

Lee forced herself to study the numerous purplish, bruise-like marks on the exposed forearm. They were larger even than yesterday. Her mother's words confirmed her fears.

"Dr. Stone said there'd come a time I'd only go three days between transfusions. Must be there. I don't believe I can make it past tomorrow without one."

Panic pulled at Lee's insides. "I'll call and tell them to expect us in the morning." She dialed the number and occupied her frantic mind with thoughts of the last doctor's visit. The nurse probing with that damn needle looking for a vein almost did her in.

"It's becoming such an ordeal; I hate for you to have to go through it." She transferred the receiver to the other ear. "I'll tell you one thing. I'm going to ask for the doctor to insert that needle. I can't believe someone up there can't do it without poking around for thirty minutes."

"Here, here. Remember? None of that, it's just part of it. I must admit, though, I miss those good veins. Now, they not only hide, but Rosa said they were starting to roll." She shook her head. "I'm sorry. What am I thinking about? You were there."

The receptionist answered. Lee made the arrangements then hung up. "Want to sit up and let me brush your hair?"

"No, think I'd rather rest."

"Mom, what do you mean future decisions about the marriage? It's over."

"You wish! A marriage may only last a few months perhaps, years, but divorce, when children are involved is rehashed over and over. You made another decision a few minutes ago, for the baby's sake, and you'll go on doing that the rest of your life. Besides, I know Ira Walker. He runs that family, and he never turned loose of anything in his life." Evelyn made an impatient gesture at the TV set, and Lee turned it off.

The older woman took a deep breath, fluffed her pillow, then allowed the back of her head to sink into it. She stared at the ceiling and shook her head. "Jesse nearly killed him several times. Your daddy even got his gun once, but we won't go into that.

"Anyway, your grandmothers grew up in the twenties, frequented bootleggers and speakeasies, and flapped out the hypocrisy of prohibition. My bunch kept the paint on our faces and the cigarettes in our mouths in spite of gossip and raised eyebrows, but we really didn't change things much.

"We did help our men win the big one. Oh, we proved women can have fun without being all that loose, but it remained for you and yours to put wedding chapels and divorce courts in the same category as used car lots. From booze to rouge and second-hand sex, three generations have brought us a long way, Baby."

Evelyn waved her hand feebly in the air then let it drop to her side. "I'm sorry, Lee. Guess I'm just full of self-pity and hating to leave my grandson fatherless and hanging around as some kind of neglected house pet for a stepfather dad. Still, his real daddy's a bum. I'm just so tired."

Lee didn't know what to say. She didn't know this woman. "Momma, are you changing your mind? Are you saying I should try to get back with Lane?"

"No, no, child! All I ever want for you and John Robert is happiness. I'm just in a funk. Fed up with ugly sandstorms, this wind and dust blowing all the time. Everything I've touched today has tried to electrocute me. Sometimes, I wish I'd been born in New England." She met Lee's eye. "Since your grandmother died, I've spent the years wondering if she looked down on me with approval or scorn. Don't do that. All I meant to say here is, I've quit second guessing your decisions."

Wes Hodges introduced Guthrie to the first-night,

Santa-Rosa-Roundup crowd, set the scene, and started the performance before relinquishing the microphone. A fit of coughing left the narrator of ranch-life mayhem breathless. For the rest of the show, he acted as Guthrie's assistant, available more as a sounding board than an announcer.

Strangely, in spite of a natural tendency toward reticence, Guthrie found his tongue flapping loose as a shaggy dog shedding water. The mike was his mount and like Sammy with music, he just let it roll. It was good to be working. He knew the arena, some of the people, most of the contestants, and had a first-hand acquaintance with a lot of the stock.

He ended the last event of the final show summing up Orvill Tilghman's good bull ride and butt-busting dismount. "Tomorrow ole Orvill may have to take off his Stetson to scratch his behind, but he looks okay. Heck of a ride, Tilghman! Give him a hand. Wal, that winds her down, folks. Thank yawl for coming, and on behalf of your favorite big-little city, Vernon, Texas, Mr. Wes Hodges and this ole cowboy hope yore trail will be downhill till we see you back here next year. Good night, folks."

The next morning, he put the sun at his back and headed the station wagon toward Saddle Horn. Excitement generated by his chances for developing a career in announcing buoyed his spirits. For the first time in days, a freshet of confidence irrigated the fear he buried and moved aside the maudlin waste of idle despair.

A concern about Wes' condition gnawed at his sliver

of optimism, and beyond that, familiar demons stalked the banks of his mind, muddying the happiness of seeing Lee. He'd called yesterday, and she and John Robert were out. Worse, Evelyn's tone seemed too cautious. She was holding something back. He tried to shrug off the doubts. Perhaps, her condition had worsened. She certainly had reason to seem strained. Still.

That evening, Guthrie knew it had gone to hell before he'd escorted Lee three steps toward the station wagon. He'd just picked her up. Already, words were unnecessary. Lee walked beside him. She'd never make it at poker. He held the passenger door for her and tried to act ignorant of the fact that this affair had ended.

Gloom shackled him. He shuffled around to the driver's side. His head grazed the top of the car door, and he grimaced as he sat. He shook out a Viceroy and pointed its butt at her. She refused. With both hands gripping the top of the wheel, he let his own cigarette dangle a moment before lighting it.

He couldn't look at her. "So, what is it? My reckless ways, lack of promise, or did Mr. Deep Pockets wander by?"

Her glare was more sad than angry. "It's John Robert."

Blow out the light. It's over! The one thing in the world he couldn't fight. Blazing streaks of smoldering embers ignited the western sky. He'd thought of catching the last light at Wild Mule Canyon, but its appeal vanished. Beauty in his world seemed out of place. He craved ugly, dirt, gore, anything to improve this image called reality. A case of whiskey or the most vulgar of whores, there had to be something worse.

Lee shrank against the far corner of the seat expectant, looking hurt, waiting. Guthrie made a conscious effort to relax his jaw. "For ten years, my life has been about you. For the last eight it's been waiting, wanting you back. Then it happened, and for a couple of months I've been on top of the world. Now, this!" He started to throw away the partially smoked cigarette, but she motioned for it.

She took the smoke from his hand. "Me, too."

He started the car, headed for the highway, then lit another Viceroy. Sheer hose accentuated the sculptured perfection of Lee's small ankles, the curve of her calves, and highlighted the shape of her knees. A glimpse of inner thigh slammed him in the gut like a physical blow, and the totality of her beauty made him want to cry.

Did she know what she did to him?

Of course she knew.

"Where are we going?"

"Where you wanna go?"

"Home pretty soon."

"Okay, let's just go somewhere and let me catch my breath."

"Guthrie, I'm sorry. It isn't what I want."

"Uh huh, you told me. A friend, yeah, a friend was what you wanted."

"I did, but I got a lot more. I got back the man I love, Guthrie. You haven't got a clue what all you have going. You're a panther among men. You are a woman's wildest fantasy, the one she dreams of. But I can't have you. There's more here than just the two of us."

He looked at her. She meant it. He noticed the needle on ninety and eased off the accelerator. "John Robert."

"My baby."

"You're going back to Lane?"

"I am. God help me, I am."

Guthrie pulled to a stop at the edge of the overlook. Coolness kissed the air, shadows rapidly darkened in the canyon, and the smell of kindling-dry range land mixed with last Friday's deposited dust. "I really thought we were going to make it."

"Me, too. We would have."

"What happened?"

"Mostly, I've been watching my son. I've prayed. Nine years ago I made a mistake. Yes, I was young, but that mistake created something a lot younger, impacted others. If I'm ever going to be worth a damn for anything, I'll protect that boy. He wants a father, not any father—his father. So far, Lane is not a bad daddy. If that were the case, it'd be different. He's just not much of a husband. Please, don't ask me not to. I can't fight you, Darling."

This was the bottom. No, Lee's sobs proved him wrong, carried him to the real depths. He blindly reached for her. She sank into his arms, shaking violently. "He wants us back."

She rested in his arms. She lowered her head, rested

her face on his chest, wiggled closer. Her tremors lessened, slowed, but her breathing remained rapid and shallow. He squeezed her, rubbed her back, gently, high above the waist. He softly kissed the top of her head and fought a sneeze as sprayed hair tickled his nose. Passion conquered tenderness, swept away restraint. His hand dropped lower. He pulled her hips closer.

"Please, I need to go home. I don't trust myself. We shouldn't." She pulled away.

Guthrie released her, mentally cursed himself for a fool, and twisted to slumped back against the seat. His fingertips machine-gunned the steering wheel. He stared into the void of darkness. There was no moon. "Remember the night I learned of him putting the make on you?"

"Don't."

"We weren't far from here, over on the Talbot road, parked in Jesse's old pickup. Remember? Talk about an execution." Guthrie mouthed a cigarette from the pack and held the rest toward Lee.

"You told me you'd broken up with him, and it was me you wanted. We were talking how we were meant to be together."

"Guthrie!"

He removed the car's lighter, held it for Lee, then puffed his own smoke alive. "That son of a bitch comes screeching up beside us and jumps out into his headlights with a pistol in one hand and your panties in the other. Remember! I should have run over his ass right there. Why, Lee, why?"

182

"Finish it, you bastard. A few weeks later, I, along with everyone else in Saddle Horn, knew I was pregnant with a Walker kid in me. And the wedding bells rang!" Lee snapped on the radio and muted the sound, obviously for enough light to see him by. Her face twisted with anger.

She stared. A soft buzz came from the radio. "You wanna know why? Have you ever played tennis on the Walker courts, seen their pool, swam in it? I was only seventeen. Ever tried to hold off a twenty-two year old man when you're still in high school? Why! Oh, Guthrie, how could you ask me that?"

She threw herself at him. He first thought in anger, then her kiss revealed his error. She offered it all, and he itched with lust and cried inside with fear, knowing this to be her gift, her appeasement to him. He knew her too well. Willing to destroy herself over and over on the altar of giving while trying desperately to not hurt others. She'd be his once more, for this briefest of moments, then be lost for eternity.

He pulled back. He'd been here before. "Sorry, I ain't sure this is proper for friends."

"Bastard!" Her slap stung then rang in his ears. He sensed blood rush to his face, and tears wet his eyes. He reached awkwardly, and she came back.

Later, she lay on the seat, naked, illuminated by the pale, green glow of the radio dial. Her head was on the driver's side. Her breasts rose and fell with each rapid breath. Strands of damp hair clung to her forehead.

Guthrie tugged at his Levi's, buckled his belt, then

fumbled to remove the wooden toothpick from the door's automatic, interior light switch. Lee held up her hands. He knelt beside her, offered his arms and helped her to a sitting position. She grasped the back of his head, tangled fingers in his hair, and kissed him gently. He forced himself to release her knowing he and this lady had just written the final chapter to a worn-out relationship.

He picked up his shirt, stepped from the car, and walked to its rear. With his foot on the bumper, he leaned with his back to the Chevy. Lee's dressing movements gently rocked the vehicle. The end of his cigarette glowed brightly. Beyond it, only darkness. From somewhere inside, an amplified voice welcomed him back to hell.

22

Down in the mouth and following the precedent set when Lee left during high school, Guthrie returned to his Wild Mule Canyon vigil each of the next three after- noons. Sammy shared the moments. The two ritualisti- cally snuffed out the lights at their eroded altar. The musician added his soft magic to the sliding shadows. Bitter gall diluted the fire of ninety-proof Guthrie downed.

Except for his songs, Sam only spoke one word the first night. "L . . . Lee?"

Guthrie nodded and held the bottle toward his friend. The musician shook it off. After that, a solemn look, a wink, a slight smile, or a raised fist for a particularly sweet note sufficed. In moments of great happiness, or times like this, when one or both dealt with sadness, their ability to communicate surpassed words.

He gave the canyon his thoughts. From its harsh features, softened then hidden by the light's retreat, ricocheted a whiskey soused, restless sense of limbo, a refuge between peace and futility.

They were a pair. If ever there was a couple of misfits, he and Sam filled the bill, a simple-minded, tongue-tied musician with a lot of talent and no promise, knocking himself out for a master bronc rider grown afraid of horses.

On the third night, Guthrie used a quarter of a pint trying to figure which was the most useless, a soldier after the last battle, a horseman afraid of his mount, or a lover without a woman. A flood of guilt engulfed him. He thought of the dead he'd left in Asia and realized he'd momentarily forgotten his own burning experiences of the preciousness of life. He'd dawdled in self-pity. Sam didn't do that. Sam smiled.

Wes Hodges' wife called the following day. After a few words of greetings, she broke into tears. She was en route to Dallas for Wes to have a series of tests. The doctors suspected throat cancer. He could only whisper now, and his cough had grown worse.

Mrs. Hodges said Guthrie would likely be getting a call from a Denver man. The Pikes Peak Roundup opened shortly, and they needed someone to replace Wes. She'd given them his name. Her voice died, still the phone lived, made soft, nerve shattering, insect-like, electronic sounds.

He swallowed and leaned against the wall trying to focus on Irene's childhood picture. His older sister held an Easter basket and wore a pink bonnet.

No telling how many times Wes Hodges had given him a boost. They must have caught each other at a hundred shows, and the man always built him up to the crowd, bragged on him. Now, he'd practically launched Guthrie into the announcing game.

Around the circuit, the Hodges name held head-stud status on the master-of-ceremony side of rodeo. He covered events from the Garden to the Cow Palace, from Coyote Hollow to the Finals. Wes announced Guthrie's first ride out of high school. Years later, back in the saddle after Vietnam, Guthrie heard the announcer do a biographical review for the crowd, lauding "The cowboy from Saddle Horn's" war record. The man always did his homework.

"Guthrie? You there?"

"I . . . I don't know what to say." The white around the numbers on the phone's rotary face had aged to yellow. "Course I appreciate you giving them my name. I'll try and do a good job. Bernice, your man has been sorta like a second dad to me. You tell him I'll try to make him proud—and—tell him not to worry. He's just like an old weaned calf that's bawled too much. His voice'll come back. Tell 'em I said that, and I'll . . . I'll ask Momma to pray for him."

The man from Denver called that evening. He wanted

186

him. Thing was, they needed him to come up a week early and work with a camera crew. The show would be televised. He packed that night. The next morning, he headed the old Chevy north.

Two weeks later, with money in his pockets and the distant smell of high country in his nostrils, Guthrie took his time on the way back from Denver. Armageddon might just wait another couple of days. He looked at new pickups in Amarillo thinking he might trade the old crate.

Hell, he had a handle on this TV thing. Howard Cosell, watch out.

However, the old fifty-seven ran better after getting a look at a couple of sticker prices. If he could get a gig for one of the next big two, Fort Worth or Houston, maybe he'd go back and talk a little turkey to those wranglers of chrome and glitter. Meanwhile, he'd just see how long this poke lasted.

Guthrie pulled into Saddle Horn on Tuesday. The following Friday had been designated homecoming. Saddle Horn's starting six were pitted against the Sage Wildcats. The football game kicked off an every-other-year class reunion. The class consisted of anyone who'd ever lived near or been a student in Saddle Horn. This was the year, Saturday night, the dance. The paved part of Main Street would provide the floor, and Sammy would take care of the music.

Guthrie managed to survive the backslapping, hand-shaking Friday preliminaries feeling halfway decent. Only when he glimpsed John Robert run down the sideline toward him did he sink back into his what-might-have-been routine. The nickname Flap no longer fit the boy's movement. His gait was fluid, not unlike Guthrie's own. Lee watched from thirty yards away as he lifted the boy. Lane stood beside her. They each raised a hand.

"Guthrie, I'm running track at the Y."

"You're doing what? Boy, it's the wrong time of year for track."

"Not if you're going to be an Olympian."

"I guess not. How's Houston? Did you see me on TV?"

"Houston's great. I gotta go."

"Good luck, John Robert." The boy dodged around adults, then finally disappeared behind the corner of the stands. "What did you say, Hanks?"

"That's Lane Walker's kid, ain't it?"

"Yeah, yeah it is. He's a Cracker-Jack." Guthrie might just skip tomorrow night's torture.

Saturday morning, the Sawyer breakfast table hosted more talk than usual. The whole place had seen a conversational drought for weeks. This morning both Sawyer parents spewed gossip more easily than Sammy would a worn verse. The chatter of so-and-so married a such-and-such and wonder if they'll go by the old home place even carried over into Jesse's last coffee and first smoke.

His folks were hard to fathom, and their common bond as difficult to see as a rattler in dry grass. Still, the marriage lasted. Easy to tell these two were back in times before his birth. Beside Cora's new dress hung Jesse's Levi's, having been pulled from the stretchers, starched, and ironed for the evening.

That afternoon, Guthrie made several trips to the Dodge pickup, but stopped himself short of killing the bottle. The old Remington twenty-two in the gun-rack probably hadn't been fired in five or six years. Still, no need making a man killing mad, he'd leave a snort in that pint.

Near dark, he decided to join the world and check out the doings uptown. He parked near the courthouse then strolled through the throng of friends and onlookers surrounding the dancers.

Sam's amplifiers plugged into an extension cord on the corner sidewalk near the drugstore. The singer crouched with one foot on a chair, bending toward his guitar. His left ear tilted toward the instrument, and he raised and lowered his face, alternately hiding then revealing sensitive scales of emotion. His music might create calluses on his fingertips, but not his heart. Someone had rigged a spotlight. Saddle Horn rocked. A woman's voice helped Sam shake the cradle.

Guthrie moved closer, trying to identify the lady who more than did justice to Sammy's music. He came to the edge of the dancers. His mom swayed in Jesse's arms. On the high sidewalk, next to Sam, stood a slender girl. She seemed to absorb the brilliant light then dust it out like a 4th of July sparkler. Dressed in a pale green thing that clung and revealed cleavage and curves and everything good; she had no bad.

The mike was in one hand, the other thrust up and outward then came back to rest over her heart. Her painted lips parted to form a perfect oval and cords of veins, or muscle, or whatever, protruded on either side of her long and shapely neck. She was beautiful and carried the Walker brand—Karen Walker.

Of all people, Lane Walker's kid sister. You might know it. Karen's voice carried above the music, over the crowd, and into the night. Her body gyrated and moved gaily with the beat, and she laughed and tossed her dark hair. Guthrie longed to show her his own flying dismount. The girl was beautiful and grown. Oh man, how she'd grown!

He tried to remember. She'd been about a sophomore when he went to Nam. When he got back, she was away in college. During the past few years, he'd only seen her at a distance. Damn, she was pretty.

Guthrie smoked then danced with his mother. He sipped Jack Daniels with Billy Hanks while modestly bragging on the quality of an old schoolmate's government issued artificial leg. He took a nip with another, younger friend whose face was familiar, but whose name escaped him. He heard about children he'd never seen and self-consciously explained away his own bachelorhood when dancing with a young mother who graduated after him. Mostly, he lounged close to Sammy and Karen. His gaze kept returning to the singer. She noticed him, mouthed hi, smiled, and resumed singing.

Guthrie reached for the makings. His fingers touched

the cellophane wrapping that encased ready-rolls. He removed the pack, shook out a smoke then idly spun it in the fingers of his left hand, trying to separate paper to prepare it to receive loose tobacco. His eyes followed every move of the girl in green.

Karen abruptly broke off a high note and bowed to the audience. She turned back to Guthrie, dropped her hands and curtsied, smiled, then leaned forward. The V of her neckline graced him with a tantalizing glimpse of hidden promise. Strands of bronze tinted dark hair partially covered pools of lively brown beneath her lashes. Sammy's music drew her back. Her body coiled, and her toe tapped.

Guthrie held the cigarette to his lips, pulled it horizontally across his mouth and licked it heavily with his tongue. He absentmindedly smoothed the ready-roll with the fingers of his right hand, still studying her. He stuck it in his mouth and lit up. Smoke curled. He raised his left hand and forked the cigarette between his fingers. Paper, wet as a rainy day shirt, alerted him to his stupidity. He glanced at those nearby, relieved that no one noticed. He flipped the smoke to the street.

Boy, where'd he been? Erilee—Erilee who?

The singer finished a song and planted a kiss on Sammy's head. The guitarist pointed a finger at Guthrie and said, "Pa . . . duc . . . ah". He laughed.

Karen joined in his laughter. She looked a little puzzled, like maybe she'd missed something.

"I . . . it . . . it's just down the road."

Now her laughter broke sincere, honest, and happy.

"Yeah," she said, "Paducah, Guthrie, all the same." Her smile spoke volumes. Said she liked Sammy, herself, this night, and most of all, life. For a moment, she reminded him of Flint, but only a moment. She was unique.

She walked toward him. "Hi, Cowboy, buy me a Coke?"

"I'm Guthrie." He moved to the edge of the sidewalk and offered his hand.

"I know you. How about that drink?" She took his hand and stepped to the street.

"A Coke? Sure, you name it, you got it." He put his hand on her arm and guided her toward the dancers. They danced their way through the couples to the throng on the other side then he guided her toward his car.

"How about the Dairy-Do?"

"Dairy-Do'll work."

"You're Karen Walker, but how'd you know me? There was a pretty big gap between us."

"Not so big. And from the reports I've been getting, it sounded for awhile like you might become my nephew's step-dad. Besides, you were swoon bait when I's fighting pimples and training bras."

Three-weeks of lonely and a fair size knot loosened in Guthrie's gut. "I'd say you won the war."

He held the old Chevy's door, thought of the Corvette he'd last seen her in, and restrained an impulse to apologize for not being rich. Walking around the station wagon his resentment grew. She was a Walker. That alone meant she probably sat there thinking of some way to hide her identity from the rest of the world while out slumming with the cowboy, as she put it. He knew her kind. Come down to the smelly freak show on Saturday night to have something to whisper about to her snobby friends on Monday.

He seated himself behind the steering wheel, caught a quick glance of her profile, and mentally stored the details: straight nose, generous but not too full lips, her forehead sloped slightly back with a slight oval shape to be graced with that thick shiny dark hair. She might be a Walker, but she resembled Sybil more, beautiful, and those eyes put the lie to any label of snobbery.

"You a Houstonite, too?"

"Until recently. I graduated from Rice in August."

Good, except for the kid waitress, they had the inside of the drive-in to themselves. Karen sipped Coke through her straw with her elbows on the table and let her eyes range over him. Totally uninhibited, she examined him like he might a strange draw. "So, my ex-sister-in-law dumped you again? Men are like a bunch of old drunks."

"What?"

"Always go back to the bottle that started the headache. You probably aren't real fond of us Walkers, huh?"

"Have to admit there's some in the family I ain't real partial to. Then I ain't acquainted with all of you, and I try to stifle my prejudices." She taunted him, and

193

still he found her easy to talk with. "What have you been doing since graduation?"

"A group of us spent some time hiking around Europe. Did you know they're getting married again next month?"

"Who?"

"You know who, Erilee and Lane, of course."

"Look, Karen, right now I'd much rather talk about you than your brother or Lee. Matter of fact, you'd be surprised at how much time I've spent trying to not think of either of them."

"That rough, huh?"

"You got ears, Little Girl?"

"Okay, okay!" She looked out the window then back. "So, I hear you're about the most flashy thing a horse-back when you're working." She propped her chin on the knuckles of both hands, waiting.

He didn't know what to say. If he admitted his new-found fear of the snakes he rode, he'd sound weak. If he lied, well, hell. That was no good. He'd never been one to color the truth. He'd rather squint than wear shades any day. No need going into the sun bareheaded, though. He did wear hats—dodged that glare. "I'm currently working more at announcing."

"Really? That was my major, speech and media communications."

"Hey, I need to talk to you. I did a televised show in Denver a couple of days ago."

The next several minutes flew by. She wanted to know everything about the show and laughed as he relived his embarrassment at being powdered by make-up people. She explained why the Denver camera-crew performed some of the tasks he'd wondered about. Her interest and enthusiasm excited him. Perhaps flying dismounts were becoming a little obsolete. She glanced at her watch, and he returned her to the corner and Sammy.

Karen danced with him twice during the remainder of the evening. Afterwards, he and Sammy loaded the sound equipment into Guthrie's station wagon for the trip back to Rita's. Karen waved then crawled into the backseat of her dad's Cadillac. Ira stared, a strange expression on his face, but he gave no sign of recognition.

23

The next morning, cemetery silence returned to the Sawyer kitchen. Stolen glances passed between his mom and Jesse. Each commented on how pretty Karen looked, and his mother mentioned seeing them dance. She blanched when he mentioned he'd likely see her again. Jesse, always attentive to a full plate, attacked his food with increased vigor. His folk's deep regard for Lee was understandable, but they knew he was no longer involved with her. Strange.

Guthrie pushed back from the table, wiped his mouth with a paper towel, then lit a cigarette. "Yawl going to church?"

"Huh? Uh . . . yeah, why don't you go with us?" His

mom seemed to ramble, searching off out in the sage somewhere distant.

"Naw." He looked at Jesse. "Thought I'd take Maude back out to Bud's if that trailer's got air in the tires."

"Good, that'd be good." Jesse had joined his wife, taken up the hunt.

A couple of miles from the highway turn-off, Maude started nickering, acting like a schoolgirl home from college. The dogs, with tongues lolling in the heat, greeted the car before it reached the ranch house. Bud and Jean weren't home. Church, most likely.

Guthrie unloaded the mare and led her to the band grazing behind Bud's barn. He released her. She circled the herd, touched noses with two then squealed and pawed. Her quick reflexes, striking out at a gelding, brought him a sense of nervousness. He'd known what they would do before they responded, and previously, would have enjoyed only confidence and curiosity. Now, he sensed a chill. He raised his jacket collar and buttoned it. The mare lowered her head and began to graze.

A light breeze stirred, raised a fine powder of decades-old horse manure around the barn. The locked windmill creaked, and the scent of dry range permeated the air, drifted with his thoughts.

Getting Bud's horse home wrapped up the final episode of his fling with Lee. He'd miss the boy. An image of the swift, sure-footed youngster dodging adults at the ball game Friday crossed his mind. It hadn't all been a waste. He certainly received more than he'd given. Yeah, the taste wasn't so bitter, put in its proper perspective. Karen's entering the picture certainly lightened his load.

Back at the house after lunch, his mother went to the bedroom, Jesse dozed in his chair, and the Dallas Cowboy's put the game with St Louis out of reach. Guthrie phoned Karen. She accepted his offer of a beer and burger at Rita's. His spirits rose. He returned to the living room, sat and stopped halfway to his mouth with a lit match.

"Who was that?" His mother marched to the TV and turned it off.

Jesse's chair straightened, and his feet hit the floor. "What?"

"On the phone, Guthrie? Who was it?" She looked sick.

"Mom, what's wrong? It was only Karen Walker."

His mother put her hands to her face. "Are you going to see her?"

Searing pain stabbed Guthrie's fingers, and he dropped the match into an ashtray. He licked his fingers, shook them. "Yeah, I'm going to buy her a burger tonight."

His mother's body shook. She moved to the front door and looked out. "She's too young for you."

"Mom. She's twenty-one. There's more than four years between you and dad."

"Things were different then."

"I don't think so."

She turned faced him. "No, that's just it, you don't

think. You didn't think about staying in college, making a doctor. You don't think so. Humph!"

Jesse rubbed his eyes. "There's lots of others out there, son."

Guthrie looked at his dad. "You, too?"

"Wal."

Cora tilted her head. "He ought to know."

"I don't want to fuss with you two. I'm old enough to know what I'm doing." He started to rise, move to the TV, anything. "What quarter is it anyway?"

"You're gonna see her, aren't you?"

"Mom."

"She's a Walker."

"You think I don't know her name? Hey, I don't like Ira any better than you two. Lane's a spoiled punk. I don't know Mrs. Walker, but what I see of Karen, I like."

His mom threw both hands upward, her face contorted. "You can't do it!" She pointed at Jesse. "For all you know, she could be kin to you. You know what a fence jumper he is."

Jesse came to his feet. "Now wait just a blamed minute."

"What do you want me to do? Move to Australia for a safe date? How about it, Jesse? You never crossed the water did you? For God's sake, what's got into you two?" Guthrie stood.

Jesse pointed his finger. "Be careful, boy."

Cora dropped her hands. Tears ran down her face. "You two stop it. Stop-it! Stop-it! Stop-it!" She slapped

198

her knees. "Guthrie, you can't. She's your sister!"

Jesse stood, turned new-calf white. His fist clenched, and his expression shouted volumes, unmistakably clear. Accused again? He stared at his wife.

Guthrie sensed his chin drop, his mouth open. He closed it and leaned forward. Tornadic winds tore at his thoughts. What did she mean? What did Jesse think she meant? He tried to chuckle. Surely, she joked. Nothing came out. Ridiculous. What the hell was going on?

"My what?"

"Your sister. Karen Walker is your half-sister. You can't see her socially." She turned imploring eyes from Guthrie to his dad and sobbed quietly.

Jesse sat. He cleared his throat, refused to look at his wife. He fumbled for a Lucky, slapped his pockets looking for a light.

Guthrie needed action. He spied Jesse's Zippo on the stand between them. He flipped it to life then shakily held it for his dad. "Mom, I don't understand."

Cora bent forward trembling. Tears still flowed down her face. "It ain't all that complicated. Ira Walker's your father. I am so sorry. Both of you, please, forgive me."

Jesse stood, bolt straight, and reddened. Then the red gathered purple splotches. "The dirty—I thought the money was because of Christina." He walked out the door, headed toward the pickup.

"Get the, keys, Son, get the keys. He'll kill him."

Guthrie couldn't move. Ira Walker was his dad? His father? He moved to the front door. Ira Walker! Jesse stood by the driver's side of the pickup. He tilted his bottle. Life came back to Guthrie's legs, and he trotted toward the old Dodge.

Jesse obviously spotted him coming and jumped in. The truck roared to life. It lurched backward just out of Guthrie's reach. Its brakes locked seconds before its back bumper jarred into a tree across the street. Gears ground, then it came toward him, wheels spinning, spewing gravel. Jesse zoomed past. The twenty-two rifle rode in the rack behind him.

Guthrie sprinted for his station wagon. Cora slumped inside the screen, one arm raised, holding the doorsill. He reached for his keys and swung open the Chevy's door. Where were they? The dresser. They were on his dresser. Seconds later, keys in hand, he bolted past his mother.

"Stop him. He'll kill him, then die in jail."

"Don't worry, I'll catch him. He probably ain't got enough gas to get to the Sawhorse."

Guthrie backed onto the front lawn. The station wagon swerved onto the street, and he turned the wheel hard. His foot pressed the pedal against the floorboard. The aging engine coughed, but caught hold. Wheels spun, and the car tilted, teetered, then righted.

Houses flashed by, and a fog of dust reflected in the rearview mirror. His mind groped, sucked quicksand-strong at wandering thoughts, and rebelled at rational thinking. At the moment, he rode another runaway. Had no notion where it headed. Then it hit him. Karen had mentioned her folks going to town.

My God! Saddle Horn was town. Saddle Horn was

the town. Ira Walker! His father! It was too much. Whatever. If somebody didn't stop Jesse, Ira would be history.

He roared down the street. There. A block away, the Dodge sat on the apron of Blake's combination service station and general store. The driver's door hung open. The Chevy slid to a stop beside the pickup. With a sigh of relief, he removed Jesse's keys from the ignition then walked toward the building and waited outside the door.

Voices came from inside. "Jesse, you can have all the shells you want—tomorrow. You're in too big a hurry. You been hitting the bottle or what?"

"Who set you up as my conscious? Damn-it, Blake, gimme a box of them hollow points."

"Not today. You come back tomorrow."

A moment's silence settled, then Blake's hard cold voice came through the screen. "Jesse, don't! Don't try it. My scattergun's under the counter. I'll sell you all the shells you want tomorrow."

The screen door banged against the wall, inches from Guthrie. Jesse's giant stride carried him toward the pickup. He stuck his hand through the open window and rifled the contents of the glove box. Papers, pliers, tobacco, matches, everything but shells spilled from the small compartment.

Jesse finally looked at him, flung his hands skyward, and slid to a sitting position on the truck's running board. "The scum, escoria, how do you kill your only son's daddy?" He stuck a cigarette in his mouth

201

and fumbled for a light.

Matches were all over the truck's interior. Guthrie picked one up and handed it to his dad. "What's escoria? Wanta go home?"

"Played with Mexican kids. Don't know, but it ain't good!" Jesse wagged his head. "The bastard deserves to die. He's got it coming. She never had a chance. He's run roughshod over this whole egg-sucking country all his life." Guthrie took his arm and led him to the station wagon. He seated him on the passenger side and felt like a traitor for having so often called him Jesse instead of Dad, or Pop or something.

He walked to the pickup, leaving Jesse staring at nothing and mumbling. "The son of a bitch—the son of a bitch." The truck started on the second try. He parked it by the building then returned to the station wagon. This slumped old man beside him was his dad, no matter the biological-whims of creation. This man he'd held at arm's length had proved himself every day of his life.

The station wagon moved slowly down Main Street. Guthrie watched his dad from the corner of his eye. "You know you can't shoot him."

"Yeah, no bullets."

"You know what I mean."

Jesse didn't reply. He studied Guthrie like he might a colicky yearling. "You okay?"

"Okay! Okay? Just about the time I get used to being known as the son of an over the hill, sagebrush Romeo who always took good care of me, I find out he ain't really the one. No, I ain't okay. Look at me, the unwanted get of the baron of bullshit.

"A mesquite sprout in a heap of horse apples is more wanted. I'm tired of feeling sorry for myself, but right now, I'd say that thorny bush is a pretty good description. Far as that bunch out at the Sawhorse is concerned, I'm just something else to be sprayed, cussed, or bulldozed under." Guthrie made the last turn and slowed.

"Don't let this thing blow you away. There's things that ain't just the way they seem, yet. Keep your powder dry." Jesse opened the door, moved slowly toward the house.

A sense of guilt slapped at his conscience for having rejected Jesse for his trifling, hating him for the embarrassment he caused. Guthrie pushed all the doubts aside. It was okay, the world knew he loved this man. Dad may not have fit, but Jesse wore the word's meaning like a glove. Hell, Jesse sounded better, anyway. His mom's shadow moved from the front door.

He got out and walked back toward town. Someone had to get the pickup, and he needed space. He called Karen from the pay-phone booth on the corner of the square. "Karen, something's come up."

"That sounds interesting."

"No, I'm serious. I can't make it tonight. I'll explain later."

"What? Don't bother!" A loud click connected him to nowhere. He traced "G. S. + O. O." just below B. D. + M. A. in the layer of sand on the booth's shelf then hung

203

up and cursed when the phone robbed him of his quarter.

How could he tell her? He only half believed it himself, and he'd heard it from the only person in the world who'd know. His mom wouldn't lie about something like that. Why would she?

Cora and Jesse sat in the shade of the house. A five-foot utility company wooden reel served as a picnic table. Jesse worked on water and a fifth of I. W. Harper. She sipped ice tea.

Guthrie walked to her and put his hand on her shoulder, looked across at the empty horse pen.

She reached and grasped his hand, but didn't look up. Again the apology, "I'm sorry, son. I should have told you. And your fa—" She looked at her husband. "Jesse, can you ever forgive me?"

He stared into the amber liquid. "I ain't no angel, myself."

"You were, till I tore you to pieces with my craziness."

"Mom, don't. You don't have to explain." He wasn't sure she heard.

Her eyes were glazed. "It's natural you and Karen would feel an attraction. I always knew this day would come. I guess I hoped you'd be happily married and away from here before she grew up."

Cora stared at the discolored wood of the makeshift table. "You've a right to know, and I've a need to tell it." She looked at Guthrie. The words came rapidly. "I'd just learned I was pregnant with Christina when Jesse and I met. Ira and I had seen each other a few times. He was a magnet to every girl in the county old enough for make-up. Certainly, he was a ticket out of the doldrums for whoever proved lucky enough to snare him.

"The worse he treated me, the more I thought I loved him. When I told him I was going to have his baby, he hit me, called me everything in the book. Said I'd never prove it was his. I was such a fool."

Cora grimaced. She lowered her face to her arm, wiped at her tears. "Jesse and I started seeing each other on weekends. He worked on the Rocking Sevens then, and before long, like everyone else in the county, knew all my secrets. We got married, and Christina was born five months later. When she died, I knew it was my punishment. I was to blame. I hated myself. It didn't take long to turn that hate on the one good thing in my life—that man right there." She pointed at Jesse. "We never voiced it, but reached an agreement, a barren, lonely agreement."

Jesse perched on the edge of his chair, downed a shot. His eyes, sad and concerned, never strayed from his wife's face. His body appeared to strain with her every word. "It was the night Booger got killed, wasn't it?"

Cora nodded. "You and Booger had that bet on who'd win the Talbot Fourth of July Shindig." She looked at Guthrie. "Ira was supposed to act as pick-up man. Instead, he came by here. Jesse and Booger had already gone. They had to help at the fairgrounds. Just Irene and I here when he came in. It was a warm day, house was open. I had my back to the door, sweeping. The baby

205

napped. Ira never stopped at the porch. Had me in his arms before I knew he was on the place."

"You two are probably the only ones in town who don't know about this. Inez Webb saw his pickup parked outside. I couldn't show my face for months, still can't as a matter of fact."

Jesse squirmed. Like Cora, it was as if a dam had burst. The words tumbled out, pushing the part of the story he knew. "When Ira didn't show, they asked Uncle Walt Malone to take Ira's place as pickup man. I took off back here to see if Irene and your mother were all right. Turned out Uncle Walt was drunk. I passed Ira on the road out by the Shelby's."

Jesse nodded at his wife. "She never let on anything had happened. When she and I got back to Talbot, we learned Booger had been killed. The old man got his horse tangled up with the Bronc, and they all went down. Malone wasn't hurt, but Booger never regained consciousness. I always knew I owed Ira for that day, but it's only now that I know how much."

His mother stood, placed herself in front of him and grasped both of her husband's hands. "Jesse, you've got to promise me. You just can't kill him. I couldn't stand losing you."

"It's okay, Hon. I'm over that now. If he leaves me and mine alone, I'll behave."

Maybe okay for the old cowboy, but Guthrie made no promises regarding Ira Walker. All his life, the arrogant bastard had missed no opportunity to belittle his every endeavor. What the man didn't tarnish, he spit on. The

trait made an acquaintance detestable, coming from a
father, it was more than he could take.

24

Walker's Livestock Sale Barn sat beside the highway a
couple of hundred yards west of Rita's place. Huge and
white, it broke the horizon of the flat plain like a ship's
sails at sea. Behind the barn, several acres of pens connected with alleyways to elevated loading chutes. Used
oil field pipe, welded strong and high, formed fences
for the lots. Today, vehicles covered the parking area.
Only Friday-night football gathered a larger crowd.

The sale operated each Monday. It started at noon and
finished when the last head was sold. Hogs sold first,
feeder yearlings last. The order buyers didn't like the
sequence, but Ira owned the nearest competition in all
directions, and his dictated terms kept the buyers on the
premises and the market active for the entire sale.

Guthrie knew the place well. He'd spent a lot of Mon-
days here working the alleys, picking up running
money during holidays and the summer months. At one
point, he'd even participated in boxing matches held in
the auction ring inside the barn. The oval ring had an
eight-foot steel fence facing auditorium seating on one
side and an even higher wooden auctioneer's bench on
the other. Doors opened at either end of the ring. One
led through a chute opening to the alleyway outside and
the opposite to the scales.

A drive-through lot served as a farm trailer unloading

207

facility. It was located near the raised loading area and next to squeeze chutes that served to regulate stock movement through brand and health inspection points.

Guthrie pulled to a stop and stepped from his Chevy. Nearby, two men stood on a raised platform near the squeeze chutes. One raised his voice. "I can't make it out, Al, can you?"

The man across the chute shook his head.

"No, it's too haired-over to read. I've seen Mr. Thornton use that ear-notch, though. Wally, run your shears over that brand." Wally did as directed.

Guthrie spoke to a man holding a gate. "Where's Ira?"

He nodded toward a wide alley running toward the barn. "Somewhere up there with Elmo moving hogs."

Guthrie stepped halfway up a fence, vaulted over, and walked rapidly toward the two men near the other end. They moved in his direction. One was Ira. Guthrie knew the black man with him. Ira's helper opened a gate.

"Not that one, Elmo, number twelve." Ira held a thin ring-man's whip in his hand.

Elmo erased his error by closing the gate and opening number twelve.

Guthrie stopped within a few feet of Ira. "Hear you're my old man."

Ira looked startled. He opened a gate and let five black and white shoats into the alley. "I ain't never denied it."

"You ain't never advertised it neither."

208

Suddenly, he knew Jesse wasn't the one. Here was the one who created the funnel that sucked a hole in his childhood. He'd lied—denied his part in his own son's life then made it worse by demeaning him.

The accosted man turned, placed his fists on his hips. "What are you after, boy?"

Elmo took the whip and moved the hogs up the alley. He looked at neither.

"Not a damn thing. Thought I'd look you in the eye and hear you say it."

"You go to hell." Ira turned and followed the group of Hampshire toward pen number twelve.

Guthrie grabbed him and swung him around just as Elmo closed the gate. "Say it! Let me hear you say it."

The auctioneer's chant resounded from speakers under the open roof and above the pens. "Inside boys, inside. Sales starting."

Ira turned and strode rapidly up the alleyway toward the sale barn. He grabbed the whip from Elmo and popped it wrathfully in the air. He lowered his head, turned, and sidestepped several feet through a narrow alley before he ducked through a steel-fenced walkway.

Guthrie hesitated, he'd hoped to keep this between he and the slime before him. Private, hell, his pain proved the fallacy of drawn blinds. A quarter-century of hypocrisy and pious whisperings had only created a pus-pot of hurt. His mom said everyone over twenty-five knew the story anyway, so why not clean house? He followed at Ira's heels, stepped inside the barn, and into the auction ring.

Stragglers took their seats deliberately causing as much distraction as possible. Order buyers tilted neighbor's hats, slapped others on the back, and by their actions, told everyone in attendance that the doings could start now that they'd made their entrance.

The auctioneer loosened up, tested his mike, and waved at friends in the first row. He looked higher and touched his hat. "Mr. Hefner, how you been? Ira, you ready?"

"Just a minute, Ray." Ira pointed at the stands. "Okay, Guthrie git. I got work to do."

Elmo opened the swinging door and two large sows entered the ring. One stopped and turned in circles. Its ears stood straight, and it blew air loudly through its nose. The other circled the ring squealing.

Guthrie lit a cigarette and waved his hand. "Ray shut that thing off a minute." The second sow's voice joined the other. "Naw, here, let me have it."

Ray handed him the mike.

"Fellows, when stock hits this ring, somebody's supposed to identify it. Well, I'm here and looking to be branded." He pointed at Ira. "A lot of you've known this guy for forty, going on fifty years. Most of you've known me all my life. Likely you know, he fathered my dead sister Christina, and now I hear he's my dad." He walked to Ira, stuck his finger in front of the older man's nose. "Is that right, Mr. Walker? Are you my papa?"

Ira shoved with both hands, and Guthrie stepped backward. Something slammed into the back of his knees, a hog squealed. He went down. His shoulders scooted the ring's soft sand. A second hog jumped over him, then he was on his hands and knees. Ira's whip lashed out. Pain slashed across Guthrie's cheek. Blood gushed.

He grabbed the whip with his left hand, pulled, and came erect in one rapid movement. Three quick steps brought him in front of this man he'd always disliked. He feinted with his left, saw the twisted face, his target. It moved into range, but his right wouldn't budge. The fist hung, cocked near his ear and ready to slam into Ira. Why wouldn't it respond? The older man's eyes were large. They showed fear.

Strong arms grabbed Guthrie from behind, held him. Two order buyers reached through the fence and held Ira. Elmo spoke from behind him. "That's enough, Mister Guthrie. You behave now."

Guthrie struggled, uselessly. "Okay, Elmo, turn loose. I'm leaving." He climbed to the top of the high fence. He sat on the top, twisted, and looked down on this man his mother claimed sired him. "It was your money set aside for my schooling, huh?"

"It was, and when I'm gone, you'll get the same as the rest of the brood. Just stay out of my life."

Guthrie took his handkerchief out and held it to his cut cheek. "Count on it." He hooked his thumb over his shoulder toward the ring. The raw lash mark stung from an embryonic, twisted smile that died on his face. He scanned the crowd and wagged his head. "You boys may want to keep a keen eye on them scales."

He dropped to the floor on the seat side of the ring and walked out of the barn. Behind him, Ray claimed to have "thirty cents, who'd make it thirty and a half?"

Guthrie exited the sale with a mental image of Ira's fear-streaked face before his fist. Soft intonations of honor thy father welled from the outfield fringes of his mind. Who made that rule? He'd had trouble with it and Jesse, now this. Hard as it had always been, the honoring part might be less difficult than identifying the target. Seemed impossible he'd restrained himself. How he'd accepted the sting of Ira's lash without hitting back was a mystery.

His heart pounded, and the whip-cut cheek continued to color his handkerchief. Head down and dejected, he forced heavy steps. His boot heels dragged out his tracks in the traffic-powdered dust. Maybe he'd have felt better if he'd hit him. A simple case of fact defeating denial said he sprouted from Walker seed. Ira acknowledged it, and the truth showed in Mr. Hefner's face, a face with no starch, sagging in sadness.

Why would it matter so much to that old man? Then he remembered Booger. Mr. Hefner, torn with grief, probably left no stone unturned, learned all the details of the night of his son's death.

Guthrie gunned the old station wagon and headed for the house. Lies branded as fact drummed in his mind, vied for a Sammy title, something like Slow Towns and Fast Secrets or Small Towns with Big Pasts.

May have been a bullheaded way to do it, but at least he'd gotten his answer. He'd thought Ira would really deny the whole thing. He turned onto the highway, and the wind whipped dry dust from the car's wheels. The plume rose then diminished in his rearview mirror.

Keep your powder dry, Jesse had said. What did that mean? Poor old Jesse, always turning over another shovel full, looking for a pony under the pile.

Down the road the sun reflected, and a red spot grew larger, approaching from town. The car took on form, then zipped past. Karen's wide eyes had locked on him and her head twisted around.

His face became clammy, and a sickness grew upward from his stomach. Roast 'em all in hell, he'd flirted with his own sister. What if they'd gotten together?

Oops, sorry! We forgot to tell you!

In the mirror, he watched Karen whip a U-turn. He pulled toward the shoulder. She might just run over him. Her car bore down on the station wagon. Its brakes locked, too late. The Vette slid, continued skidding toward him. She whipped the convertible into the ditch, did a three-sixty, and came to rest nose to nose with his fifty-seven.

The door swung open. She raced toward him with energy that did justice to any world-finals roper. He half expected her to pull out a pigging string and wrap him in a three-legged half-hitch. He doubled his fists, crossed his wrists, and with the bloody handkerchief, held them out the window. "Here, I'm yours."

"What happened to your face? You're bloody all over."

213

"Our father gave me a spanking."

"Our what?"

"Karen, you better get in and sit and listen."

"I don't want to, and listening is not what I do best."

"Please."

She walked around, sank into the passenger seat, and waited while he lit a cigarette. "Let me have one of those."

Guthrie shook a smoke from the package toward her then shoved in the lighter. He leaned back, dabbed at his cheek, and pushed up his hat brim.

Karen pulled out the lighter and lit the cigarette. "I hate Viceroys. Who hit you?"

He looked at her and suddenly, for some reason, the whole monstrous deal of deception, confusion, and their brief relationship seemed almost comical. He was twenty-five and a mental infant. Didn't even know who to call momma and daddy. He laughed. It wasn't a happy laugh, but more a what-might-have-been, cynical laugh.

"You bum. Where'd you go last night? Why'd you bother if you didn't want to see me? Who came along?"

"No one. Karen, when I saw you Saturday night, you gotta know, I was smitten. There was something about you, and we talked; and the chemistry was there, and I knew I'd found something so special, so wonderful. I thought I knew what it meant. I didn't."

Karen shoved the door and leaped to her feet. "So much for first impressions." She flipped the cigarette to the pavement. Tears shone in her eyes. She tossed her hair and took giant strides toward her car. Her broken voice trailed behind. "So long, Cowboy." The Vette's door slammed.

"Wait, Karen, I don't want to hurt you." He bolted from the Chevy, ran to her window. "I've got to say this right."

She backed a few yards, slammed the shift into low, and started forward.

"You're my sister!"

The corvette's wheels spun, pelting Guthrie with gravel. Tires squealed across the pavement then locked and left heavy marks leading onto the shoulder. The car came to rest on the opposite side of the highway. A cloud of dust obscured its back bumper, swallowed the Corvette, back to front, then drifted across the ditch and disappeared. Karen jumped from the car, facing him.

Guthrie trotted across the road then stood before her.

She had a wounded look and stomped her foot like a startled doe. "Our daddy? Your sister? What's the deal? What are you talking about?"

Guthrie shifted his weight. "Well." He looked down the pavement then switched directions. "Mom heard me call you yesterday. She sort of went to pieces."

Karen took a step toward him. With a hand on each of his arms, she tilted her head, peering up into his face. Curiosity replaced her look of anger. "Your mother doesn't like me?"

"Ain't that. She said Jesse's not my dad. You and I can't see each other. It's true. Ira's my father, too. I've been flirting with my sister."

215

"That's a sorry lie."

"He admitted it. I just cornered him, and he admitted it—just before he cut me with that whip."

"Daddy did that? Why? Lane's older'n you. Momma and Daddy have been married longer than that."

"Uh-huh."

She wilted to her knees then dropped to the edge of the pavement and sat cross-legged. She looked down and held her hand up. "Gimme another one of those nasty Viceroys."

He lit a cigarette, examined the barren road in both directions, and handed her the burning smoke. Folding his legs, he sank into a sitting position.

Neither spoke for several moments, then Karen turned toward him. Her eyes were misty. "We don't look alike."

"Your good luck." The whine of a distant engine caught Guthrie's attention, and Billy Odom's old cattle truck loomed down the road, moving toward them. "We gonna move or just let Billy finish us off?"

"It's a wide road. He's got plenty of room."

The truck's noise intensified then lowered. It slowed and sounds of downshifting overpowered the tire's hum while it inched slowly in their direction. By the time it reached them, the mammoth rig barely moved. Air brakes vented, and the vehicle came to a rocking halt. Heat from the engine enveloped them. The heavy bumper guard towered above the Corvette.

The driver leaned out of the passenger side window. "Yawl need help?"

"Naw, thanks, Mr. Odom. We're okay."

The trucker looked at Karen. "You're sure?" He nodded at Guthrie. "Ain't ever day I dodge a couple of squatters in the middle of the road."

Guthrie nodded. "Herd it on along. We're sitting here fiddling with our pedigrees."

"Your what?"

"Go on. Git! You gonna fool around here and miss a load at that sale. If we ain't up by the time you come back, start worrying."

Karen smiled. "Thanks, though, for checking, Billy." The truck groaned away. Her lips quivered. She clamped her jaw. Guthrie reached for his handkerchief, but then remembered leaving it on the floorboard. Karen wiped her nose with a wadded tissue. She searched his face then stared across the rolling grassland. "You think it's really true?"

"Why would anyone lie about a thing like this?"

"It's strange. Like you said, I felt drawn to you when I first glimpsed you. I don't feel like your sister, but then I've never felt very close to Lane either." A car took form down the road. "We better move to the Vette."

They stood beside the vehicle then seated themselves after the car moved past. Karen found a second tissue. Guthrie looked at his cheek in the mirror.

"Your eyes. That's it! Gray and piercing like those in the picture of Granddaddy. And John Robert's are the same. I guess it is true. We'll be close, Guthrie. I don't want us to be like Lane and I, or Daddy and I. Let's talk

217

about things that matter, important things—you know ambitions, dreams, and things like that. Part of me wishes it weren't true. Isn't exactly what I had in mind, but I'd as soon put off that diaper thing awhile anyway." Karen put her hand to her mouth and made a hurt sound. "Does Mama know?"

Guthrie shook his head. "I don't know. Jesse didn't."

She twisted toward him. "How'd he take it?"

"Like a bull takes a hot iron. He headed for his gun. He'd have stormed the Sawhorse if he'd had any shells."

"Guthrie, that scares me. There's no telling what he or Daddy will do if they get together."

"You're right. There's a storm brewing, and somebody could get killed."

"I better go. Somehow, I gotta find out if Mama knows. And the men, we've got to figure a way to keep those two apart. Will you meet me at the café for breakfast in the morning?"

"How about eight?" He stepped from the car.

"Eight it is."

25

Guthrie tilted his cup, toying with the half-empty, half-full dilemma. Alvin solved the problem by filling the mug. Karen entered, and he sensed an initial excitement, but reminded himself they were kin.

When the eggs arrived, she leaned over the plate and used both hands. Sitting there, working the breakfast,

218

she resembled a roundup cowboy more than a Rice graduate. She made the napkin a thing of utility, not a stage prop for femininity. She chewed quickly and talked around the movement. Her bunkhouse manners detracted not an iota from her stunning beauty. Sister or sweetheart, a fellow had to like what he saw.

Her soft words reached only Guthrie. By the end of the meal, he learned that Sybil offered no resistance to Karen dating him, so she obviously knew nothing of Ira's philandering.

He recounted going to both stores that carried ammunition and asking them to not sell Jesse shells. Used a made-up story to tell them the old man was cussing mad about all the male dogs hanging around the pump house. Guthrie lied that Coach Weaver's young collie bitch trailed a canine corps of cupid-struck mongrels. The merchants agreed to refuse the sale, but expressed surprise, mentioning they'd have thought the waterman would be more sympathetic to such a cause.

He paid the check and followed his newly discovered sister to the sidewalk. They hunched their backs, raised their collars, and turned from the wind. Karen refused his offer of a smoke. He lit a cigarette. "Get in, and we'll talk in the car, out of this norther."

She walked to the passenger side of the station wagon. Her Corvette sat a few parking spaces away. He reached for the driver's door handle and looked over the top of the Chevy. Jesse's Dodge came down Main Street.

Karen faced the other direction. "There's Daddy."

He wheeled, saw Ira's new Ford dually on the driveway of Blake's station. "Get in."

Jesse's old Dodge rattled closer. It accelerated down the street. The bronc twister turned utility man looked neither left or right. His eyes focused on the Ford. Guthrie burned rubber backing out and turning, yet remained a hundred yards behind his used-to-be dad.

At the station, he slid to a stop beside Jesse's pickup. The old cowboy approached Ira. The twenty-two, pump rifle dangled in his right hand. Blake twisted the Ford's gas cap and walked toward the door of the station. Ira followed.

Jesse's voice cracked across the cool breeze. "You cut my boy's face."

Ira stopped mid-stride. He put both arms up, hands outstretched. His eyes locked on the rifle. His face whitened. "Jesse, don't be a pig-headed fool."

"Who do you think you are? You got too big for your britches thirty years ago, Ira Walker. I should have gut shot you then. Now, you dare lay a hand on that boy."

Metal slapped against metal. The snapping, business-like action of the pump sounded sinister, loud against the quiet. Jesse brought the barrel of the rifle waist high, pointed at Ira.

Guthrie rounded the front of the station wagon, headed for Jesse. "Dad, don't."

"Jesse, for God's sake, don't kill me." Ira turned and ran for the door of the station. The loud crack of the twenty-two almost absorbed both his and Ira's pleas.

Ira grabbed his hip, spun, and fell. "No more, I'm hit. You son of a bitch! You've shot me." He rolled from his belly to his side, twisted, looked at the widening, wet spot beneath his hip pocket.

Blake stood with his mouth open, looking at Jesse. Guthrie stopped just short of the man he'd called Dad.

Karen rushed to Ira and knelt.

Mr. Hefner screeched to a halt straddling the highway's white line. He leaned across the seat, fished in his shirt pocket fingering for his eyeglasses, then peered out the passenger window toward the station.

Jesse walked, gun in hand, to the old settler's vehicle. He opened the passenger door and placed his rifle on the floorboard. He spoke loud enough to tell the world he'd laid down his rifle. "Mr. Hefner, would you call the sheriff. Tell him I'll be home, probably in the kitchen. I'll have some coffee ready when he gets there."

"I'll tell him, Jesse." The old man pulled to the phone booth at the edge of the park.

Jesse walked slowly back to Karen and Ira. He looked at the small spot of blood on his victim's trousers, touched the fallen man's butt with his boot-toe. "You ain't bleeding much, Ira. Reckon you'll make it."

"You bastard. It hurts like hell."

"Yeah, wal, times are tough."

Ira struggled to his hands and one knee. The leg of the hurt hip projected straight behind. "Why'd you shoot me in the ass?"

"You turned. I'uz pointing for your gonads."

"Sawyer, you're crazier than a bat. I'll get you for this."

"Bring help. You got all that unfinished business. Maybe we better get you to a doctor. Guthrie, back your wagon over here. I'll give you and Karen a hand loading him. Then reckon I better go wait for my company."

Blake patted Karen on the back, looked nervously in all directions. "He'll be okay, honey." He nodded. "It's gonna be okay."

Guthrie moved the Chevy as directed. He and Jesse helped Ira to his feet. With support under either arm, Ira hopped and dragged his hurt leg toward the fifty-seven.

On her dad's second hop, Karen stooped to retrieve a small object that fell from Ira's Levi's. With her finger only a few inches away she pulled back. "Ugh, it's the bullet."

Blake picked it up. "I'll swun, must have gone through his billfold. Ira, maybe you ain't too bad hurt."

"Feels bad."

Guthrie shoved his saddle out of the way. Ira groaned and squirmed his way into a facedown position in back of the station wagon. Karen jumped in with her dad.

The highway bisected the town of Talbot a short drive down the road from Saddle Horn. Its Medical Center recently emerged from bankruptcy, and now served as a County Hospital. Voters brought it back to life with their hard earned tax dollars. An Odessa, Texas immigrant served as administrator, and two young transplanted doctors, one from the Philippines, the other, Iran, qualified the facility for Medicare.

The speedometer registered eighty coming out of the long turn east of town. Guthrie straightened the vehicle into the arrow-straight road beyond and pushed the accelerator down until the pedal met the floor mat. Karen's voice reminded him of her presence. He raised his foot slightly.

"Guthrie, maybe I should pull his pants down, look at that wound. What if he's bleeding to death? Maybe, he needs a pressure bandage."

"Whatever you think, but it sure don't show to be bleeding much."

"What if it's all internal?"

"Well, look then."

"Daddy can you unbuckle your belt?"

"You leave my britches be, little girl. Just take that billfold out of my pocket. It's burning like the devil. Sawyers, just a couple of saddle bums, the both of you! Bigger pests than Johnson grass. Guthrie, you got a bottle in here anywhere?"

"Naw, I generally mooch off Jesse."

"Figgers. Ouch. Oh, that's better, Hon, thanks."

"Guthrie, don't you look, but that bullet did cut through this billfold, his cards and a wad of bills."

"Ira can you move that hip?"

"Now that my wallet's gone. I think part of it was sticking in my—Say, what the hell you two doing together this time of morning? My God, yawl ain't been—together!"

"Daddy, we know. We know we're brother and sister."

"Oh, yeah. Well, look, Guthrie, I'm sorry about that whip. You got a right to be chaffed about all this."

"Save your breath, Ira. Who knows, maybe you got a doctor or two to cuss yet today."

Upon their arrival at the hospital, the Walker luck held. No babies were being delivered. Dr. Acuna was free to see the rancher.

The nurse pointed to the waiting room near the hospital's entrance. Karen phoned her mother. She returned to the lounge, stuck the fingers of each hand into her pockets, and sprawled into a stuffed chair. "Well, we really kept them apart, didn't we?"

"We did good for a couple of hours." Guthrie's mind whirled, fixed on nothing. He idly watched miniature dust devils swirl and eddy into the corners of the covered entrance outside the glass doors. Time moved slowly.

A few minutes later, the doctor appeared. Karen jumped to her feet and met him. Guthrie followed.

"You his kids, right?" The doctor's smile was the biggest thing about him. "Okay, relax. His hurt is pretty good, not too bad. He will be okay, I bet. The bullet only go in this far." Dr. Acuna held his finger and thumb apart about a quarter of an inch. "The bone was not scratched. My nurse will clean the wound, then I'll put in stitches. We'll give him a tetanus shot and send him home after, oh, maybe one hour." The doctor smiled even bigger, nodded, and turned back toward the emergency room.

Sybil's Cadillac stopped in the front driveway. Her heels beat a rapid rhythm to Karen's side. They hugged.

"How is he?"

"Mom, he's okay. They're giving him first aid and then plan to release him. His billfold and that wad of stuff he carries took most of the impact."

Sybil seemed to notice Guthrie for the first time.

Karen nodded at him. "He brought Daddy over here in his station wagon."

"Guthrie, it's good to see you. Thank you."

He shook her hand, nodded.

"You said he was shot. Who?"

"Jesse Sawyer."

"Oh, my God! That again?" Sybil melted onto the couch. She unsnapped a pouch, took out a cigarette, then lit it with a lighter from the same case. Karen joined her mother on the couch. Guthrie sat opposite her.

Sybil placed the cigarette in an ashtray and took Karen's hand. She extended the other to Guthrie. He took it, unsure of his next move.

"And you kids, what do you know of this whole nasty mess?"

Karen's eyes were on him. They filled, and she brushed at the tears with the back of her hand. "Cora saw we were about to get together, you know, date. She told Guthrie and Jesse about . . . about Daddy being Guthrie's father, too. I'm sorry to tell you like this."

Sybil released their hands, took up her smoke. "It's okay, Karen, I know about that."

"You what? I don't understand."

"No, there's no way you would. Let's go see Ira. You say Jesse shot him in the butt?" She seemed to almost smile as she said it.

Guthrie stood. "I better get on back to Saddle Horn."

Karen wiggled bye with her fingers. Sybil spoke. "Thanks again, Guthrie."

He shrugged, reached for the door.

"Guthrie, don't get too down about this. Things aren't exactly straightened out, yet."

"Yeah, you're telling me."

Forty minutes later he pulled to a stop behind the sheriff's black and white Ford.

Otis Wright had held the title of sheriff of Sage County long as Guthrie could remember. Fortunately, their paths had not crossed often, but he knew the man's reputation. The lawman was saddle leather tough, gun barrel straight, and knew when to talk and when not to. He smiled just often enough to get re-elected and never put force on a man unnecessarily. In the old days, he, Booger, and Jesse rode for the same brand. The sheriff's face was as solemn as those of Guthrie's folks when he entered.

Wright stuck out his hand. "Guthrie."

"Otis, how you been?"

The sheriff held his hat in his hand and walked toward the front door. "See y'all after supper."

Jesse followed, closed the door after him then went to his chair. "I should have finished Ira while I had him down."

Guthrie looked at his mom. "What's he talking about? Ain't he going to jail?"

His mother wiped dust from the TV cabinet with the corner of her apron. "Otis called the hospital and talked to Ira and Sybil. Ira says he may not press charges. Told the sheriff to bring the three of us out to the Sawhorse after supper tonight. Sybil says we have some talking to do."

"Wants me to beg. I should have finished it."

"Jesse, be quiet. For God's sake, haven't you done enough for one day?"

Guthrie wondered about his hearing. "They want all three of us out there?"

His mother seemed near the end of her rope. "That's what the man said. I'm going to lie down."

26

The Sawhorse ranch house did for Panhandle society what Tara did for Atlanta. It provided a place to be, or at least, one to be seen. The home seemed out of place in this flat, treeless landscape. It was as though Walker number two planted it a thousand miles too far west. Cora labeled it Georgian Revival style—quite unusual in Texas. Guthrie agreed. Anything with seven chimneys poking out its roof and six thirty-foot limestone columns flanking its entrance was definitely a little rare.

In days past, he'd visited friends at the bunkhouse, and eaten at the grub shack, but had never been inside the main house. Lee described the interior as rich with beautiful hardwood wainscoting, ceiling panels, and moldings. She'd mentioned the main entrance opened into a foyer that in turn led to a horseshoe staircase massive enough to support hay wagons.

The sheriff's car stopped in front of Jesse's. Sybil, with Karen at her side, met them at the front steps. "Cora, it's so good of you to come. Jesse, Sheriff, Guthrie, we meet again."

Each acknowledged Sybil's greeting. The party followed the two Walker ladies inside. As he stepped onto a beautiful, foreign-looking rug, Guthrie wondered if all his earlier scrapping and kicking had cleared his boots. They passed through a large formal room, down a short hall, and into a huge den. Lee had not exaggerated. The scent of burning mesquite came from a stone fireplace.

Ira lay on his good side, on a couch. "Well, Otis, good. I see you gathered them up."

"Ira, shut up. You all have a seat. Let me bring you some coffee. Just tell me how you take it. Sugar, cream?" Sybil filled cups then handed them on saucers to Karen, and she, in turn, distributed them around the room. "I gave Flo the night off, you know, since there may be things said that are better kept private."

Guthrie noticed a hat rack, took Jesse's and the sheriff's Stetsons, and placed them with his own on the man-made tree. He sat and aimlessly stirred his black, sugarless coffee. At Sybil's reprimand of her husband, Otis turned and made a pretense of examining a collection of rifles encased in a glass cabinet.

Karen distributed the final cup to the sheriff. "Thank you, ma'am." He looked at Ira. "Well, Walker, looks like we're all here. Have to say, ain't sure what this is all about, but here we are. What's on your mind?"

Sybil answered for her husband. "Mr. Wright, this is all sort of awkward. It's my idea that calls for you being here. Just seems to me there's been enough violence, and I wanted you here."

"That's what I do best, ma'am, keep the peace." Ira seemed a bit miffed at a woman attempting to neck-rein him. "Ira, you say you're not pressing charges?"

"Need a word with Jesse about that." Ira pointed his finger at the elder Sawyer. "I'm prepared to drop this whole rotten thing on your word that you'll never again try to do me harm."

Jesse stood. "You do what you want about charges, but I'd have killed you while you were down if I'd thought of ever doing you more damage."

"Good enough. Okay, that's it. No, I ain't gonna press any charges. Otis, do I need to sign something?" He didn't wait for an answer. "Us older ones here know how it used to be. You know, when you're young and full of vinegar. Lord knows I did Cora a disservice then, later, both she and Jesse . . . uh, and Guthrie. When I saw that rifle pointing my way, well it started me thinking. It ain't that I wanted to do you mischief. Hell, I can't explain it."

Otis moved to the hat rack, took his John B. "No, there's nothing to sign. Guess my part in this is over.

Jesse, hope you've learned something. You may not like him, but he saved you doing some time." He nodded toward Ira then the ladies. "Well, y'all got your car. I'm gone."

Sybil raised her cup at the sheriff. "Just a minute, Mr. Wright."

The lawman stopped, turned his hat, slowly, by the brim, an inch at a time. His impatience showed.

"Sheriff, I don't mean to be high-handed, but please, stay another moment. You may, yet, be needed. Jesse, you and I have something to say. I want the sheriff here while we do."

Jesse sagged in his chair. His cup rattled on the saucer. He sat it on an end table. "Sybil!"

Mrs. Walker looked at Karen, sitting near her dad, then at Guthrie. "It's you kids that have been misused here. As always, you pay for our foolishness. Cora, Ira, there's no reason Guthrie and Karen shouldn't see each other if they want."

His mom's speed took him by surprise. She shot to her feet. "You pompous old biddy. Save your prattle for something you know about."

"I know the same thing about my daughter that you know about your son."

"And that is?" Cora's words rang through the high-ceilinged room.

"Who her father is, and Ira, darling, it isn't you." Sybil's gaze rested on Karen. She ignored her husband. Her stony look of humor-shaded irony vanished. Anguish replaced it. "Sweetheart, forgive me. There's only one way to say it. Jesse Sawyer is your father."

Cora sat. The sheriff's hat picked up prop-wash, and he eased into a straight-backed chair. Jesse cleared his throat. Somewhere, a clock chimed. Karen gasped, put her hands to her face, and her body shook.

Ira hollered. "Sawyer, you son of a bitch." He leapt to his feet, stood poised on one leg, started forward, then fell, facedown on the floor. Otis went to him and helped him back on the couch.

Sybil moved to her daughter, squatted, and embraced her. Without turning, she spoke firmly, "Jesse."

He stood and slowly clumped across the room to Karen and Sybil. "It's true, Karen. She told me early on, but made me promise not to say anything." He put his hand on Karen's shoulder. "I've always watched you with pride."

Guthrie stood. "Damn." He wandered to the front room, started up the stairs. Halfway, he realized where he was and moved back toward the den.

He heard his mother's voice. "How? When?"

Sybil was visible through the doorway. She stared dispassionately at Cora. "You remember me calling and telling Jesse they wanted him to help with the vaccination that year. Of course, I knew about you and Ira. I just failed to mention that he and the hands would all be at the south pasture. Jesse came here. He arrived more innocent than he left."

Otis walked toward the door. The sheriff raised both hands, rolled his eyes at the ceiling. "We had more sense in grade school down at Brushy. You people need

231

Dear Abby, not a lawman."

His mother stood. "Guthrie, take me home."

He made eye contact with Karen. "I'll call."

She nodded.

Jesse followed them to the car and climbed into the rear. The ride back to Saddle Horn was quiet. His mom stared out the window. Jesse's smoke drifted up front. Guthrie gave up trying to think. There wasn't a horse in Sage County fast enough to put him in range of his thoughts.

The phone rang shortly after eight the following morning. An exchange of pleasantries, including a short discussion of the weather followed the caller's introduction of himself as Chairman of the Fort Worth Stock Show Committee. He asked if Guthrie would be interested in announcing their forthcoming rodeo. Guthrie agreed in general to contract wording and hung up as soon as professionalism allowed. He sensed juvenile, candy-store enthusiasm worming into his voice.

The man said five-grand. Maybe, he meant five hundred. This must be what weightlessness felt like. He had to tell someone. Who'd give a rip? Maybe Sammy? Naw, he didn't seem to relate much to anything he couldn't touch or hear. His mom and Jesse would be out of commission for another week after yesterday. They'd have to taper off the day's excitement by staring at a week of television with little or no conversation.

Karen! He'd call Karen, but which one? Karen the almost sister, or Karen the almost-dateable doll. Hell, he didn't care which one showed. He just needed someone to brag to.

Sleepy responses, made up of meaningless grunts, yawns, and I-guess-sos exposed the falsehood of Karen's statement "oh, yes I'm awake". She finally admitted the lie and said she and her mother had talked until a few hours before daylight. She agreed to breakfast at Alvin's, but asked for an hour.

Alvin liked to tell that football had not been invented when he attended school. As a matter-of-fact, most of the Texas Panhandle had only sponsored four grades of school when Alvin graced the halls of learning. Guthrie figured the short-order cook had not missed much on the scholastic side of the ledger. The lack of football opportunity was a more serious matter. The café man tended toward big—real big. His son came along and added new meaning to the word. Alvin Jr. attended West Texas State then moved to Chicago and played for the Bears. Football dominated the conversation at Alvin's.

While waiting on their eggs, Karen held her own with the big man's good-natured banter, taking the Oilers' side of the debate concerning Texas' best pro-team. Alvin served their breakfast, leaned with his arms resting on his counter, and clumsily fished between his teeth with a toothpick. He turned the conversation technical with talk of options and platoon substitution. Tiring, Karen surrendered by admitting the only kind of split-ends she knew about came from bad hair-dos.

Alvin became serious. "It's none of my business, but

I hear you two had a rough day yesterday. How's Ira doing?"

"He'll be okay."

The big man turned his attention to Guthrie. "And Jesse, what about him? Otis take him in?"

"Alvin, you know about this cut here, don't you?" Guthrie pointed at his face. "And you know about what the doctor said. How many reports you get on that shooting down at Blake's, seven or eight? Well, Jesse's home, and there's not gonna be charges filed. Now, why don't you put that nose back in joint and let me and my girlfriend eat in peace."

Alvin's face turned blank, his expression akin to that of an anvil. He seemed intent on a coffee stain.

"Yeah, girlfriend. She ain't my sister, but you gonna have to get that story somewhere else." Guthrie held the café man's eyes.

"Listen, Sonny, I whipped your ass regular right along with Junior's when you were growing up. I can still do it. Don't get smart with me."

"You're probably right, but you'd need some cleaning up around this joint afterwards."

Alvin lumbered to the kitchen, mumbling to himself. Guthrie heard a cabinet door open. He stood, bent over the counter, and caught a view through the doorway of the café man tilting a bottle. He spoke quietly. "Why'd I do that?"

She gave him a you're-just-an-ass look and went on eating.

What could he say to ease the sting? Old Alvin was

all right. It just seemed the Sawyers had carried scandal sheet headlines long enough in this burg. They finished their meal in silence, and he left money on the counter.

The bell on the door tinkled when Karen opened it. Alvin's voice carried from the kitchen. "Didn't mean to step out of line, Guthrie. Yawl come back."

"No offence, Alvin. I'm just wired a little tight right now. See yuh. Tell Junior, hey, next time he calls."

Karen motioned to the Vette. The morning air was cold, and she had the top up. She started the car, drove slowly toward the canyon.

"You all right?" he asked.

"I'm so confused, I can barely think. Talk about a flip-flop. Your daddy's mine—mine's yours. I don't know whether to flirt with you or tattle on you. How do I go about getting acquainted with Jesse?"

"That won't be hard."

"He is nice, huh?"

"Top drawer."

"Lee says you were always embarrassed by his . . . his reputation."

"That's true. It took a lot of distance and considerable time for me to realize how important he is to me. And to be honest, it still hurts."

"Tell me about it, accepting him I mean."

Guthrie lit a cigarette, motioned with the pack. She shook off the offer. "Nothing much to tell. I'd been in Na'am about six months. Written Momma a few times, but couldn't bring myself to really make contact with

Jesse. Then one day we got caught out in the open. I got cut up pretty bad. Had a concussion or something. A couple landed pretty close. Anyway, after it was over that night, I was dizzy and throwing up till the wee hours. Finally, I went to sleep. Woke up later crying like a baby, calling Jesse's name. I wrote him next day. It's been a lot better since."

"What did you say?"

"Don't know. Think I talked about the monsoons mostly. He wrote me back. Said it was dry here."

"That must have been something."

"It was. I still got it."

"May I read it sometime?" Karen pulled to the rocky shoulder of the overlook.

"Sure. Say, guess what! I got a call from Cowtown today. They want me to do the stock show."

"That's great, isn't it?"

"Great? It's more'n that. A six month paycheck is about what it is."

"Maybe I'll join you for a performance or two. I have friends in the Mid-cities."

"Swell. I'd like that."

"Guthrie, you said something back there about being wired tight, and you don't mention riding anymore. I heard that was a big thing with you. What's going on? Lee had me thinking you were going to be the next World's Champ. What's the deal?"

"How come you picked this spot?"

"Somebody said you liked it."

"Lee? You didn't give me much."

236

"Sammy?" She snapped the name like a dog fighting flies.

Ice formed in the brown pools of her eyes. She'd mentioned Erilee, but apparently the name was off limits to him.

"Speaking of not giving much, neither did you—the horses?" She'd thawed some.

"It's a long story, and not one I'm proud of. The bottom line is since that wreck at El Paso, broncs and I ain't friendly. Naw, more honest is, I'm getting afraid of them. You been around enough horses to know they smell fear."

"Is it a big deal? I mean since you're serious about this announcing thing anyway, aren't you?"

Guthrie squinted into the sun. His view roamed the vastness of the canyon, rested on the dark green of nearby cedars, then meandered across to the deep blue miles away. Tamed by frost, the canyon's brighter colors had blended, transformed to diluted browns and straw colors. Clay banks of red and umber drained to the deeper valleys of chalky-white.

"The answer is, yes, to both. It is a big deal, and I am excited about announcing. Bronc riding compliments commentary well though. Maybe not now, but soon enough television will demand World Champs at the microphones. Look at baseball with Pee-Wee and Dizzy, and football's going the same way.

"Besides, rodeo's who I am. There aren't many of us, and I like it. It's just that sometimes it hurts so lamed bad. Bucking is the high wire act, the top of the crop, and for my money, broncs are above the rest. Bulls make a good show, but riding them has never had a purpose. Man's been riding—or riding at—horses since he crawled out of the cave."

"It is important to you."

"Guess I'm learning how much."

"You mentioned El Paso. I know you were almost killed out there. Mom followed the story in the paper. She read the Radcliffs were awarded a quarter million dollars. Said the last article mentioned your case having been settled with undisclosed conditions. Why all the mystery? Did you get money?"

"I didn't want money. I get paid to ride, not roll around in the seats. They took care of some hospital bills. All I asked of them."

"Speaking of hospitals, I talked to a friend of yours last night who was in one not too long ago."

"I didn't think you'd feel like talking to anyone after we left."

"That's the reason I called Flap. He's always been my hero, the one person who can pull me out of the dumps."

"Me, too. We got pretty thick last summer. He's a good boy. Now I know why, got it from his uncle."

"Strange, us sharing a half brother and having the same nephew. Guthrie, he looks like you. Hey, tell me there's no secret there?"

For a moment, he thought she meant John Robert's hospital bill, then he realized she referred to the boy's ancestry. "Nope, not concerning me. Those days I was too green to cause secrets. We just happened to get the same Grandpa's eyes I guess." He'd often cursed his earlier naivete. Relating it to Karen, it didn't seem to matter. "No, we were just friends. Now, I'll be Uncle Guthrie."

"Friends? Friends!" Karen's mouth opened. "Erilee told Lane that both the doctor and the business office at the hospital said the benefactor on Flap's bill wanted to remain just an anonymous friend. Lane thought it was Dad . . . um, Ira, but he says no. Sure! It was you! Had to be. You did that and didn't let anyone know. Who else could it have been? It was you."

Guthrie pumped both palms at Karen. "Okay, okay, let's just keep this to ourselves. There's enough bad blood between Lane and me."

She threw both hands around the back of his neck and pulled him forward. Her kiss carried too much seasoning for siblings and too little for passion. It fell into the you're-a-hell-of-a-guy category. Whatever, it fit well and made him laugh. Seconds later, with rising blood and a desire for more, he realized there was definitely no carryover of brotherhood.

Karen's eyes flashed. She smiled, bounced on the seat, then sat on her hands. "You're so incredibly nice."

He chuckled.

27

Karen started the Corvette, backed from the rocky overlook, and turned toward Saddle Horn. "I guess we share a half sister, also."

"What? Oh yeah, Irene. I'll be."

The Vette's windshield magnified the sun's heat, warmed the small interior. Cattle grazed the frostbitten pastures with backbones arched against the early winter chill. Saddle Horn itself gave the impression of huddling, back to the wind, head down with gusts of dust dancing like foggy breath down Main Street.

Karen turned from the highway and stopped at the corner phone booth. "Gonna call Mom and tell her I'm on my way to visit Jesse."

"Okay. There's old Sammy. That breeze has him woke up. Boy, he's hooking 'em. Karen, I'll walk across."

Sammy biked down the highway, coming from Rita's direction. His legs supported his weight, and he leaned forward, pumped, and tilted his head into the crosswind, looking to the side.

From the opposite direction, the whine of a large truck sounded, straightening from the curve and picking up speed. Metal sideboards rattled, and chains clinked. The engine's familiar roar said Billy Odom.

Guthrie stopped mid-stride. An eerie sense of disaster tore at him. Time slowed. He'd seen Sam do it a thousand times. He screamed. "Sam! Sammy, no, no, don't!"

The musician's trademark was to wheel onto Main Street, as fast as the bike would go, wave and show off to those catching the act. The monster's noise of acceleration ricocheted from storefronts and smothered Guthrie's fear into panic. It was horribly plain that there were no plans for the truck's slowing. He made two steps toward the highway, waving his arms and hollering.

Sammy leaned to his left, started his turn. Karen's scream joined Guthrie's. The bike angled directly toward the huge bumper. The scene unfolded like a chronic nightmare. He'd envisioned the rehearsal, and reality played to its tragic end, uncut, unaltered, too horrible for his brain to accept.

The rig's brakes screeched. A thud, more sickening than loud, accentuated the din. Bile surged in Guthrie's throat. The giant trailer yawed, jackknifed. Dirt and smoke and terrible sounds filled the air. The cab skewed sideways. Sammy's guitar flopped, hanging by its strap from the right-side mirror of the truck. A twisted ball of pipe and chrome careened to one side, bounced, tumbled to a vacant lot. Sammy's crumpled body dangled about the bumper.

Guthrie reached the front of the truck. Billy wheeled around the opposite fender, blood streaking from his lower lip. The driver fell to his knees, grabbed his face, and groaned. He removed his hands and his haunted eyes searched Guthrie's face, screamed silently for hope.

Karen's boots pounded behind him. He turned, grabbed her. "Honey, don't look."

Dust drifted at their feet. In his arms, she cried. Nearby, a car crunched to a stop on the road's shoulder. The noise seemed distant. Footsteps approached, and words drifted with the dust. People gasped and cried.

Guthrie sensed the small crowd, but it, like the sound, moved in another place.

He wrapped his arm around Karen's shoulders and walked her toward the Vette. The street was cold and lonely. The wind bit. The drone of a high-flying plane added mystery to his shock. He looked up and followed the jet stream to its source. Sammy's favorite song haunted him. It talked of El Paso, of thirty thousand feet. Did anyone up there gaze below? Did they know that Sam rested in this desert sand? A tear worked at the corner of his eye. He brushed it away and looked at his feet.

"Where will I find Daddy? Jesse?" Karen asked.

"At the pump house. Want me to come?"

"No. Oh, Guthrie, no. I need to talk to my daddy."

"Understand. I'll see you later." He watched her drive away. He clamped his jaw and looked back at the wreck. Bud hurried with a blanket toward the truck. Guthrie moved to the station wagon, eased it to the highway, and turned away from the crowd toward the canyon.

An hour later, he returned to his parent's. He drove slowly. His mother knew of Sammy's death. Her eyes were red. She talked of the little man who'd brought smiles and light with his music to the lives of so many.

Sam held no church membership. In the past, on various Sundays, he might have been found with the Baptist, then a week later with the Methodist. Perhaps, the next week he'd honor the Church of Christ. Once or twice a year he caught rides to Talbot and joined his Mexican friends at Mass.

His body rested Thursday and Friday at Talbot Memorial Funeral Home. The services would be held there and then his remains would be returned to Saddle Horn for burial. Friday morning telephones began to ring and pickups stopped nose-to-tail on nearly every country road and most of the town's streets. The word was being passed that calls, cards, and flowers were inundating the funeral home. Space demanded the funeral be rescheduled for ten Saturday morning at the Saddle Horn High School combination gymnasium and auditorium.

Mr. Hefner called shortly after noon Friday and asked Guthrie if he'd say a word or two for Sammy the next morning. The three Saddle Horn preachers and the priest from Talbot would each deliver a short sermon, then he as Sam's unofficial guardian, would say a few words. The community thought that as Sammy's best friend, it would be nice for Guthrie to say something then have Brother Hempstead close the sermon with a prayer. By Friday night, Jesse had raised two thousand dollars for expenses.

Saturday morning, the curtains on the stage behind Sammy's casket were drawn. It sat on the sidelines of the basketball court. To one side and at mid-court stood the Baptist Church's pulpit. The coffin was to remain closed. A white guitar rested on top of the bronze casket and the length of the auditorium was a solid array of flowers.

Guthrie watched with amazement from the steps of the school as the crowd gathered. Vehicles filled the shallow parking space between the school and the highway then spilled onto the shoulders of both sides of the road.

He expected a crowd from folks in a fifty-mile radius, but found it surprising to spot road-weary company cars with oil drilling equipment signs and New Mexico license plates. If their plates were hidden the white desert dust still spoke of the Land of Enchantment.

Vans and pickups that carried brands from distant ranches mixed among the neighborhood vehicles. Some marked with red mud and Oklahoma tags suggested Sammy's popularity extended to at least parts of the three-state area.

Apparently, cowboys weren't the only hard working, lonely, and dry-throated lovers of music and cool shade. These tough men of the oil patch must have shared both with their beer and, perhaps, found a little meaning to a hard-life before tossing their metal hats at Rita's dance floor. Guthrie felt of the paper inside his coat pocket that held the words he'd struggled with last night. Sammy had to be proud.

Later, Guthrie shifted his weight from one hand to the other on the podium, tried to speak. No sound came. He raised his eyes, gazed from the dim paper to the audience before him. Beyond Mr. Hefner and the preachers, over the heads of the crowd in folding chairs on the gym floor, the benches of the basketball bleachers were packed. He thought of shadows painting the canyon at

244

the overlook. Still the words balked. Sounds of soft sobbing reached him.

Guthrie tried to imagine Sam's face, tried to let it drift before him. It was no use. But then through the open windows, the hesitant chords of a guitar floated into the gym. Emanuel, Sam's protégé. Young and poor and Sam had said, "a quick learner". He lived a half block away.

Guthrie's voice rose above the sounds of the instrument. "Folks, I'm sorry. This is harder than I thought. . . . Sam Bolstien's life and his music will play in my memory forever. All of you, I'm sure, received your own special treasures from Sammy. He loved to tease me about my name. Liked to call me Paducah. Said it was up the road from Guthrie. We all know he was correct.

"Sammy was one of my closest friends. Fortunately, for me, I was born here in this town where friends like Sam abound. Still, like many of you, when I needed comfort I sought out Sammy."

A man's dry cough carried across the room. A baby cried, and its mother's heels tapped across the hardwood. The child's cries echoed in the cavernous room. Guthrie looked left at the exit where overflow people stood staring silently toward him and the casket. The child ceased crying, and the quiet hollowed caverns in his head.

"Mr. Hefner told you how he brought Sam here and acted as a sort of father to him. These men of God told you how Sammy inspired them, enforced their faith with his simple goodness and uncomplaining manner. Still, no one has, nor probably can, explain why God chose to touch Sam as he did with a dash of gift, a pinch of handicap, and an over abundance of soul.

"He was like the little train that said 'I can', and he did. He surpassed every obstacle life presented him, shoved back every fear that attempted to torment him. With a guitar in his hand and a smile on his face, he helped us be better. I, for one, will try harder to follow his example. Now, Brother Hempstead."

The crowd stood, with heads bowed and at the end of the prayer gradually dispersed. Guthrie breathed deeply, let the inner peace spread. He knew what he had to do after the burial. He looked for Bud.

Karen joined him for the ride to the cemetery. She'd smiled, thanking him with her eyes, but said nothing at the front of the school. She studied him. Perhaps, she wondered at the contrast between him and his friend. He certainly had no explanation.

Rita's portable, marquee-type sign rested near the road. The two-wheel trailer supporting it tilted toward a flat. That would have been Sammy's job. Someone had replaced the menu with the words "Prevent Grass Fires, Stomp Butts". Was it Sam's last joke or just an over-boozed cowman expressing a real fear? Somehow it seemed a little out of character for the gentle musician.

At the cemetery, Guthrie parked and Karen laced her wrist between his elbow and body. They walked together through the metal gate. Frost had long since killed the stickers and grass burrs. Dry winds followed and sucked them dry, forced them to the ground. Harmless, they crunched underfoot.

The slow moving crowd passed Christina's grave and moved on to the hearse and green carpet identifying Sammy's last resting place. A troop of uniformed Boy Scouts from Talbot acted as pallbearers and stood rigidly nearby.

Afterward Bud and Jean joined Karen and him as they left the site and made their way back to the cars.

"Appreciated your words there at the schoolhouse," Bud said.

"Yeah? Well, thanks. I'm sure he'd have played a tune for me." Guthrie delayed the others until the hearse passed then shut the cemetery gate.

"Bud, that young sorrel you had snubbed up when we brought John Robert out, you ever get him busted?"

"Funny, you mentioned him. Gonna carry him to a sell in a couple of weeks. I messed him up, Guthrie. Let him slip his halter and get loose in the round pen while saddled. When he finished, I took that saddle off a piece at a time. Without a rider, he learned all the tricks—all the bad ones, that is. Shame, he'd have made a good'un." Bud chuckled. "I open the back door now, he starts quivering."

Guthrie held the car door for Karen. "Is he up?"

"Yeah, there in the stomp lot by the barn. He pens easy."

Guthrie crossed to the driver's side. "How about me trying him?"

"I heard what you said up there about Sammy, you know, him not backing off, and all. But, Guthrie, you sure you want to do this? You know, the world's full of ole stove-up cowboys. But think about it, they ain't a lot of nice-looking young men with straight noses and a set of teeth that can crawl up to a microphone and talk to a crowd about rodeo, not and make sense doing it.

"You can have a go at him anytime you wish. Just be blamed sure. With my past, sleeping ain't what I do best. I got all the what-ifs I need without picking up pieces of old friends."

"Bud, you're a real bundle of inspiration. Friends like you, it's a wonder I get out of bed in the morning. I'll be out soon as I get changed."

Karen had left her car parked at the school. Nearing it, Guthrie asked. "You want me to drop you off here?"

"You're gonna ride, aren't you?"

He nodded.

"Let me go with you."

"That's what you want?"

"You're what I want. And I intend to see you stay in one piece till I get you."

No fake modesty, no blushing or averting of the eye. This girl shot straight. No question she was, for a fact, Jesse's daughter.

28

The sorrel snorted through flared nostrils and circled, crowding the outer confines of the corral. He seemed to float. His hooves barely kissed the ground, and his ears were erect. Not a scene to conjure visions of hospitals and the scent of antiseptic, but in Guthrie's case, it did.

Probably, a lot of jobs failed to stir such thoughts. The little accountant at Talbot wore thick glasses, but his hands were nimble, his joints in line, and his work precise and efficient. He exhibited no fear of his office machines. Odds were, he'd never experienced a broken bone in his life.

And the old baggy-pants lawyers going in and out of the courthouse seemed to live a tranquil life that offered little wear. Guthrie clamped his jaw, stepped through the gate. Hell, he might as well shoulder this war-bag, he'd been packing it all his life.

Bud's saddle, bridle, and rope rested atop the fence. He followed Guthrie through then shut the gate. The horse jerked his head up and down, pawed the earth. Guthrie reached for the rope and carefully studied the length of Bud's stirrups. He'd fit.

"You want, Guthrie, open that chute gate, and we'll run him in there and saddle him. Beat roping and snubbing him. Your call, though."

"Good, no need riling him. What you say, he's already got bad memories of that post."

Karen and Jean stood talking a short distance away, outside the lot. Their elbows rested on a railing, and they peered beneath the top board. A moment earlier, he heard mention of "wedding dress", but now their conversation did not carry.

In the chute, the sorrel spread his legs and tensed, but took the snaffle bit with little resistance. Bud gently pulled the bridle over the horse's ears and fastened the

249

throat strap. He stepped back, but continued holding the reins near the bit. From outside the fence, Guthrie eased the blanket onto the animal's back. He followed it with Bud's saddle then reached through and threaded the latigo through the buckle. He climbed to the second rail, bent over the gate top, and tightened the saddle. White widened in the gelding's eyes. He sucked in air and humped his back. His ears lowered.

Guthrie's throat tightened. This ride might determine if he would continue forking broncs. If beat by this pup of an outlaw, his career ended here. If he rode, maybe, just maybe, he had a chance of coming back. He wanted that feeling of completeness again. Wanted it so bad, it tickled his taste buds and raised the short hair at the back of his neck.

Something about the animal, maybe its energy, stirred him. Everything in view came into focus, created a unique awareness. This was all about life, and somehow, he'd forgotten. Every part of his body signaled him. Even the hair on his arms measured the weight of the sleeve around it.

Afraid and anxious at the same time, he wanted the exhilaration of being loose, alive, and on top of more of an animal than most ever encountered. There would be no flying dismount today. If the horse won, he would decide the ending. If he stayed aboard, it would be until this outlaw gave up and allowed him to step to the ground. There'd be no buzzer.

"You want to mount him in there, where you can get a good seat?" Bud's face was serious, his eyes worried.

The guy knew what was going on, all of it. Who'd he been talking to? Jesse, maybe? He'd always known the small town grapevine he so hated moved as surely, though not as nimbly, with real caring as it did with gossip. This whole country knew him better than he knew himself.

"Naw, let me have him. I'll lead him out. We've pampered him enough." He opened the gate, shoved it back.

The colt sulked, legs spread, back arched.

Guthrie slapped the two-year old on the butt. The horse shot forward, but had sense enough to wheel on his back legs and turn at the end of the reins. Guthrie took hold of the bit, pulled the animal's nose to its near shoulder and grabbed the saddle horn with his right hand.

The horse blasted air through flared nostrils and tilted the rear saddle skirt higher with each breath. He seemed prepared to launch in any direction.

"You gonna blow, or buck?" Guthrie jammed his knee into the horse's belly.

The sorrel shied, spinning in a circle. Guthrie stayed in the center. His hand held the horn and enabled him to spring forward into the stirrup and let the momentum of his own leap assist him aboard. He stayed low and with the action.

In the saddle, he kept the near rein short. He hoped to keep the horse circling, but it overpowered him. The animal ate slack and soon had its head down and his body working in moves without rhythm. The horse squalled, leapt forward with fear and fury. Guthrie's head snapped backward and the animal changed leads and rolled to the left.

Excitement overcame fear. Fun was back, and Guthrie relished its return. Sure this colt was green, just a rookie, nothing like the professional buckers in the big time that carried a more celebrated reputation than most cowboys, but he bucked well, and had no book of what to expect. This baby might not be a final test, but he was a good indication. Cold sweat and dizzying fear vanished. The air was fresh and his newfound confidence, a balm.

The horse grunted, crow hopped, and his breathing grew louder. He tired. The animal carried good flesh, but he'd grow stronger for another couple of years. This ride neared its end, and the taste of victory washed away the dregs of fright.

The colt gathered himself and lunged skyward, twisting his body as he rose. Guthrie hollered and fanned the sorrel's rump with his hat. Inches before they landed, fear stormed back. Off balance the animal came down at a crazy angle. His feet touched ground and his front knees buckled. The sorrel's nose drove into the ground, his head turned, and he rolled onto his side.

Karen's scream registered, and Guthrie fought desperately trying to jerk his leg free of the stirrup and at the same time, get out of the saddle. Only his foot failed to clear the fall. The fashioned swell of the bucking saddle's old pommel trapped his ankle. Instead of standing astride the downed horse its weight forced him to sit, trapped and writhing in pain. The horse lurched to its knees, flailed his lower legs, and rose, front first. Guthrie came up in the saddle. His left foot dangled, free of the stirrup.

The horse shook, slowly walked a few steps dazed. Guthrie pulled on the off rein and it circled right. He let it walk.

"You all right?" Fear crackled in Karen's voice.

"Fine, fine," he lied, speaking soft, hoping to not startle the bronc.

"What about that foot?" Bud asked.

"Hurts."

Guthrie circled the colt to the left then the right. With a little coaxing it moved in figure eight patterns then came to a stop. He let the animal stand, rubbed his sweaty coat, and spoke soft encouragement. Silently, he cursed the torrent of pain surging from his foot.

The boot grew tighter over his swelling arch and again he tested the injury with the stirrup. A groan escaped, and he kicked free of both stirrups, slid from the saddle. On the ground and supported by only one leg, he almost fell as the horse shied.

Bud took the reins, slapped Guthrie's shoulder. "Hell of a ride, cowboy."

The gate seemed farther than he remembered. He hobbled to it and leaned there, looking down while moving the boot. The foot twisted and bent okay, perhaps it wasn't broken. Applying weight brought doubts. Hurt and disgusted at having come so close only to have total victory slip away in pain was disheartening.

Karen grabbed his wrist and placed his arm over her shoulder. Her other arm surrounded his waist, and she looked him in the eye. "That liked to have been a mess, huh?"

In spite of the pain, he had to chuckle. She had it back together, determined to prove her toughness. "Touch and go there for a minute. Set me over there and help me get this boot off." He nodded toward a cord of mesquite firewood. "Uh, and put a please on the end of that."

Bud hollered. "Think it's broke?"

"Just bruised, I'm hoping."

By the time he'd settled on the wood, Bud had unsaddled and released the colt. Jean hurried toward the house promising over her shoulder to be right back.

Guthrie tugged, pulled, and twisted on the boot, but he'd waited too long. He grimaced in pain and bit his lip with each effort.

"We gonna have to cut the boot?" Bud asked.

"Costs too damn much."

"Got a sharp saw. You want, we'll take the leg. Once it's drained, it'll probably slip right out, save the boot."

Karen gave him an angry look, raised her fist.

"Leave him alone, maybe he'll laugh hisself to death."

Jean returned. In one hand she held a bootjack, in the other a plastic freezer bag of ice. She placed the bootjack on the ground in front of Guthrie's good foot, and Bud helped him rise. Karen got under the other arm, and the two of them supported him while he placed his weight on the jack and got the sore heel in its opening. A moment later, the boot came free.

Guthrie remembered an elastic bandage in the station wagon and soon they had his foot wrapped in an ice pack.

"What do you think? Will he buck next time?" Bud nodded toward the sorrel.

"I'd bet on it. Like you said, he'll be rough straightening out, but we took him quite a ways today."

"I'll probably just take him on to the sale. Too much work around here for casualties."

"Karen, if you're up to driving, we'll git."

Bud's two dogs escorted them halfway to the blacktop. A moment later, Karen turned onto the highway, settled back, and glanced at Guthrie. "Well, how'd it feel?"

"Rough at first, then great till he crashed. Believe I can pull it off though."

"When's Fort Worth?"

"Two weeks."

"And Erilee and Lane's wedding's this next week."

He couldn't read her thoughts. "Thanks for reminding me."

"Does it really scare you?"

"Everything about the Sawhorse scares me."

29

For the past three mornings, Guthrie awoke dreading today's events. The first two-day's of anxiety were followed by relief upon his realization that the wedding wasn't until later. This morning, the dread turned to a dead stump in the gut. He'd run out of calendar. The bells rang today.

A face to face meeting and talk with his half-brother lurked in back of his mind like a bad dream. And Lee. Now, she'd become a half-sister-in-law. That should be fun. He smiled wryly into the mirror and smoothed wrinkles from the tie's Windsor. If nothing else, the day should prove interesting.

He moved to the bedroom, sat, then winced pulling on his boot. Both the wedding ceremony and reception would be at the Sawhorse headquarters' main house. Invitations had gone to all of Saddle Horn, much of the Panhandle, and to dignitaries statewide. Sybil called and talked with his mom for thirty minutes the day the invitations arrived.

Guess he'd never know what they discussed, but the conversation seemed to settle some of his mother's nervousness. At supper that same evening, she told Jesse they were going to that wedding for the sake of our children. Jesse was to understand she expected nothing less of him than gentlemanly behavior and a civil tongue. He said he understood. His chewing didn't slow, but it didn't take a mind reader to see he was having trouble sorting yours from mine to ours.

He winked at Guthrie. "I'll comb my hair and change underwear."

Guthrie couldn't decipher the look his mom cast at her husband. Later with silverware gathered on his plate and heading for the sink, he noticed a kind of softness in her eye while she absent-mindedly turned her wedding band with her thumb. It seemed Jesse's magic still worked. The man endeared himself to women even while eating beans.

Now, the aroma of his mother's bath powder filled the small house. The sounds of Jesse moving about the bedroom signaled he shared Guthrie's uneasiness. A closet door opened then what sounded like a hatbox being placed on top of the chest of drawers followed. Tissue paper rattled then Jesse said, "Cora, this thing needs to be blocked."

"A little late to be thinking of that, now."

Guthrie moved to the front door, opened it.

His mother's voice came from the bedroom. "You gone, Son?"

"See yawl out there."

He turned onto the highway and marveled at the warmth and stillness of the day. It was mid January and almost hot. Not a breeze stirred. He picked up speed, let his gaze sweep the range. Last summer had been dry and hot, carrying into the second year the previous twelve months drought. In early fall, rains had come. By the first hard freeze of November, the lightly stocked pastures had shot grasses and broom weeds knee high.

Now, dry again and ten weeks after frost, all hints of moisture had disappeared. The pastures were like kindling and knee high with twisted, brittle fodder. The positive side was that a little cottonseed cake would see cattle through the winter, keeping them in good flesh with light hay cost. The downside offered disaster. Nature had primed the Panhandles' flash pan. It awaited the spark.

Karen and Lane met him at the front steps. Lane wore a black and maroon tuxedo. Karen's low cut formal flowed behind her. Its ruffled short sleeves somehow defied gravity. Burgundy, it enhanced her every shadow and reflected in the highlights of her hair. Guthrie took a deep breath, moved toward her. Sybil and Ira stood by the door.

Lane stepped forward. "Brother, good of you to come. You can scrape those boots right over there." He pointed at a sharp edged piece of metal imbedded in the concrete.

Karen shoved her older brother's shoulder. "Lane, you ass!"

Lane smiled, stuck his open hand out.

Guthrie took the offered hand, smiled. "You take care of what you annex around that horse lot, and I'll look out for mine."

"Stated like a true Walker." Lane lowered his voice. "Stay away from my kid sister." The fake smile vanished and raw hatred showed in his face.

Guthrie allowed his shoulder to brush roughly against that of his older brother. "Go to hell."

Karen took Guthrie's arm. "C'mon, say hello to the rest of this wolf pack. Then I'll show you around."

He bent and whispered in her ear. "I'd rather see the bar."

Ira's gaze followed him. John Robert streaked through the entrance and vaulted to Guthrie's arms. He stopped, lifted the boy higher.

"Mom and Dad are getting re-married, and you'll be Uncle Guthrie." The boy's face exuded happiness.

Karen patted John Robert's back. "He's already your uncle, Puddin.'"

"Uncle Puddin?" The glint in his eye added humor.

Guthrie lowered him back to the steps. "Like weddings?"

"Hate 'em, but Mom said I could change and ride old Zapata after the ceremony."

"How's track?"

"I'm the fastest kid my age in Pasadena."

"Good boy." Astonished, Guthrie took Ira's offered hand then Sybil's.

She shook his firmly, patted his shoulder while giving her husband an icy stare. "Remember!"

Ira paled. "Guthrie, I'm glad you're here. You and Karen come with me. Want to show you something."

He followed Ira into the foyer, Karen at his side. An arch, decorated with yellow roses spanned above the lower step of the horseshoe stairs, and plants and other flowers funneled out from the banisters. Tall candelabra stood at either side. Ira limped around the decorations and led them upstairs. At the end of the hall, he entered the study then turned and pointed at the picture of his father.

"Guthrie, your grandfather."

Piercing gray eyes stared over a prominent nose and

handsome face of the patriarch. The resemblance to his own mirrored image startled him. He'd not expected this. Lane's greeting had been true to form. This from Ira, well, it'd take some getting used to. Maybe, Jesse should have butt-shot him years ago. It seemed to have tempered the man.

"What was his name?" The question was unnecessary, but he had to say something. In a droughty country, where many wore poverty as proof of piousness, it was hard to be wealthy and popular. The wealthier you were, the harder others looked for misdeeds. If the current generation wouldn't provide them, they just went further back or made them up. Most locals grew up on lore that linked bankers, Walkers, and Red Riding Hood's rabid-wolf with equal billings. Guthrie knew the Walker lineage.

"Arthur, Arthur Walker. A good man, but a hard father. You're a lot like him."

"Understand he helped tame the country."

"He did that. Kids, I was fifteen and relieved when he died. He's near fifty when I was born. Like you, I had an older brother. Lane will tell you, and you know better than him, us Walkers are hard on sons." He glanced at Karen. "More so than daughters.

"Told old Lane this story yesterday, thought you two had a right. Don't know if it's age or John Robert that's turning me soft." He rubbed his hip. "Jesse may have had a hand in it.

"Anyway I had this older brother. He died of TB on the Comanche reservation over in Oklahoma ten years before I learned of his existence. According to Mr. Hefner, Poppa saw my brother twice. He took him a horse for Christmas in 1898. Then, in 1902 he went back. This time he carried an extra saddle."

"Sounds like he was trying to make contact." Karen looked from the picture to Guthrie, back again.

"I guess, but it didn't work. The kid stabbed him with a splintered piece of pine picket. Excuse the language, but I've decided I'd rather not have folks piss on my grave when I'm gone, especially kin." Ira stopped and put his hands on his hips, looking neither relieved nor sad, perhaps a little puzzled.

"I'm glad you showed him to me. Far as that other's concerned, ease up on yourself some. A fellow's bound to start thinking, once he's shot, 'specially if he's hit near the brain." Why'd he say that?

Ira's expression turned blank then a hint of anger died an early death, and he laughed. "So how you two hitting it off?"

Karen grinned. "Pretty good in spite of the generation gap." She dropped off at one of the upstairs rooms saying she needed to check on Erilee.

Downstairs, Jesse leaned on the bar talking to Judge Wheeler. The judge practiced in Lubbock and owned a couple of ranches joining the Pease River. The two talked low, seemingly intent on the other's input and oblivious to the crowd. Guthrie moved on down without interrupting and had the bartender pour him Bourbon and Seven-up. He proceeded on through side doors opening to the barn side of the house.

261

His thoughts bolted, scattered, and refused to be penned. Some moments, he struggled through hell and at others, denied if he didn't think he was beginning to enjoy the day.

Erilee had weighted his thoughts for years. Today, she was remarrying, and he didn't care a whit. Lane insulted the hell out of him, and it really didn't make him all that mad. His father of the week, Ira, acted half-decent for the first time in memory. Guthrie certainly had no slot for that experience.

Two women were upstairs. Both were beautiful. He sipped the drink, chased it with a drag from his cigarette. Thinking of them produced a moment of quiet in his inner stirrings. Both were important to him. The first had helped him become a man. The second made him proud to be one. A voice at the door said, "Everyone inside, please."

Mr. Hefner escorted Lee down the giant stairs. His age and dignity seemed to enhance the beauty of the woman on his arm. Karen waited at the foot of the stairs on one side and Lane on the other. The preacher stood in the center. John Robert stood beside his dad, arrow straight, and his face a mirror of happiness. The two descending the stairs moved slowly, in step with the wedding march.

A flicker of distant lightning flashed across the room, adding a touch of discotheque to the atmosphere. All eyes followed Lee—all but his. He luxuriated in, drowned in Karen's beauty. He wished he stood there, next to her, making the wedding a double header.

The solemn air of the ceremony turned festive as Lane kissed his bride. A murmur washed the crowd. Ushers escorted mascara-streaked women out behind the departing couple then the band hit a dance beat. Some milled in the crowded room while others moved outside. White-jacketed busboys hurriedly removed folding chairs, rolled back the rug and dodged anxious dancers. The crowd thickened, couples swung to the music, and the air grew heavier with heat and dampness. Ceiling fans were turned on, and people wiped sweat and laughed.

Guthrie and Karen danced near her mother and Ira. He grumbled. "Who'd a thought of this heat? To think we decided to have it indoors afraid of snow."

Guthrie smiled, moved his hand slightly lower, enjoying the supple movement flowing from above Karen's hips. Talk about a panther!

Jesse and Cora swung by. He dropped his wife's hand, spoke excitedly. "Guthrie, the judge offered me and your mom a job."

"How's that?"

"Asked us to move to the Lazy K, down near Padacuh. Said he needs a ramrod, and he'd match Mom's teaching salary if she would keep me sober and feed the hands. It'd amount to about twice what we're doing in Saddle Horn."

"Gonna take it?"

"Do prairie dogs live in holes?" He twirled his wife.

Karen laughed. "He's gonna kill your mother."

"Don't look like she's minding."

Jesse leaned back toward them. "Old Ira's gonna need a bumper calf crop to pay this bar bill."

Guthrie nodded. "I'd say."

Bud swirled Jean nearby. "If booze kills drought, the Panhandle'll be swamp by morning."

A few minutes later, John Robert tugged at Guthrie's sleeve. He wore Levi's. "Help me saddle old Zapata."

"Go on." Karen waved him off. "We've got all evening."

Moving toward the barn, John Robert kept up a constant chatter. He carefully explained the importance of a good stance in the starting blocks then demonstrated proper breathing during a race. At the moment he had three ribbons, but the blue one eluded him.

"I'm going to get one next time." He swung his fist like he beat a table.

John Robert caught the horse. Guthrie checked the saddle's stirrup length and in a moment pulled the cinch tight, buckled it, and tucked in the loose latigo. To the northwest a mountainous, dark storm front rose high in the sky. "Hey, Tiger, don't go beyond that section the other side of the landing strip. Fixing to get some weather."

"That's through the gate and all of the next pasture?"

"You got it. The one with the old diving board in the stock tank."

The boy got high enough on his third try to grab the saddle horn with one hand and the cantle with the other. He pulled himself up, got a foot in the stirrup, and grunted his way aboard.

"Atta-boy."

Later, Guthrie watched from the veranda on the east-side of the house. John Robert and Zapata rounded the far end of the paved runway, passed through the open gate and grew ever smaller. He found himself mentally riding with the boy, seeing details absorbed by youth and ignored by age, sensing the freshness of life with each deep breath. The imagery comforted him, gave meaning to the confusion of an adult world.

He'd had his time when every prickle pear, every mesquite bush and twig of sage was a new experience, a time when you searched the ground beside your horse's hooves and marveled at your own shadow, a time to crease your hat just so and straighten in the saddle. Yes, this was turning into a good day.

John Robert rode over a rise and dropped from sight. A breeze swept the patio, lifted Guthrie's collar, and washed him with chilling cold. Lightning streaked across the sky and thunder scoured the dark heavens.

"Let it rain," someone shouted.

Karen stood in the door, searched the crowd, and then spotted Guthrie. "The photographer wants to get the family's picture out front before this cloud hits. You know which way J. R. rode?"

"Yeah, I'll go get him."

"No, you stay. I need a chance to visit with him. Which way?"

"The pasture east of here, joining the highway."

A few minutes later, Karen appeared below, rounding the corner of the house in an old battered jeep. She still

265

wore her formal, but had apparently thrown a blanket over the jeep's dirty seats.

Mr. Hefner appeared beside him. "That kid gets prettier every day." He watched Karen fighting gears and zigzagging toward the pasture gate. "Rare to find looks and brains together. The time comes, who's gonna give her to you, Jesse or Ira?"

Guthrie's cigarette bobbled in his lips. "What? Mr. Hefner, there ain't another man alive could get away with that question."

"I know, son. It's my age saves me. Whichever, when the time comes, I'll put in a good word for you." Across the pasture, dry forage formed waves of troughs and swells that raced before the front.

Guthrie looked at the old gentleman and laughed. A blue-green glare of light transfixed him, almost blinded him. The wind rippled his shirt. Heavy thunder followed, prodded him to movement. He stepped forward. His heart pounded. A plume of smoke and dust and fire billowed at a point along the fence a half-mile north of Karen's position. He grasped the banister and hollered. "Fire! Grassfire!"

The east veranda was also the roof of a three-car garage. At Guthrie's cry, everyone went into action. Most repeated his words and pointed. Some turned in circles. Others crunched into a pile of immobile flesh at the doors to the house. Guthrie saw the blocked entry then looked over the railing directly below. Too high to jump. A TV-antenna's triangular mast fastened to the house, anchored in the corner of the veranda. Its braces formed a ladder, and in seconds, he hit the ground.

Sprinting for the nearest pickup, he looked toward the fire as he ran. The heavy wind supercharged the flame, and the single lightning stroke had now exploded into a blazing mass of madness. Acres were already blackened. Surging drafts sucked flames skyward. Tongues of fire leaped, twisted, thrashed about like a great beast. It sped, spilling its fury before the gale.

Keys dangled in the truck's ignition. He started it as others spilled from the house. No telling where John Robert had ridden, but the fire raced directly toward Karen. It took only a second to cull his memory for the lay of the land that made up the pasture. He had a lifetime habit of mapping such details automatically.

The tank's construction only required pushing a mound of dirt across a low waterway with a bulldozer. The principal reservoir consisted of the hole created by the dirt's removal. A creek wound across the far side of the pasture and the blacktop highway skirted the south. The fire streaked from the north side, spreading laterally as it surged forward.

Guthrie's head banged into the top of the truck. He'd hit a wash, now remembered others. Hidden by high growth, some were large enough for the truck's whole front end to drop into. Such a happening would spell disaster. He dropped the four-speed from third to second and told himself over and over to be smart. He had to get there, but to do that he had to be smart.

At the gate, a horn's faint honk beyond the fire brought tears to his eyes. She was calling, and he was helpless! So close, so damn far. Concern overpowered control, and his vehicle literally flew through the air only to slam and shudder into the earth then roll crazily on. Listening for the horn, he heard only the fire's crackle, its roar.

Heat thermals generated great rushes of air. Fire whooshed over and upward. He tried to quell the panic, thought of Karen. He loved her. He'd never known this feeling before. Had he lost her?

The wall of fire, now a half-mile wide, raced almost as fast as he. Somewhere on the other side was the girl he loved. God, why, why? Let her live, and the boy, for God's sake, the boy.

Ahead the fire burned. Guthrie raced through its aftermath. He tore across blackened earth and blazing branches of mesquite bushes. Embers glowed in the remnants of pack rat nests. Strewn in every direction were smoldering cow patties sending up plumes of smoke, and always the roar of the fire beast taunted, threatening. He drove directly for it. The truck bounced, it's bumpers almost digging into the scorched earth.

The explosion slapped him in the face from fifty yards away. The blast came from the midst of the burning mass. The noise rent the air, deafening. A fire-ball mushroomed sixty feet, and a jeep's hood flew toward him.

Dear God. She was gone. No. This wasn't possible. This was America, not Na'am. The heat chased away his ability to think. The front of the pickup neared the fire. He hit the brake and turned the old truck's wheel.

It veered sideways with two wheels locked and stopped. He stepped out, kicked the door, and fell to his knees.

Soot and embers burned his face. He slapped and wiped at the heat. Zapata screamed, almost a human sound, terrible. The horse reared, a shadow in the fire, then emerged a blazing ball from the wall of flame. He crumbled to the ground and thrashed, became a smoking heap of horror.

Guthrie stood, watched the fire retreat, and dug for his handkerchief. Sobs racked him. He was again in the dying field. He shook his fist skyward and sank back to his knees. Through tears, he watched the straggling back fingers of fire march away.

A weakness formed in its center. Water appeared surrounded by red dirt and deep cattle tracks. No blaze burned in that spot. Seconds later, the earthen dam and a dilapidated diving board became visible through the shimmering heat. Waves lapped white against the dam.

Guthrie looked in awe, afraid to believe. Then he saw them. There in the water, in the middle of the tank. Two heads bobbed above the water.

He hollered. He didn't know what, but he hollered.

Karen moved toward him. She was waist deep holding a bedraggled John Robert. Fright mixed with determination on her face.

Guthrie raced forward, stumbled, fell. A live ember burned his hand. "Darling, my darling." He neared the water.

Karen reached the shallows, her formal now brown,

stretched, floating behind. Her hair hung in strands, but she smiled. She released John Robert and splashed forward laughing and crying, her arms outspread. "Sweetheart!"

Guthrie splashed to her, embraced her, and they fell. Their bodies parted, but their lips remained joined. Seconds later, braced on one arm, he continued to smother her with kisses.

John Robert tackled him from behind, and he went face down into the mud and shallow water. Guthrie stood, helped them each to their feet, and led them to the shore. He stopped, put his arms around them. Their laughter softened, turned to sobs, and both their bodies shook. They huddled together watching the fire snake toward the highway.

Two men bounced to their side in a Cadillac, then Lane and Erilee slid to a halt at the water's edge. Laughter interspersed Lee's bawling. Tears dripped down Lane's face. He pumped Guthrie's hand. "Oh, man, thank you. Thank you."

"Hey, it wasn't me. I just got here. Karen and old J. R. did it for themselves. Fast thinking, huh?"

"Thinking comes fast when your butt's sizzling, doesn't it, J. R.?" Karen squirmed closer to Guthrie.

"Come on, Sis, y'all get in, and let's go get you some dry clothes. This wind's turned cold." Lane opened the car door.

"Take them on to the house, Lane. I'll drive over to help the boys start that fire line. Won't take long to dry off over there. Go that way." Guthrie nodded at, and pointed away from, Zapata's carcass.

Light drizzle and calming winds combined with three hours of back breaking work to bring the fire under control. Men stumbled back to the main house dragging wet gunnysacks, raggedy, frayed, and scorched suit coats, and tools of every description. Most took up stations near the bar and punch bowls, spreading black mud and dripping water in their wake. Jesse brought up the rear. He clanked up the road on the bulldozer he'd driven to drag out firebreaks.

Ira greeted the returning men from the steps. "Come on in, friends. Don't mind them floors. We'll clean 'em or replace 'em. Can't thank you enough. Jesse, inside here! The bar's still open. You boys saved this place. If she'd crossed that runway we might have lost all of headquarters. Those of you ruined those suits, there'll be credit at the dry-goods store for new ones tomorrow morning. Old Henry may have to back order, but we will, by God, get 'em for you."

Karen, freshened up and wearing jeans, sat on the hardwood floor beside Guthrie. She leaned her back against the wall.

He turned up a glass of punch, tasted the fruity mixture, and savored the flavor of Vodka. He winked at Bud. "One thing about it, we must have started out the best dressed fire dogs to ever spit at a flame."

Karen laughed. "Maybe so, but Lee's photographer snapped a post-pond picture for my bridesmaid finale that left a hell of a lot to be desired."

271

30

Houston had indoor baseball. Dallas sported banks, Dandy Don, and America's team. Fort Worth bragged of being Cowtown, home of the first indoor rodeo. Guthrie sensed he owned it all. He'd just finished an evening's performance announcing the Fort Worth Stock Show Rodeo at Will Rodger's Coliseum. Yesterday, he'd been invited to host the upcoming Houston Rodeo, and beside him, Karen drove the Vette. She'd gotten into town near noon.

A few miles out of Fort Worth, little traffic moved along Texas Highway 121. It was past midnight. Guthrie leaned back and studied Karen's face in the soft glow of dash lights and the intermittent glare of headlights.

"How far out there?" He referred to the on-site veterinarian living quarters of her girlfriend, quarters that Karen had invited him to share for the night.

"Cathy said an hour-and-twenty-minutes from the coliseum."

"And she normally lives there?"

"Yep, except like now, when they're running out of state."

"These people she works for must be pretty rich, huh?"

"Yeah, sort of like my folks—well, your dad and my mother—but not Cathy. She got lucky enough to hire on doing what she always wanted. Course, being first in her class at A & M Vet School helped some."

"Taking care of running horses?"

"Exactly."

"So how we gonna get in, barging up at two in the morning?"

"The foreman, Mr. Blanton, has a trailer near the front entrance. We'll wake him, get a key, and let him know we're on the place. He's expecting us."

He handed her a half-smoked cigarette. "I still think we should have gone to my room."

"Gripe, gripe, gripe. You'd think a cowboy with a chance of getting lucky would be a little happier about it." Smoke filled the gaps between her words.

"Just anxious. An hour-twenty can be an eternity."

The car shot forward. The needle hit ninety, and she smiled. "You did good tonight. Had them on the edge of their seats at the right moment then relaxed and happy in between."

"Wes and Mrs. Hodges will be there tomorrow night. You'll enjoy them. I told you, didn't I? Ole Wes ducked the bullet. Least for awhile. They say it's emphysema, not cancer."

"Guthrie, I'm glad. I know you two are close."

"We are."

"Did you hear about Evelyn?"

"Yeah, talked to Mom yesterday. She said the service would be day after tomorrow. I won't be able to make it."

"I know. I'll have to leave tomorrow afternoon to get back myself. Won't be able to meet the Hodges this time. Maybe at Houston."

"Express my sorrow to Lee and John Robert."

Karen shook her head, tossed a strand of hair from her face. "Okay. Boy, they sure shuffled our dominoes, didn't they?"

"I'll say."

"It's just so strange. Here we are, a few days after swapping life-long fathers, going along like nothing happened. Like, maybe, we'd traded cars."

"I don't know about that, then again, I ain't ever traded cars."

Her look showed disbelief then acceptance. "You know what I mean. You called it the other day. How'd you say it?"

"Said we'd always been slick eared and botched branded." He reached, caressed the back of her neck.

The Corvette streaked through the night. Ahead, red taillights grew in brightness then disappeared as she passed to be replaced by glaring brilliance that rapidly dimmed. Karen rounded a long curve rising higher until finally, near the hill's peak, millions of lights from the Metroplex twinkled in the distance.

Guthrie flipped a thumb toward them. "How many strays you reckon are back there?"

"I don't know, half as many as the number of hurt parents, I guess. You know, until driving down today, I'd been so caught up in my own embarrassment that I'd given little thought to the years of pain and misgivings the four of them must have gone through. I'd always taken them for granted. They were there—just a part of the landscape, corner posts marking boundaries. What about you?"

"That about covered it earlier on, but later, Jesse kept things stirred up, made me realize parents were real, not always perfect. Never dreamed he wasn't my dad, though. Mom and Ira? Yeah, that was a shot in the gut.

"Karen, they're our folks, but they're only people. Like all the rest, they're wandering around toting some of the past, hoping for a tomorrow, and looking for a handhold on a fast turning world. Least we found the truth."

"And each other." She reached and touched the hand he rested on her shoulder.

With time, the last of the traffic disappeared. The headlights probed full bright down the highway, touched darkened homes and vehicles parked in driveways. The world had banked its fire, slept. They alone stirred embers.

Karen turned on the inside light and glanced at a crumpled paper from her purse. She turned from the main highway to a narrow, paved lane, then stopped. White fences extended either direction from a huge stone arched entrance. A gate secured it.

Karen read from the note and pressed a code into a panel. Nearby, a sign declared the site to be "Prentess Farms, Standing Sun-Deck, Johnny's Rush". Down the lane and beyond the car's beams, outbuildings returned dim reflected lighting from nightlights around a massive home. Inside the gate, a side drive led to a large mobile home.

Minutes later, Mr. Blanton, clad in a house coat and rubbing his eyes handed them a key. "Been expecting you." He pointed to a small house between the large home and the lighted barn. A horse's frantic nickering drifted from the barn area.

"Sounds like ole Sun's riled. One of them fillies must be coming in. I'll put on some britches and drive up that way in a minute. Durn pest's liable to keep you awake all night if I don't put more distance between them. Make yourself at home. Ought to be plenty of grub. Cathy likes to eat, but she keeps it worked off."

"How many horses did they take to Florida, Mr. Blanton?" Guthrie asked.

"Bob, just make it Bob. Flew one and hauled five. Talked to him Saturday, so far they'd taken two places and a show. The big run comes up Sunday. Caught your ride in Fort Worth last year, Guthrie. How's announcing?"

"Good, thanks for asking."

Cathy's bungalow sat only a few yards from the barn. Across the road and extending from the larger structure, a fenced run-a-round protruded. Inside the pen, Sun Deck battled the earth, challenged the night. Beyond the fringes of light, shadows of two or three horses flitted along a fence, and it was in that direction that the tormented stud directed his calls and interest.

Karen parked, and Guthrie took her suitcase and his overnight bag. He followed her to the front door. She put the key in the opening, turned, and smiled hesitantly. He grinned back, tried to be reassuring. Did she have second thoughts?

Behind them, Bob's pickup lights circled then grew brighter coming their way. The stud trumpeted, charged the high fence, then wheeled and kicked. A metallic bang came from the area. Karen found the light switch, and led him inside.

She crossed the small living room, skirted the breakfast bar, and walked to a door opening to a hallway. She entered, turned on the light. He followed. She studied Cathy's bedroom. To one side was the bathroom.

Outside, Bob hollered, "Sun." A whip cracked. Guthrie crossed behind Karen, set the bags on the bed, turned, and opened his arms.

The aroma of perfume preceded her across the room. Her face tilted, eyes closed, and she tiptoed, bringing her lips to his. He bent, crushed his mouth against hers, tasted her lipstick, and shared her breath. Strong fingers dug into his back. She alternately nibbled and pressed her lips against his. Her mouth partially parted, worked hungrily.

He released her, struggled to remove her coat, and she wiggled free of the garment. Outside, a barn door slammed, and Sun's nicker became more muffled. Karen came back into Guthrie's arms.

Her dress was knit, something with tiny holes and little loops, soft. He explored its texture, tested the flesh beneath the garment. The cloth rolled, but beneath along her back, the skin felt taut. Lower, his hands explored areas of softness, delicate dips, and maddening curves.

277

He wanted to inhale her, solve the mystery of her moves, write the book on how to make it to the buzzer. He pressed his leg between her thighs, gripped her butt, and pulled her closer. She moved against his leg. Her firm pelvis pressed ever harder.

She separated from him, put her hand against his lips. "Wait, let me bathe and change."

"Now?"

"It'll only be a minute. I've driven from the Panhandle."

"Okay, okay, I'll wait, but me and ole Sun are aging fast."

"There's probably wine. Cathy's the only valedictorian wine-o I know."

Guthrie moved to a window and peeked through the blinds. Sun had disappeared from the outside area. His nickers grew more faint. Bob's pickup started, moved toward the lane out of view. Guthrie sat, removed his boots then poured a small glass of Rose he found in the refrigerator. He leaned against the cabinet and listened to shower spray hitting tile or plastic or both.

The pattern varied, and he tried to envision Karen moving and soaping her body in the wet spray. The image came easily. That door was the problem. He alternately stepped on the loose toes of each sock and pulled one foot after the other free. His shirt took a second, and he stopped a step from the bathroom door.

"May I come in?"

"What?"

"It's lonely out here."

"Poor baby."

"Is that a yes?"

"Does it sound like no?"

Guthrie dropped his pants and hand paddled through clouds of steam to the sliding doors of the shower. She opened them. He stepped in, slipped, and almost fell toward her. Karen grabbed him around the waist. Water ran warm on his body. She pressed against him, and spray bounced from her shoulders into his eyes and nose. He kissed her.

Sensuality replaced thought. She raised a leg, and he felt her thigh around his wet skivvies. He unsnapped the shorts, allowed them to drop, then eased her around as he struggled downward, fighting to not fall. Finally, his back rested on the back of the tub.

His embrace tightened. Spray pelted. The shallow water sloshed with frantic movement. The tub, awkward and confining, accentuated the perfect union.

He closed, matched, joined, threw his body at her and she threw back. He thrust deep and probing, crazy to be a part of her most inner self. Fascinated, he watched as she sat erect, then hypnosis denied all but the movement of her breasts, the unbridled pleasure of her body.

She gasped, chewed at her lower lip, and fell forward against his chest, moaning, settling around him. She pressed closer.

Guthrie exploded into fragments of rigid bliss then collapsed, exhausted. Karen lay quietly for a moment. She raised on her elbows and smiled. "I heard the six second buzzer."

"Ten."

"Well, you know what they say about flying time?" She put both hands on the side of the tub, stepped out, and pretended to turn the knob to cold.

"Don't even think of it." He turned off the water and caught the towel she tossed. From the pasture, a shrill whinny answered Sun's neigh.

31

"Ladies and Gentlemen, welcome to the nineteen-seventy Houston Stock Show and Rodeo. Let's all please stand for our colors and the National Anthem." Guthrie's amplified words echoed, and he raised both arms in a sweeping motion. In the alleyway beneath his platform, two mounted standard bearers raised in their saddles.

An entry drum roll preceded the sound of percussion instruments. The loud music excited him. The first of two girls released her eager mount, and Old Glory streamed into the arena, blown by the wind of a fast pace. After a few seconds, the Lone Star banner of Texas followed, moving in the opposite direction and traveling on the other side of the arena. At the far end, each girl doubled back through the middle of the oval then made a sliding stop at center ring.

The Houston Rodeo was underway. With his hat over his heart and strains of the Star Spangled Banner in his ears, Guthrie stole a glance at a group of seats to his left. The box belonged to Wes Hodges. Jesse, his mom,

Bernice, and Wes stood at attention. Two empty seats remained beside Jesse. She'd said she might be a little late. He looked toward the entrances. Nothing! Ghosts of old pain and loneliness played with his mind. The young beauty standing by the band got through the final 'brave' note, and the music settled into a parade march for the Grand Entry.

Guthrie introduced Houston's mayor for a short welcoming speech. Later, he signaled Sparks who reduced the lighting and put the spot on the Governor's box.

The State Executive stood, bowed, and silently presented his lady to the crowd. The Governor ended his short greeting by pointing to an area near Wes' seats and mentioned his pleasure at being in the company of the next crew to set their sight on the moon. Sparks moved his spotlight to the three indicated men. Wives and children accompanied them. The astronauts stood, waved, and received a standing ovation.

The crowd took their seats, the din lessened, and he spotted Karen moving toward Wes' box. She made her way down a now empty aisle. Cowboy boots, Levi's, red shirt, and an outlaw black hat said 'look-out boys, country's come to town.' Bad and beautiful, she swung down the passageway like the queen of the cowgirls.

John Robert trotted beside her. His free hand held a souvenir, perhaps a pennant. They took their seats beside Jesse and Cora, and Guthrie reluctantly directed his attention back to work.

The show moved quickly making his job easier. Had it not moved well, he'd prepared to give this crowd from the cradle of Texas independence a history lesson. Let them know that cowboys were here before oil workers and space walkers, but covering the action took full time. He ran with the flow, touched on bits and pieces of the story.

Wes Hodges' doctors said he could work part of one event. He made his way to the announcer's platform during the bareback riding and prepared to take over while Guthrie moved aside to perform as the second saddle-bronc rider of the night. Color had returned to the older man's face, and he grabbed the mike like a kid after candy. Guthrie winked, tucked in his shirt, silently cussed the knot in his stomach, then hurriedly made his way to the chute area.

"Folks, I'm Wes Hodges, and you don't know how good it is to be here." If loud meant welcome, Wes received it. The rider before Guthrie stood on the chute fence, took off his hat, and waved it at the announcer. The crowd gave Wes a bigger ovation than that of the governor.

Minutes later, Guthrie looked down on his bucking rig and the bronc beneath it. He gingerly worked himself into the saddle, found his stirrups, and took the single rein. He checked the slack and again became aware of the familiar voice of his friend.

"You've all met this next bronc rider. Except for this ride, he's been your announcer. Don't worry, if he's able to walk and talk when the buzzer blows, he'll be back. He's fast becoming known as the twenty-five year old father figure of Pro-Rodeo.

"Look's like he's about ready down there so, I'm gonna have to cut this short. Want you to know it's his first ride back after a bronc wrecked him in the stands at El Paso a few months ago. I've seen a lot of these ole tough country boys come back, but this waddy takes the cake. If anybody can do it, he can. He's drawn a good one. Give him a hand, ladies and gents, Guthrie Sawyer down in chute three on Saturday night."

Guthrie tugged his hat brim down, caught a brief odor of oiled leather then horse. He moved his stirrups forward, leaned back. The crowd rumbled. The bay's nostrils rattled, and cold sweat needed wiping. Fear's sick taste filled his mouth. Yeah, he'd been here before, but not like this. He must be crazy. He felt the bronc settle, balance, saw his ears go forward. His own voice, dry and scaly, rasped across the chute. "Turn him out."

The gate swung open, the horse crouched then exploded. He started skyward, cut it short, twisted, and came down hard, spun left. Guthrie raked his spurs, swung his leg groundward, and braced for a jolt. The bronc's legs churned, fought for balance moving ever lower to the ground. Dirt buried his left rowel. The animal leaned then caught himself.

Air replaced leather beneath his butt and under his chaps, then the familiar form of the saddle settled around him. He'd weathered the worst. The horse gathered himself, reared, and stood on his back legs. He leaped higher and forward.

Guthrie bent his knees, leaned forward and pushed

against the stirrups. The bay lunged earthward, lowered his head and bawled a hollow guttural scream of desperation. Guthrie knew the sound, though heard it only rarely. Almost an equine death rattle, it was reserved for that moment the panther's fangs connected with nerve, when defeat was inevitable.

Guthrie sat straight, enjoyed the rush, and worked his spurs. He was the rooster responsible for the sun, the stag bellowing and echoing down the valley, the bighorn ram guarding the mountaintop. He was Guthrie Sawyer, son of Texas, and a couple of others. He was back.

The horn sounded, but instead of letting Saturday night relax, he continued to work the bronc. Old sounds from a war-torn jungle crashed in his ears, and an image of Flint Payne fighting his last bull crossed his memory. There was one more move to be made. It was all about living. The mount went up, and Guthrie left him at the apex of the leap. He removed his hat floating high above the horse, waved, somersaulted, came down on his feet, and bowed to the crowd.

To his left, Karen sprang through the air and cleared the top rail. Her face beamed happiness, her smile, love. She hit the arena dirt running. John Robert dropped from the fence to the ground behind her. Three uniformed officers started after them, but Wes' words stopped them. "Let 'em go, boys, they're part of the act."

Karen never slowed. She went airborn several feet away, and her arms encircled Guthrie's neck. Her legs wrapped around his waist. She relaxed and slid down until her lips met his. John Robert tugged at their shirts. He waved a blue track ribbon in Guthrie's face. On the ribbon gold letters said "First Place".

Guthrie picked the boy up and carried him on his hip to the fence. Karen took long strides in the deep dirt, partially trotted to keep pace beside them. The crowd was on their feet applauding, yelling, and whistling. He helped both over the fence then headed for Wes.

"Folks, chalk up a ninety-one for old Guthrie. Sorta puts on a show, don't he? Okay, bronc-busters, you got something to shoot at now."

Across the arena, Guthrie spotted more familiar faces. Other fragments of his kaleidoscope family stood, all but one, smiling. Ira particularly had a big grin. Sybil applauded politely. Lee's smile blended some with sadness, but definitely delivered the message, 'I'm happy for the two of you.' Only Lane's features expressed boredom.

Regaining the platform, Guthrie took the mike and shook his friend's hand. "Thanks, Wes." He gestured toward the older announcer. "Folks the best pardner a man ever had, my friend and yours—I've always wanted to say this. Please, a hand for Wes Hodges."

The next rider scored seventy. Determined to keep the crowd alive, Guthrie pulled out an old Flint Payne description for the hammer-headed bucker that followed. After he stated the animal was sired by a hard scrabble stud and out of a bad mannered mare, the bronc turned traitor and did more running than bucking.

He decided to hold comments until after the ride in the future.

His ninety-one held, and after the final ride, he unplugged the mike and wound the chord for Sparks. He climbed down the short ladder just in time to slap a flying five on John Robert as he raced past on his way to the Walkers.

"See you, Pard."

"See you, Uncle Guthrie."

As he approached Wes' box, Karen slipped her arm around his waist.

Jesse patted him on the shoulder. "Good ride, son. But that chatter, you been saving up all these years?"

"How'd I do?"

"Windy as a barbed wire fence in a blue norther."

"I'll take that as good. Ole Hard Scrabble sorta fell flat, though. How about it, any of yawl want to join us for the dance?"

His mother put her arm on Jesse's. "No, I'm going to take him back to the hotel, make him buy us a good bottle of wine, and look out at all those downtown lights."

"Good for you." He and Karen waited in the aisle while the others stepped out in front.

Karen looked up at him as Jesse and Cora stepped away. "You ever seen those Houston lights?"

"What? No. No. I never have. I love lights, 'specially from thirty floors up."

She touched her head to his shoulder. "Sounds better than dancing."

Ahead of them, Jesse put his arm around Cora and laughed. The man seemed different, looser. Probably the foreman's job played a big part of it, but it looked like other things contributed.

A child younger than J. R. waited with his parents at the opening to the NASA reserved seats. The kid wore Khaki pants and a big white hat with red lacing around the brim. A leather loop dangled from the hat beneath his chin. One of the astronauts held the boy's hand. The young woman beside him smiled at Karen. The youngster remained deadpanned studying Guthrie.

The kid's eyes roved from the big black hat down to the silver buckle and end-tipped belt then on to the high-heeled boots. His eyes grew bigger. Still, his face showed no expression.

Guthrie nodded and stepped past the trio. Something touched his hip. He turned, and the boy stood behind him, his face now alive with boldness, curiosity.

"You got a six-shooter?" The boy held both parents by the hand. He tilted his head, awaiting the answer.

"At home, keep it in the holster. . . ." Concern covered the young mother's face. "Keep that locked in the safe. The county sheriff keeps the key." A touch of sadness tugged at the happiness in Guthrie's heart. He'd switched generations, turned his own beacon on, marking the shoals, making up new lies.

Center Point Publishing
600 Brooks Road ● PO Box 1
Thorndike ME 04986-0001 USA

(207) 568-3717

US & Canada:
1 800 929-9108